Praise for *One More Day*

"Beautifully dark, totally devastating, and so riveting you might find yourself gripping the pages, *One More Day* is about the holes in our lives and how we struggle to fill them, the love of parent for child, and the secrets that define us. Absolutely mesmerizing."

—Caroline Leavitt, *New York Times* bestselling author of *Is This Tomorrow* and *Pictures of You*

"*One More Day* is an absolutely riveting book. It's a rare novel that combines intrigue and suspense with so much heart—but that's what makes it one of my favorite new books of this winter."

—Sarah Pekkanen, bestselling author of *Things You Won't Say* and *The Opposite of Me*

"Kelly Simmons's *One More Day* casts a spell over the reader from its tantalizing first pages. Twisty, psychologically deft, and wildly original, it'll have you guessing until the very end. Utterly mesmerizing."

—Megan Abbott, Edgar Award–winning author of *The Fever* and *Dare Me*

ONE

MORE

DAY

ONE MORE DAY

KELLY SIMMONS

sourcebooks
landmark

Published by Sourcebooks Landmark, an imprint of Sourcebooks, Inc.
P.O. Box 4410, Naperville, Illinois 60567-4410
(630) 961-3900
Fax: (630) 961-2168
www.sourcebooks.com

Library of Congress Cataloging-in-Publication Data

Simmons, Kelly.
  One more day / Kelly Simmons.
      pages ; cm
  (softcover : acid-free paper) 1. Mothers and sons--Fiction. 2. Missing children-
-Fiction. 3. Psychological fiction. I. Title.
  PS3619.I5598O54 2016
  813'.6--dc23
                                   2015009793

          Printed and bound in the United States of America.
                     VP 10 9 8 7 6

For my parents, who believed

MONDAY

C arrie Morgan's kidnapped son came back while she was at church.

Later, when she told a few fellow Episcopalians in Bronwyn, Pennsylvania, about this miracle—and she would, eventually, be brave enough to tell the whole story to a few new friends—they would point to this salient fact, gently insisting it was the linchpin. The cause, the effect. As if her faith had conjured a delicate simu- lacrum of her baby, truly ephemeral, wafer thin. She was taken aback by their steadfast view, the quietest version of fervor she'd ever witnessed. Most of the WASPs she knew—her mother, her in-laws—seemed able to take or leave their religion, abandoning it in favor of science, suspending church attendance for golf season. Or, as her Gran used to say, *as income rises, faith falls.* Indeed, when she pressed her own husband, John, asking him with tears in her eyes how he could have been an acolyte, how he could have been vice president of his youth group and *not believed* in what they both had seen with their own eyes, he had blinked at her and said, *Religion was sort of something we did, not something we believed.* An activity, a sport. A club.

Yet even after the whole week was finished and her deepest fears and faith confirmed, she would still shake her head and insist firmly that being at church when it had all been set in motion was merely a coincidence. She would try to convince everyone it was actually *ironic*.

Because she wasn't there at Saint David's—the soaring stone cathedral set high on a hill as if lording its wisdom over all the Philadelphia suburbs—kneeling, weeping, praying for her son's safe return; she'd stopped doing that months ago. No, she was mindlessly assembling brown boxes in the basement for their annual clothing drive and keeping track of her donated hours in the back of her mind so she could log it in her little notebook, as if she could hand over the evidence someday at the pearly gates.

It was early October, the part of the month still clinging to the grassy excess of summer, still warm enough that people were donating sweaters instead of coats, cottons instead of woolens. The boxes they packed were light. There were three other women: Anna, Joan, Libby. Carrie was stronger than the others and much younger. They were grateful to have her, happy to have someone sturdy and yet fragile. Someone who could be useful but who was still in great spiritual need herself. She looked so pretty and neat, her clothes always pulled together and her tortoiseshell hair perpetually shining in the stained glass light, but she still made mistakes, took risks, like a child. Defiant in her own way, headstrong as a toddler—they could tell by the set of her jaw. So much to learn! How often does a perfect volunteer like that come along?

It took a while, but Carrie had finally thrown herself back into volunteering. At first, she showed up whenever someone asked for volunteers—church, preschool, even bake sales at the nearby tennis club—trying not only to take her mind off her missing son, but also to create a new engine of purpose for her day. She hadn't just lost a child, she'd told her husband; she was a full-time mother—she'd lost her *job*. His face had twisted at that choice of words, and she'd been furious right back at him, in his face. *Oh, so I can't say that anymore? That raising a child is work? It wasn't all tickling and tossing the ball around, John!*

But more than the anger and the emptiness, there was the

crushing sadness, sadness that was held back by some kind of societal seawall until it gathered fury and sloshed over everything. After a few breakdowns at school in front of women who managed to comfort her while also raising their eyebrows at the intensity of her sobs, she'd settled in at the church, where no one seemed to judge her. That she could go from competent to sniveling in a matter of seconds had no place at a school. Plus, she still looked so pretty when she cried. No reddening of the face, no smearing of mascara. *That's not real crying*, everyone whispered.

The children at school were always bubbling with questions, especially about adults who acted strangely. And the school was full of boys. Boys who didn't want to be stared at by a woman they didn't know who occasionally tried to touch their hair. The day she was asked to leave, the volunteer coordinator sat with Carrie in an empty science classroom, squeezed into the taut plastic chairs, and stared at the periodic table of elements while Carrie sobbed as if there were some chemical shorthand for what was happening to them all.

No, the church was further from the living, closer to the dead and the unforgivable. The church was where she belonged. The women there weren't like the young teachers and young mothers at school. They didn't believe anymore in perfect outfits, perfect homes, even perfect afternoons. They'd chipped their china; they'd buried their parents. They *knew*.

Some days, like that one, the hard work and convivial camaraderie did too good a job. Carrie almost forgot for whole blocks of time—hours sometimes—that Ben had been stolen from her car while she struggled with a parking meter outside Starbucks. Ripped from his car seat, leaving only a damp pacifier and one pale-blue sneaker. It haunted her for so long, wondering where the other shoe was, and then, suddenly, she could stop thinking about it. A miracle.

For weeks, the car smelled like Ben. John would come outside in the evenings and find her sitting in the backseat, breathing in the lost perfume of motherhood. The swallowed milk and damp hair, the aroma that lingered at his neck, around his ears. Even cranky, even tired, even with mud streaked on his face, Ben was never truly dirty. He smelled like milk and teething biscuits, wet paper straws and terry cloth bibs and fruity jelly. The finest combination of sour and sweet.

Months later, when John had her car cleaned and detailed, Carrie flew into a rage, pounding her fists against his chest, as if he'd been the parking attendant, as if he'd worn the uniform that made her scrabble through her purse for more money. As if he were the silver meter flashing a red flag demanding another quarter, starting the fight over twenty-five measly cents that had cost her everything. John held her, soothed her, made her dinner. Then he brought it up again. *We should move.* A few towns to the east, closer to his parents. So they could help them, so Carrie would have a change of scenery. And she shook her head so vigorously that the tears flew off her cheek. *We can't leave! What if Ben comes back?* And then, just like that, Ben did.

She floated between the boxes. Ben had been missing more than a year. It had been almost fifteen months, and only in the last few weeks had Carrie finally experienced the ability to separate from herself, suspended from her awful history, and forget—forget that she hadn't left her house or yard for weeks, that she'd been almost catatonic; forget that she once heard John telling his mother on the phone, *It's like she was taken the same day he was.*

She forgot how she sat in the dark, rewinding Ben's crib mobile over and over again, the path of the stuffed stars and quilted moon circling for hours above her head, the lullaby always in her ears. John had finally taken it down and told her the mechanism had burned, the battery sparking. She'd found it, days later, in the basement, tucked inside a pail full of rags. Hiding the evidence. Proof that John couldn't take it; he just couldn't take it anymore. But she could. She could take it forever. She'd come upstairs with the mobile, wagging it in his face, telling him, *Hang it back up, damn it! Now!*

"Sometimes I think you want to stay sad," John had said as he'd grabbed it out of her hand. "Like you deserve it or something."

And she'd gone in the bathroom and whispered to the mirror, "Maybe I do."

But after so much time, the tasks she'd assigned herself sometimes took over, as they were supposed to, distracting her, and then—realizing they'd done so—threw her into guilt. Distraction, guilt, distraction. But sometimes, for a few hours, that distraction brought a level of comfort. Not happiness exactly, but something close.

She moved lightly, fluidly, as empty people tend to do. A ghost in a coral cotton sweater and gray lululemon tennis skirt, moving through the dusty corridors, someone with nothing, carrying other people's cast-off things. If there had been baby clothes in a bag in that narrow basement, she would have thought of Ben, surely. If, while driving there, she had passed the new groomed playground, all curved edges and bright colors and wood chips, and seen a ball being kicked across the short, mowed grass, she would have ached inside. His first words, *ball* and *bat*, and not, as she loved to joke, what she kept training him to say: "Thank you, Mommy." But instead of dwelling on her boy, she worked swiftly while discussing innocuous subjects like golf. Whether Libby should start playing with her husband during his impending retirement. Anna sharing her belief that several ladies in the congregation cheated on their scores regularly.

"I'm so glad you're feeling better," Libby said as they walked out to the parking lot. She squeezed Carrie's hand tightly, then held it as an older sister might as they stood next to Libby's dusty, dog-hair-filled Subaru wagon. Libby had always been Carrie's favorite person at the church. She came from one of the wealthiest Philadelphia families—it was embedded in her monogram forever, *K* for *Kelly*, a letter that stood wider than all the others, strong enough to withstand gossip, to live on reputation alone—but she lived her life like she had no money or pedigree at all. The oldest car in the church parking lot. Straight, blunt hair that belied her soft heart. Mothballs the only perfume she ever wore.

Libby couldn't help smiling when she was around Carrie and her husband, John. It was as if, by knowing them, she caught a glimpse of how her own daughter's life might have turned out if she hadn't been killed in a car accident at sixteen. Pious, hardworking, organized, Mary, her daughter, had been blonder, shorter, slighter, but she was just as strong and openhearted.

Libby had finally renovated Mary's old bedroom a few years ago and had given one of Mary's needlepoint belts to Carrie. Carrie had run her fingers over the tiny knots and x's with wonder, like she was reading Braille, parsing the meaning of the design, the small whales and gulls and anchors. Libby loved seeing it, peeking out beneath the bottom of Carrie's coral sweater, threaded through the belt loops of her tennis skirt.

"How can you tell I'm feeling better?" Carrie asked.

"Oh, it's plain as day."

"Because you haven't found me curled up in the basement bathroom with tissues stuffed up my nose in a while?"

"Well, yes." Libby laughed.

"They really should invent a product for frequent criers whose noses run. Like a nose tampon. There's probably a huge market for it."

"See, that's what I mean—making a joke again. There's a... lightness to you lately."

Carrie returned Libby's smile. Libby always laughed at Carrie's quips. In high school, the girls her own age had never seemed to understand her sense of humor. She'd make a comment or observation in class, and the teacher would smile, but the students would look at her like she was speaking a foreign language.

Libby got in her car and pretended to fiddle with something in her purse. She sneaked glances toward Carrie as she walked to her car, closed the door, turned on her engine. Carrie drove past Libby, waving again.

Slivers of sun still shone stubbornly on the speckled alders dotting both sides of the creek in the distance. But slate-bottomed clouds hung heavy above the green oaks and lindens circling the parking lot, shading Libby's car.

Libby watched Carrie a long time, till she was out of sight, then did something she only felt a bit guilty about. She sent a two-word text: *En route*. She thought it was sweet that Carrie's husband worried about her. Libby was a slow texter, with large calloused thumbs from gardening, and as she pecked out the message with her head bent down, another car sprang to life in the parking lot. It pulled out of a far corner, headed in the same direction as Carrie's.

Carrie took the shorter way home, via Route 30. She glanced at the rearview mirror a dozen times, but it was only to smile at the bobbing blue sneaker, Ben's remaining sneaker, that hung there. Like Dr. Kenney had suggested, she took it out of the drawer where she'd been keeping it and tried to consider it a good luck charm. But the swaying shoe mesmerized like a hypnotist's watch, and she never saw the car lurking half a block behind her, turning when she turned, veering when she veered. Even if she had noticed, it never would have occurred to her that something was amiss. Everyone on the edge of the Main Line drove the same predictable routes. She didn't worry. It had been a week since Detective Nolan came over to ask her "one more thing" that sounded innocuous but probably wasn't, days since she'd fumed to her mother that no one ever asked John more questions, only her. He'd been in Ardmore that day too, hadn't he? Said he went out for a run after lunch, but had anyone tracked down his route, asked for the DNA on his sweaty clothes? What would they say if they knew how jealous he'd been in college, how he'd followed Carrie when she went alone to fund-raisers or parties and watched as she went inside? But she didn't think about this. And it had been hours, two at least, since she had thought about her son. Because she was getting better. She was coming back to life. *She was.*

She took the last winding curves of Sugarland Road, passing the moss-dappled houses in the distance, the endless driveways up green hills, everything weathered and nothing glittery, no agate twinkling between the low fieldstone walls. She turned onto her street, a dark macadam slash flanked by piles of faux stone. She pulled into the abbreviated driveway and got out of her car. She opened her hollow red front door, and she heard it then, that babbling half language only babies and toddlers know. The sounds she wished she had recorded more of, remembered better, once they were gone. She put her hand up to her mouth and walked slowly up the stairs. She sniffed the air for traces of him—powder, shampoo—but smelled something that reminded her of a soiled diaper. The sounds grew louder, unmistakable, and she couldn't decide if she was thrilled—or deeply afraid.

—o—

T he mothers of the older children at the YMCA had noticed a man hanging around the previous summer, watching the kids burst through the doors after swim class. Sometimes he followed them the few blocks over to Starbucks afterward, eyeing the children's seal-slick hair, their tiny bottoms popping out of their bright, squeaking suits.

Ben was still a baby then, not quite two, so Carrie was always in the pool or locker room with him, but she still let him have some freedom, some space to run and explore. She didn't hover, no; sometimes she was making a shopping list or chatting on Facebook with her few college friends—the only time they seemed to communicate anymore. Maybe if she had looked up from her phone or her son, she would have fixed on that man more clearly. She would have been alert! Wouldn't she have? And been suspicious of someone who seemed to be watching the children and sometimes maybe the moms, yet who also looked like he may have been taking photos of the building, the paint job, almost like an inspector might, for a perfectly logical reason, on his phone.

It had been a particularly hot and wet summer, and each time Carrie and Ben had returned for a lesson, the shrubs and plants flanking the entrance had appeared to have doubled in size; tendrils had turned into tentacles, brushing against their legs, casting longer and wider shadows with every passing day. If Carrie had had to guess—and she had guessed wildly under the microscope of police questioning—she would have said that the man might have been a landscape architect, there to trim, to uproot and replant, to right nature's summer wrongs. Hadn't she had that very conversation with another mother afterward? That she'd assumed the same thing?

Oh, the mothers of the YMCA. The pool moms, the swim team moms. A little older, a little wiser than Carrie. They knew how to keep a child's hair from turning green. They always had ziplock bags for wet Speedos. She'd noticed their competency as much as they'd noticed her rookie mistakes—forgetting a towel, bringing a large shampoo bottle instead of a small one. They didn't know her at all, but they were nicer, so much nicer, than the mothers at preschool. Was it distance that allowed them to feel something? Was it the idea of Ben, not knowing him, that opened their hearts? Or was it just the lack of competition, since none of them had toddlers anymore?

Carrie knew what it was like to feel judged—she'd spent all of high school feeling that way. She didn't have the money, that wide, green safety net the other kids had, but she'd always felt she didn't have something else, some indiscernible heft, a knowledgeable weight left out of her DNA. Her grandmother had always said Carrie was an old soul. And it did seem that people her own age never understood her. In college, Chelsea and Tracie were always defending her to other people on their floor who said she looked "ironed" and was "too quiet" and "not any fun." *You just have to get to know her*, they'd say. *She's quick-witted. She loves to talk, once you know her.*

The moms at the Y never got to know Carrie, but they never blamed her either—they blamed themselves. They were so upset they hadn't written down that suspicious man's license plate number! Came up to her at the candlelight vigil on the grounds of the Y and told her so. Squeezed her hand with tears in their eyes as if they'd been buddies because they'd shared a bench at the locker room once, when Dolphins were leaving and Tadpoles were coming in. Some of them brought casseroles and flowers and balloons and stood in a semicircle around Carrie and John as if they'd been family or neighbors. Afterward, John's mother said she was so glad that Carrie had the support of so many friends. *Did you see all those candles, lighting up the night?* And Carrie hadn't corrected her. Sometimes people who don't know you still know exactly what you need. The same group of women attended the second candlelight ceremony when Ben had been gone a year.

Carrie had become more vigilant since then, more observant; maybe every swim mom had, owing to their guilt. No one could say whether the man's car was an old Honda or a Toyota or a Ford. If under the road dust, it was dark blue or green or black. If his long, almost girlish hair was brown or blond. If he went into Starbucks or merely sat outside, watching as they left their children in their cars, unlocked, while they dug in their purses to pay the meter.

As Ben grew and got heavier, Carrie moved him from the center to the seat behind her. Other boys unlatched themselves, got out of their seats. Not Ben. He was active, yes, but still cuddly, still obedient. Still loved to be carried. Easier, faster, for him to be near her own door. Except when there was a meter to be fed. The dark shadow of the parking attendant at the end of the block, the brass buckles of her uniform flashing in the sun, as if that was the person Carrie should be worried about. More money, surely, at the bottom of her purse. When the police asked her, over and over, *to think back to that moment* and whether there wasn't something she saw—a blur, a color, a hint of the man's hair or clothes—all she could conjure, contorting her face, begging her brain for more, was the dark leather cave of her purse. So big she could get lost in it. There was more at the edges of the frame, lost to time's edit. There was more she couldn't bear to tell them. But Carrie's mind froze in the darkness, the silty suede bottom, of that bag.

C arrie was more observant now. She stood outside her son's room, the door open six inches. Wide open was too sad. Closed tight, even sadder. So she left it slightly ajar always, like an invitation. John had finally learned not to touch anything, not to change anything else, lest it alter his wife irreparably.

No more babbling. Had she imagined it? No view of the crib through the opening. The *Where the Wild Things Are* poster on the wall. The pale-green rocking chair. The pastel wool alphabet rug that cost so much and never mattered to Ben, who never grew old enough to learn the ABCs, to spell, to put together sentences. Just handfuls of words, juxtaposed. *Light me*, he'd say when it got dark in his room. *Light me*.

Those words could have become a touchstone for her and John, a catchphrase to illuminate their path back to each other. But when she held them out to John once, in the dark of their bedroom, he hadn't said them back to her and hadn't turned on the light. He had simply hugged her a little harder, almost grimly. And that wasn't enough. No, not nearly enough. She was more observant now, but John was less.

"Ben," she whispered into the room from the safety of the hallway. Did she dare open the door wider?

No response. She felt silly, her cheeks flushed. Probably heard a child out back, on the walking path to the pond below her house. The sound carried sometimes, depending on the wind. She turned to go back downstairs, and then she heard it.

Squeaking. The sound of a small mattress when little feet bounce up and down.

"Ben!" she cried as she opened the door.

"Mama!"

She would never forget the sight of him, the width of his smile, the sparkle of his green eyes, as he stood in his crib. The same delight whether she had presents in her hands, or food, or nothing. A smile for a smile, always. The equation that children bring, that adults forget. She didn't need a snapshot to capture the way his golden hair stuck to his forehead on one side from being asleep. His cheeks were flushed because he was too hot in his clothes. She would never forget, because he looked precisely as she remembered him.

The same smile.

The same clothes.

The same pair of yellow socks.

Not one centimeter taller. Not one ounce heavier.

Fifteen months later.

I guess you could say I was there that day. There, with that beautiful little boy. Watching. Always watching.

I can't help it—I see children and I end up thinking about them, caring too much. Obsessed, some call it. But that seems unkind.

I still remember a long time ago at the supermarket, a tiny girl in a yellow dress, her fingers clinging to a red cart like she was going to climb it, sobbing, wailing really, as if her life were about to end. Her father stood nearby, picking lint off his green pants, ordering from the deli, ignoring her. I wouldn't ignore her. I thought about her every time I saw something yellow. How old was she now? Did her father still turn his back on her? Was she even his daughter? If I'd followed her, if I'd watched carefully, if I'd closed my eyes and let it all sink in, could I have saved her?

My mother named me Rain because I was born crying, with rain in my eyes, but now I dress up like a lady and tell everyone who comes in to call me Raina. I added the A to give my name hope, to make it always go up, singing at the end.

I was Raina when I saw that boy again from the window, where I stood between the parted curtain. Just me, alone, beneath the h *and the* i *in the pink neon sign, blinking the word* hi *above my head. A coded signal to anyone who walked by, calling out that I was friendly, even when I looked, in my mysterious swirling skirt that didn't belong on me, like I was not.*

Almost as soon as Ben had started to walk, Carrie had started signing him up for activities. Music classes, art classes. And then, as he got a little older, gymnastics, indoor soccer, private swimming lessons at the Y. Even though he had slept in a crib right up until the day he'd gone missing—even though he hadn't been particularly verbal or intellectually advanced—Carrie had recognized his good balance and motor skills, and in some ways, she'd treated him like an older child, given him a fuller schedule than some teenagers.

He was always the youngest in the class. But he could do anything the three-year-olds could do. He'd been an active baby and hadn't loved to sleep either in the beginning. FOMO, Carrie would say, laughing. *That kid has a big case of fear of missing out.* Everyone who met them—in the park, on an airplane going to Florida to see Carrie's mother—smiled and said the same thing: "Oh, you're in trouble." How they would laugh over that, the travails she'd have with outgoing and active Ben in the future.

John's family had bought him every kind of ball that existed, and John had played with him nightly in their narrow back-yard, laughing and remarking on his prowess, encouraging him. Long past his seven o'clock bedtime, when the sun was low in the sky, shadows so darkly orange it made them both look tan, they kept throwing and kicking and laughing until Carrie called them in a second or third time, insistent.

When Ben was sick and he was allowed to watch television or play games on their iPad, he would lose interest quickly. Sometimes they noticed him staring out the window, as if imagining himself out there, grass under his feet, the seam of a ball in his chubby palm.

He slept well at night, but not for very long. Seven hours. Maybe an hour nap during the day. John attributed his son's ability to sleep at all to those nights in the yard, and both Carrie and John had convinced themselves Ben needed to be engaged, that he liked being kept so physically busy. *He's not a cartoons and storybook kid*, John would say almost proudly when Ben turned away from their iPhones or squirmed when they read him a story.

Then Carrie and John would lie awake in their bed and think of all that was to come with their sweet wild boy: the broken windows, the broken bones, the stitches, the chipped teeth. They were all safe for now, but yes, everyone saw it: trouble up ahead. *We'd better move closer to the hospital*, Carrie would say with a laugh. *Put the orthopedist on speed dial now!*

But part of that engagement, that scheduling, hadn't catered to Ben's nature but to Carrie's own boredom. She hadn't known at all how dull being home full-time could be. She'd actually looked forward to Ben's activities and outings more than she'd let on to anyone—even thinking through the details of her own outfits, choosing a fringed scarf or flowing sleeves appropriate to the swishing movements of the music class, or wavy tunics and bright flip-flops at the pool. The other moms, juggling multiple kids and commitments or coming from a job, would be decked out in business casual or black workout clothes, always heading to or from something they cared about more. But she'd had time. She'd had time to always look like she fit her circumstances, even when she didn't.

She wasn't used to boredom; she was so accustomed to working overtime, studying, volunteering. She'd felt a gnawing need for something more. As Ben grew older, she'd thought about adding a demanding hobby, like gardening or needlepoint. Maybe she needed a job. Or maybe she needed another child. That would fill up her days, but the thought also paralyzed her with worry. How could she ever love another child the way she loved Ben?

John had started talking about trying for another baby just the week before Ben was taken. Carrie spent that entire week, everywhere she went, imagining the same scenario with two children instead of one. Two hands she had to hold. Two sets of needs in the diaper bag. It had seemed manageable everywhere but at the Y. *If I had another child*, she'd thought, *I wouldn't be able to enjoy Ben's accomplishments. I'd be scrabbling in my bag for another sippy cup and not see the first time Ben bravely put his face in the water and blew bubbles.* She'd miss him using his kickboard, astonishing his instructor, getting the hang of it before anyone else. It had made her so sad, calibrating those measurements. Realizing she wasn't ready to have two children in her life, she still clung to the enjoyment of one. She was bored, but wasn't that better than unprepared and overwhelmed?

But six months after Ben was taken, when she had started to feel strong again, she had gone back to the Y every week, just as she had with Ben. She had all the time and attention in the world. That was all she had.

She didn't lock her car. What did she have to lose? The old gloves in the glove compartment? The pennies she always had in the tray when what she needed were quarters? The wrapper from her gum, balled up on the floor because she never washed and tidied her car, because Ben would just make it muddy again? She could wash it every day now if she liked. She thought she'd been bored then? She hadn't even known.

At first, she had told herself she was just going to remember her son, his movements, the way he splashed with his starfish hands. Then she had told herself she was just there for the camaraderie, for the swim moms who had been so nice. And there was undeniably something calming about the light on the water at first; it reminded her of the stained glass glow of church.

But that wasn't it. She would go to see if the man at the Y dared to show his face again. If he really had been looking for her and not Ben, as John had worried, then maybe, just maybe, she could draw him out. She would feel a twinge of guilt about all the outfits she'd taken care to assemble. Had she baited him by looking pretty? If she hadn't looked so nice, would the whole equation have come apart? Still, she dressed carefully each morning she went so as not to alter the balance.

The last time she'd gone, the Tuesday before Ben came back, she'd chosen pale-blue shorts, a navy-blue button-down over a white tank top, brown gladiator sandals. A beige down vest on top of it all. A mix of fall and summer, because of how steamy it was in the pool area. She brushed her hair, then rolled a hair tie onto her wrist to pull it into a bun when it got too humid.

The warmth of the indoor pool hit her the moment she opened the door, and she was glad she'd worn the shorts. She shrugged off her vest, and the receptionist waved her in and smiled—no more asking for ID. After fifteen months of her child on a milk carton, everyone in the state of Pennsylvania knew who she was. She couldn't steal a grape without being recognized, let alone stage a kidnapping, commit a murder.

She didn't go straight to the pool this time, didn't feel like it. She stood and listened to the muted sounds she could hear even in the entryway—of basketballs pounding and water splashing. The sounds of fun. She wandered the corridors outside the locker rooms, looked at the bulletin boards. A calendar with all the swim groups marked by giant cutout fish. Photos of the Dolphins having a party for someone's birthday, the unappetizing aqua hue of the sheet cake. Pictures of swimsuits lost and found, easier than everyone rooting through the giant, moldy bins, always wondering if theirs was inside.

There was a bank of glass at the end of the corridor where the property overlooked a small stream. A few picnic benches were nestled there, and Carrie watched as a woman unwrapped a sandwich for a small child who was crying and shaking his head. The woman looked up just then and met Carrie's eyes. Carrie smiled instinctively, but the mother's face was grim. *Don't make him eat it*, Carrie thought. *He needs a hug, not food.*

Carrie put her hands up to the glass and looked around in all directions. A few trees marking the calm space, the street to the north, cars going by. Nothing else. She sighed. She didn't know why she kept insisting on coming back. If she did see him, what exactly would she do? Call Detectives Nolan and Forrester? Chase him? And what would she say if she finally came face-to-face with him, and his muted, reported, *alleged* features assembled themselves into an actual person's face?

Out of the corner of her eye, she saw someone on the sidewalk. Dark hair, a dark polo shirt. He turned suddenly and rushed out of her eyeline. She ran back down the corridor, past reception, out the front door, letting it bang behind her, not holding it for the next person. She raced to the sidewalk, looked in both directions too fast, hurting her neck. She didn't see him anymore. Just then, a dark car pulled out of the far corner of the lot, turned onto Lancaster Avenue. A black car, a Honda, she thought. It looked like her husband's.

As she walked across the large parking lot to her car, she glanced nervously over her shoulder at every acorn that dropped, every car door that squeaked open or shut. It was getting colder. She felt a mantle of fog creeping toward her, weighing on her. Finally, she stopped and whirled around. Not a single person behind her. On the sidewalk where she'd stood just a moment before—no one. Nothing. Across the street, a line of storefronts built decades ago—too new to be considered charming, too old to be considered cool—blurred together with their innocuous earth tones. A flash of red in one of them, and Carrie squinted, naturally drawn in by the brightness. A little girl standing in front of a glass door. When she saw Carrie, she raised her hand and waved. A car honked and swerved on the street, and Carrie jumped back.

Her hands shook a little as she drove home. Surely John wasn't following her again? He'd promised after that last time, before Ben was born, when he'd nearly gotten into a fight with Julie's husband after Chelsea had hosted book club, that he wouldn't do it ever again. Still, he'd looked so strong, so mysteriously different, standing behind those bushes outside Chelsea's, watching the women disperse for the evening. That night, they'd had acrobatic sex, just like the old days in college, when his longing for her, his jealousy, seemed the most potent drug she could imagine. No one had ever cared for her like John. No one had ever watched over her like that. She'd been left alone her whole life, with only a dog and a key on a lanyard around her neck. How intoxicating it was to her to have an angel watching over her. But they both knew it was wrong, that it was too much, childish and overwhelming, crossing some kind of line other men, different men, didn't cross. The next morning, she told him he simply had to stop worrying about her. That was what he called it—not jealousy, not possessiveness—worrying. That was what they both allowed themselves to believe.

She pulled her phone out of her purse, dialed her husband.

"John, were you just at the Y?" she asked.

"Yes," he said. No lie, no hesitation. Had he known he was caught?

"Please tell me you suddenly decided to take swim lessons."

He was silent, and she knew.

"John, you can't fol—"

"Carrie," he said, his voice cracking in a way that made her feel unmoored, afloat. "I miss him. I miss him too."

After a long moment, she swallowed and said okay. She said she knew that. Part of her was relieved she'd been right, that she'd known it was John. And part of her felt guilty, because a child had waved at her as if she were a lifeboat, and she hadn't waved back.

S he picked Ben up and hugged him tightly, relishing the weight of his head against her shoulder, though her first instinct, she would recall later, was to strip him and put him in a bath. Where had he been, after all? Who had handled him? What had been left behind? She touched his bottom gently, checking the weight of his diaper. Not full. But not toilet trained either.

"Ben," she said softly again. "My big Ben like the clock, ticktock."

He made that exhalation he always made when he was so content, he had no words. To call it a sigh would be to diminish the miracle of it.

She stood with him in her arms and tamped down her instincts— bath, examination, interrogation. She stuffed the questions back down in her throat, the thoughts back into the recess of her brain. Hope that he had more language in place. Hope he could tell her what she needed to know. Later though. Not now. She reminded herself that she'd learned those things weren't important. Life was fleeting. If only she could have him back again, what would she do? How many times had she said it, pleading with the universe? Just one more hug. Just one more song.

She sat down in the rocking chair and rocked him. His body curved into hers, his feet dangling, his soft socks on either side of her hips. The height in John's family was thwarted by the lack of it in hers, resulting in a son who was not particularly tall. A boy she could still rock like a baby. Thirty-fifth percentile. Those numbers that seem to mean everything but that you try to strip of meaning when you don't like what they say. His damp forehead against her chin. She put her hand against his back and patted him rhythmically. The feel of the nubby, striped T-shirt beneath her palm familiar as the skin of a well-practiced drum. She breathed in the fold where his neck met his shoulder. Sweet and almost fruity, like she remembered, but with just a tinge of something earthy and damp. *Like the green end of a strawberry*, she thought, a mix that meant he was just a little bit dirty from playing. Someone had let him play! Had let him have fun! She smiled, thinking of how he liked being outside. She started to sing a song about grass and trees and honeybees, one they'd sung at preschool, and then, seeing his dark lashes flutter, she realized she was putting him to sleep. No, that wouldn't do.

She stood him on the carpet, lifted his shirt tentatively, fearing wounds. His round belly. The dinosaur curve of his spine. His skin soft, tended. She retrieved the baby brush on his dresser, silver with bristles so soft they did nothing, and brushed his bangs out of his eyes, marveled over the curls behind his ears, the whorls that started at his scalp. Nowhere else, just there.

She held the silver brush aloft. "Did they…hurt you?"

His eyes, blinking, confused. He didn't know that word. What would he know, from his life here, of someone hurting someone?

"Owie? Did you get any owies?"

He shook his head solemnly. She'd forgotten those juxtapositions, the silly words with the serious faces.

"Are you hungry?"

He nodded. She carried him downstairs into the kitchen. Everything was clean. So anxious for distraction, she and John took every chance to do anything that needed to be done. They stayed busy, eternally busy.

"Juice?" he asked.

She swallowed hard. There was no juice in the house. John had removed it all: the organic juice boxes, the squeezable applesauce that cost a fortune, the mini carrots packaged with ranch dip. He'd found her sobbing over them, the refrigerator door open, and taken them away the next day, as if that would help. It hadn't. She'd merely moved her tears to the grocery store. She could avoid the baby food aisle, but the toddler foods, the preferences, were hidden everywhere.

"Chocolate milk?" she offered brightly.

"Chock milk! Get me chock milk!"

She smiled and got out the chocolate John kept for his ice cream, swirled it in a glass of milk, and found a straw. She held it up to the light, bent it, marveling over it. How long had it been since anyone in her house had used a straw? *Fifteen months.* She put Ben in the big chair, his booster seat long gone. Where had it gone? She didn't remember its disappearance. John, the thief of her memories.

His chubby hands on the glass, the still tiny shells of his nails. Who had trimmed his nails? Who had taken such exquisite care of him? *A woman,* she thought suddenly. A mother. Someone who wanted a child. *Why had they been thinking all this time it had to have been a man?*

"Daddy," he said, looking up from his glass.

"Daddy," she repeated. Of course. Of course! How selfish she was being! John needed to see this, needed to have his moment too!

She dug her cell phone out of her purse in the foyer, dialed John's number. He picked up right away, trained, ever alert.

"Can you come home right away?"

"What's wrong?"

"It's…hard to explain."

"Well, can you try?"

"Ben is here."

"What?"

"He was here when I got back."

"Where? Here where?"

"In his crib."

"What? Was there a note, a message? How did they get in?"

"I don't think they... I mean... Well, I don't know."

"Did you check the windows and doors?"

"No—"

"Did you call Detective Nolan?"

"John, aren't you going to ask how he is?"

A sharp intake of guilty breath. A pause. She heard people in the background. A restaurant, a store? Where was he? Out in the field, meeting a client? The world going on without their son in it, without her in it.

John swallowed hard, as if eating the question. He felt terribly guilty, hearing his wife state the obvious. Why weren't those the first words out of his mouth? In the restaurant lobby, his face turned red with shame, and he turned away from his clients, who were chatting merrily at the bar, nursing the beers he had just paid for, lest they see his face. They already knew his son was missing; everyone knew. But not everyone wanted to talk about every detail.

"Well, I assumed you would have said—"

"He's fine. It's just that—"

"Thank God. Well, you hang tight, and I'll call Nolan right away."

"No."

"No?"

"John, there's something...I can't quite explain."

"I would say there's a lot we can't explain. How did they get in? Where did they keep him? Is he talking more? Has he told you anything? You have to remember every word, Carrie, every word he says. Write it down. Take careful notes."

"John, don't call Nolan. You have to see him first."

"What? No, no, God, what if they're watching you? What if they followed you, if you're in danger? We have to call him now. I need to get off the phone. We—"

"No!"

Ben looked up for a second. The word he hated. The word

Carrie had thought back to a thousand times, wishing she could erase it and restring her memories with yeses. Give him anything he wanted if she just had the chance. There was no malice in his eyes, just slight recognition. Then he went back to slurping the last dregs of chocolate, running the straw around the bottom of the glass, searching for more.

"Listen to him, John," she cried. "Can you hear him slurping?" She brought the phone closer to Ben. "Do you want a quick photo? Should we FaceTime? I—"

"Carrie, stop! I have to call Nolan!"

"John, no! You have to see him first," she said. "Promise me you'll come home first."

"Why, honey? Why?"

"Because he's exactly the same," she whispered.

"Well, of course he is."

"No, I mean, he's not any older."

"What?"

"He's not three. He's still two."

"Honey, that's just a trick of the imagination. You just don't remember how bi—"

"I remember! I remember everything!"

"Or…he's been…confined, maybe. Underfed."

His voice didn't catch when he said those words. *How could that be?* she thought. *How could that possibly be?* The thought of it, the images—they tore at her. But she'd lifted Ben's shirt. She'd seen. He wasn't scrawny, ill-cared for. He was simply too small.

"No. He hasn't aged, John. It's like he's been…preserved."

"*Preserved?*"

She heard so much in John's intonation, in his pause. His mind, his logical mind, the gears almost musically obvious when they were turning.

She took the phone into the living room.

"Yes, John," she whispered. "Like he's not…really ali—"

"Carrie, listen to me. We should call Dr. Kenney right away, right now, then Nolan before—"

"No! No!" Half screaming, ramping up. She knew how to get his attention, how to make him listen. His fear of her breakdown was greater than his need to be right, to do right.

"How about Libby then? I'll call Libby and—"

"If you call anyone, I swear to you, John, I—"

"Okay, okay," he said. "Lock the doors."

John excused himself from his clients, saying he had an emergency at home. Oh, the looks on their faces. How many emergencies could one man have before they stopped feeling sorry for him and started wondering about him? No, these were good people. One of the women had patted his arm almost tenderly as he left.

As John raced home, he went through all the options: Whether his son was really in his house. Whether the crime was about to be solved. Whether his wife was losing her mind. And, yes, guiltily, whether the promotion to regional manager that he was up for would be affected by any of these possibilities. He was competitive, he'd cop to that, but he ordinarily wouldn't be so jaded and cold. It was only because the other top salesperson in the area, Lara, had told Justin at the convention in Atlantic City last month that John had gotten the "pity vote." She'd said this half drunk at the hotel bar, and John, who only had an occasional drink, had filed the information away.

At home, Carrie's thought process was narrower. It wasn't until she got off the phone that it hit her: John knew Libby's number? How on earth did he even know her fellow volunteer's last name?

Ben had been kidnapped on July 12. Carrie had stayed inside her house for the rest of July and the entire month of August. She'd started seeing Dr. Kenney in early September, and later that month, with John's and Dr. Kenney's urgings, she'd started going out in public again. At first, John would take her places—they'd go out and pick up dinner, go to the dry cleaners. He said there would be strength in numbers. But it was really more belief in his own strength, in his own watchdog characteristics. The world might judge Carrie, but they wouldn't dare do it with him standing nearby.

One Saturday afternoon, John asked Carrie if she wanted to ride with him—he needed to buy socks. She said yes, knowing it would make him happy, that it would be evidence of her getting better. But when he drove past the running store in Bryn Mawr and kept going, driving farther away, headed for the sports store in Ardmore, she felt her throat starting to constrict. She hadn't been to that shopping district, so close to the Y, near that Starbucks, since Ben was taken.

John squeezed her hand as they drove down the main street, looking for a parking space. They passed the Starbucks, and Carrie closed her eyes.

"John," she whispered.

"It's okay," he said. "I'm with you."

"But—"

"It can't happen again, Carrie."

"I know, but—"

"Exposure," he said. "In small bits and pieces. Dr. Kenney told me all about it. You can't get better without exposure therapy."

"Grief is nothing but exposure."

"What do you mean?"

"Don't you feel like you are missing your skin? Like every breeze, every drop of rain, is just like an assault—"

He didn't say what he thought out loud. *No.*

He spotted a parallel parking space a few blocks away, across the street, and pulled in.

Carrie released the breath she'd been holding; the car was facing away from Starbucks, toward the east, almost at the farmers' market.

"You ready?"

"I'll wait here."

"No," he said. "God, no. No, come with me."

"I can't."

"Carrie, what if—"

"What if what? Just say it, John. Acknowledge that something bad could still happen."

"That's not it! That's not it at all. It's just—"

"Just what?"

"Just…you might get sad or scared or—" He stopped, just in time. Just before he said something that would set her off again. "And what if you're alone?"

"I'm alone all day," she said.

"Okay." He sighed and opened his door. "I'll hurry," he added. "No unnecessary sock browsing."

"Yeah, no lingering over the argyles."

She managed a small smile, but his smile behind the glass of the door was so wide it was almost magnified. Was that all it took? A little teasing to make him think she was herself again?

He jogged across the street, jaywalking with his long strides, never even coming close to a car or to anything in his way.

Carrie breathed in and thought not of John or of Ben but about dinner. She thought if she could think of ordinary things—brushing her teeth, eating Chinese food—that all the extraordinary things could be held at bay.

She didn't hear the footsteps approaching. She didn't pick up on the sighing, the click of the pen. When the navy-blue sleeve appeared in the corner of her window, she jumped, the way you do when a leaf lands on your head. A blue arm, a jacket, pants. In motion, heading up the street, away from her, not stopping, but fury rose in her nonetheless.

She got out of the car. Fifteen minutes still left on her meter, but the next person would not be so lucky. She watched the young parking attendant in the navy-blue uniform with the sensible black shoes walk to a car two spaces ahead and start to write a ticket.

"Wait!" Carrie called, and the woman turned. "I'll pay the meter."

"This your car?"

"No, I—"

"Too late," she said and sighed. "Already started writing."

"You should cut them a break," Carrie said.

The woman said nothing, kept her head down.

"Do you even have a heart under there? Do you ever think what you might be doing to someone?"

The woman put down her pen, raised her eyes to Carrie, cocked her head, then squinted. Slowly putting it together.

"I know who you are," she said.

"So?"

"So I'm sorry about your baby, but—"

"But what?"

"Nothing."

"But what? But you have a job to do? That's what you were going to say, right?"

"No."

"What then?" Carrie cried, walking up to the woman. "What is your excuse?"

"Get away from me, now," she said. She gripped her walkie-talkie like it was a lifeline.

Carrie turned, went back to her car. As she reached for the door handle, the parking attendant called out.

"You should have locked your door."

"What did you say?" Carrie's eyes narrowed to slits.

John walked up, whistling, a bag in his hand. He looked at his wife, her hands clenched into fists. The parking attendant gripping her walkie-talkie.

"Does someone…need a quarter or something?"

"No," the woman said flatly.

The parking attendant's words rang in Carrie's ears the whole way home, not in a single voice, but a cacophony, a Greek chorus. Saying what everyone else was thinking, including her. *It's your fault. Sooner or later everyone will know.*

John's father had recommended Dr. Kenney, but John hadn't told Carrie that. His family had been concerned when John described his wife's behavior; they'd thought Carrie should start therapy right away, but John had waited a few months to mention it, since Carrie's emotions were still so raw.

John drove his wife to the first appointment. Carrie stared out the window and chewed on her nails, which were already short and ragged. The doctor's office in Wayne was on the lower floor of a small sunlit house that had been retrofitted for a Pilates center, a family therapist, and a dermatologist. Dr. Kenney came out and greeted Carrie warmly but merely nodded at John, as if he hadn't spoken to him already at length.

Carrie went into the office, and John sat down in the waiting room. The back of his head leaned up against the soft grass-cloth wall. He hoped to hear something, not actual words but a sense of what was happening—laughter, sobs, soothing. Something. But no voices broke through. The room buzzed in his ears, an audio stew of furnace and light, the tick of a clock. He started to squirm, as if he was the one expected to speak. As if the noisy quiet was a perpetrator of some kind, a weapon to make him cry out.

He got up, stretched, then sat back down, closed his eyes. He stayed in the too-stiff chair for over half an hour, until another man came in. He was around John's age, taller, well built. John stood up and said hello out of politeness, thinking this was another doctor. When the man finally made eye contact, his eyes were dark, long-lashed, and startling, like a model's. He looked away quickly, sat down a few seats away. He tapped his feet and jingled his change, his face angled toward the floor, until Carrie and Dr. Kenney finally came out of the other room.

On the drive home, Carrie was quiet, but she didn't cry and her eyes weren't red. The silence in the car was only slightly different from the silence in the office.

Finally, John spoke. "What did you talk about?"

"He kept asking me about my father."

"Your father? Really?"

"You sound disappointed."

"No, just...surprised, I guess."

"He said many women who marry young have issues with their father."

"We weren't that young," John replied, screwing up his face. "And you don't really, do you?"

"He asked me what my first memory of my father was, and I—I remembered the strangest thing."

"What's that?"

"He was sleeping in a hammock in the backyard, and my mother told me to wake him up. But when I did, he called me another name, a man's name, like he was dreaming."

"Well, he probably was. A sleep talker, maybe."

"But then he opened his eyes, and he looked...afraid. Like I was going to hurt him."

"Then what happened?"

"That's all I could remember."

"I mean, what happened after that with the doctor?"

"We talked about being parents and stuff."

"Did you lay down?"

"No. I made another appointment at the same time next week,

which is what he recommends to all his patients. Pick a time and stick with it."

"I guess that makes sense," John said. "It's easier to remember."

"I guess."

Outside, the clouds threatened rain again. They hung above the trees as if daring people to hurry home before things got worse, but John didn't hurry. He was never in a hurry to get home to that empty house.

"So what's the first memory you have of your father, John?"

"Mine?"

He waited a long time before answering. He tried to answer all of Carrie's questions, but it wasn't always easy.

"I don't know. Little League?"

"No, that can't be it. What about when you were younger? Before you went to school?"

"I don't know. I never thought about it."

When they got home, John went into the den and emailed Dr. Kenney. He asked if the man he'd seen in the waiting room had the same appointment every week, right after Carrie's. "If so," he wrote, "we would like to change ours."

C arrie liked staying busy. In college, she had signed up to
supervise the cancer walk—because of her grandmother,
everyone had thought. She had volunteered at the soup kitchen—
because of the lean years with her mother, John had always
thought. And she would spend one night a week tutoring kids
whose parents were divorced or had died—because of her father,
they'd all assumed. Her mother had thought it simply the safest
kind of rebellion. She, after all, had always been too busy and
volunteered in the smallest slices—cans for a food drive, a toy for a
tot. Carrie was different. And she'd been keeping a list of these differences, logged in a small, worn notebook, since her senior year
of school. It lay tucked in her drawer, beneath her heaviest winter
socks, a list of pros to weigh against unstated, unshared cons.

When Dr. Kenney had urged her to start going out again, it was
almost as if he knew about the contents of that drawer. That was
the thing about Dr. Kenney—Carrie had wanted to not like him,
to think John had merely pressured her into seeing a therapist, that
he wasn't worth the money. And then he'd pried open her heart
and her mind and given her excellent advice.

He'd even listened patiently when Carrie insisted John was
actually the one who needed therapy. *John is the one who isn't
grieving. He's the one who is in denial. He cried the first day and*

then never again! It chilled her to think of how easily he coped. Cleaning the house, detailing the car. Going out to get a haircut right after it happened. Researching alarm systems. But when she questioned him, probing the corners of his psyche before they fell asleep each night, asking him if he wasn't *sad*, she'd felt his flesh cushioning the word, absorbing it, the minute it came out of her mouth.

"Of course I miss him," he said, as if that had been what she asked. Even when she'd caught him at the Y, he didn't sound quite right. He couldn't say the word *sad*; *miss* was so much easier. John's parents had dozens of smiling family photographs clustered atop the piano, scattered on tables, lining the hallways. Everything about the Morgans telegraphed *happy*. Carrie had once told her friends the most negative thing anyone could find in that house was a needlepoint pillow with the words "I'd rather be playing lacrosse." Even in her darkest moments, when she'd been sure the whole family was talking about her behind her back, the worst she could imagine was that they simply felt more sorry for their son, who'd not only lost his baby, but also had to buttress his wife.

John had thought Carrie was going off the deep end, Carrie had believed she was having a normal reaction, and Dr. Kenney had seemed to think they both were behaving fine.

"There's no right or wrong way to grieve," he'd said.

"If there's no wrong way to grieve, then why did John suggest I come here?"

"Well," Dr. Kenney had replied, "it's not about grieving; it's about living. John wants you to start living again."

"You mean John wants to start having hot sex again."

Dr. Kenney had blushed, and she'd almost apologized.

But Carrie had been prone to crying fits that summer and fall, even after she started leaving the house. She still didn't want to talk to the legions of people who knew everything, who'd memorized the media details of her personal business. *There's the woman whose son was kidnapped. There's the woman who couldn't protect her own kid.*

There's the woman who didn't even see the kid taken. That's her. There's something fishy about her.

And, of course, there *was* something fishy. She was the only witness. There was scant physical evidence. Dozens of overlapping, smudged, mostly useless partial fingerprints on that rear car door—Ben's, John's, Carrie's, their babysitters'—along with strangers'. The window washer from the stoplight outside Philadelphia who'd leaned in close to John's window, resting his palms on the roof and the door; the dreadlocked college kid who'd loaded Carrie's groceries at Whole Foods; the older man who'd carried a table for her across the IKEA parking lot. They'd been found, fingerprinted, ruled out.

Carrie had been surprised by John's recall of the window washer, his description of his teeth as "yellow and crowded, a double row almost, like shark's teeth." Had John ever looked at Carrie or Ben that carefully? If Ben had been taken from John's car, would *he* have been able to recount what clothes his son had on?

And then, worse than almost everything, were the looks she'd gotten from Detective Nolan when the lab report came back with all the partial prints. He'd waved it in the air as if it were some kind of bad report card and sighed. "Mrs. Morgan, don't you ever wash your car?" She'd looked at the bulging buttons at the front of his shirt and wanted to scream, *Detective Nolan, don't you ever eat a salad?*

And John, dropping his head, not bearing to meet her eyes, knowing he was winning the car-washing battle—he was always on her about how dirty that car was!—but losing the loving-his-wife war. *They* should have washed it more often, not her. John should have taken the car on a Saturday, washed it himself, done it as a loving favor to his wife. Then they might have a fresh, clean fingerprint!

That same incredulous look on Nolan's face was replicated occasionally by strangers, who glanced at the name on Carrie's credit card and searched her face. If they looked at her carefully and watched the way she zipped shut her wallet and walked to her car, would that solve the mystery? Would they see something in her body language that solved the whole puzzle? If she listened to everybody whose child had *not* been stolen, well, they all had spidey sense, got a feeling, saw a look, thought they could figure it out. *It must have been someone the child knew who grabbed him! Or else why hadn't he cried? Why hadn't anyone seen? And how long does it take for a grown woman to find a freaking quarter? And why hadn't she locked her door anyway?*

Now, Carrie was standing in the kitchen entry, listening to John's car screech into the driveway, door slamming, feet running, trying to use his key and realizing the front door wasn't locked, just like the car. Knowing she hadn't listened to his repeated warnings. Carrie tensed inside, waiting for him to yell at her for that too. Everybody said the same things to her: She needed to lock the doors to keep people out but open her heart to talk to them, to help them, to let them in. But how on earth would she know the difference between who to keep out and who to let in?

Inside, John's face was paler than usual, a trickle of sweat sliding down one of his dark sideburns. He put the bag from the farmers' market on the coffee table.

"You stopped for food?" she said incredulously.

"I went out earlier," he said. "Put it in the office fridge."

She stood in the entryway of the kitchen. "He's in here," she said, as if he couldn't see that.

He stepped in. "Oh my God." His voice cracked. "Benny boy," he said softly.

"Daddy, Daddy!"

Ben ran to him, wrapping his arms around his father's khaki pants, burying his face between his knees. *Is he smelling us too?* Carrie wondered. *Inhaling the memory of metal, the steam iron hovering over the fabric?* John closed his eyes for just a moment, as if his lonely knees had missed his son, then bent over and picked him up.

Ben had a face full of John's features—small nose, dimpled chin. But his coloring was lighter, more like Carrie's, as if someone had mixed in sunlight. The best of both families, Carrie's mother said once to John's mother, and John's mother had agreed. Carrie couldn't always trace the good in her own family tree, but Ben had it. He had the sweetness, the light, that she remembered from her own early youth.

"You see what I mean," Carrie said.

John held him aloft, smiling, then tossed him, caught him, wild giggles in the air. He was both loving him and testing his weight.

He glanced at his wife but didn't say anything. Didn't want to tell her the truth: that he didn't remember, that some of the details of his son had slipped away, that he had changed the wallpaper on his phone to a picture of Ben just to help him stop that erosion but that it seemed impossible. John carried Ben past the small island, past the pantry door with the vintage *Eat* sign on it.

Carrie eyed the half-open pantry door. There, on the molding, the pencil lines that were fading and a little smudged, the evidence even John couldn't bear to paint over, to erase. They both knew they would own the molding of that door forever, with the marks of their son's height.

"Let's measure him," she said.

"Me big!" Ben said.

"Yes, you are, buddy. You're big. Come on, Carrie. He's a little bigger; he's just—"

"No. Take him upstairs, get the scale. Maybe we should call the pediatrician? Find out what he weighed—"

"None of that matters, Carrie," John said. "Let's call the police, and let's...just love our son, okay?"

John's eyes met Carrie's over the top of their son's head, and she nodded.

But when she nestled Ben back in her arms, she bounced him, trying to remember how heavy he was before. She thought of every time she'd strained to pick him up, balancing a shopping bag on the other hip, thinking he was too big to carry anymore.

Like so many things, she wanted to take it all back.

The night before Ben came back, John and Carrie had stopped at Trader Joe's to get milk and eggs, but Carrie had waited in the car. John had started buying most of their groceries, had gotten in the habit of it during the months when Carrie refused to leave the house. At first, she had thought he was being helpful, but then it had started to grate. She had asked him point-blank: *Don't you trust me to do anything? Do you think I'll lose the fucking lettuce too?* He'd bitten his tongue and told her not to be silly, that he didn't care who bought what. But the truth was that John liked to choose the spring mix with the big set of tongs, to squeeze the cucumbers, to see the eye of the fish. If they wanted half a tray of lasagna, he seemed to glimpse something in the plastic containers that Carrie didn't—as if the way the cheese was nestled in between the meat and noodles and the pattern of the herbs peeking through meant something, mattered. *It's noodles*, she'd say, shaking her head as he compared one package to another. *Not a Rorschach test.*

Sometimes she went inside with him, to the farmers' market or Trader Joe's or even 7-Eleven, and sometimes she tired of his specificity. On that particular night, she'd let him shop alone. She'd squinted through the windshield. She'd never noticed it before, but from the angled parking spot, through the line of squat trees that paralleled the sidewalk, she could see down the road, the corner of the Starbucks sign.

How long had it been? When she tried, she could still conjure the particular concert of tastes on her tongue, the sweetness, but always the bite of the acid. She closed her eyes and thought of it, felt the pull of memory and hunger.

A careful, perfectionist woman doesn't allow herself many indulgences. At least, not many they would confess to. Carrie's indulgences were occasional messiness, occasional laziness, but always, always caffeine. For her, it had started long before the current coffee craze had taken hold, when she struggled to stay awake in high school. Some days she went straight from school to her job at the Gap, then stayed up till two a.m. doing homework. She'd gotten in the habit of not only drinking coffee with her mother in the mornings before school, but also taking whatever was left over in the pot as an iced coffee for the afternoon. Add in a Coke at lunch and she was pretty much buzzed all day, nearly every day. Going to college and studying all night, then becoming a parent only exacerbated her need.

Ben had been a terrible sleeper in the beginning, always hungry, often restless. They'd tried four different kinds of pacifiers and two types of baby swings before he finally learned to settle. Back in the days before he started walking, when he was still relatively happy being in a stroller, she'd taken him anywhere there were Starbucks stores. She was comforted by the speed and familiarity of her favorite brand. She liked the little scones that fit so well into Ben's hand. She took pride in her complicated drink order, the tangle of flavor and size and embellishment rolling off her tongue proudly, as if she were reciting a long, complicated poem for an appreciative audience. She enjoyed the challenge of plucking a single balsa wood stirrer from a thick gaggle of them. She liked knowing exactly where the napkins were.

The baristas stopped writing her name on her cup—they knew her. Her order was her own, like a signature or hairstyle, quirky and telling, a little sweet, a hint of salt, complicated. She liked to think she was the only one who ordered it, but once, standing in line, she heard another woman, old enough to be her mother at least, ask for her coffee with *one pump of chocolate, one pump of caramel, sprinkle of salt, no whipped cream,* and she felt her cheeks burning. Was the woman a regular? Had she overheard Carrie ordering this before, standing daily in this same long line, and just thought to herself, *Gosh, that sounds good. I'll try that too?* And then, just as quickly, she felt a long finger of shame pointing, burning. Why couldn't she be more generous? She had invented the drink, yes, but it didn't belong to her, and even if it did, why couldn't she share it? She considered changing her order, tinkering, trying something new, and then tried to put the incident out of her mind. After all, if she baked a pie from scratch, without a recipe, wouldn't she be glad if someone else liked the way it tasted?

Her response to this, the jealousy topped with shame, bothered her at the periphery for weeks before the realization began to creep in, slowly, that her daily ritual was all too important to her. She had no job and no direction—and happened to be blessed with a happy, healthy child who didn't need a whole lot from her. Other people, yes: his father's roughhousing and sporty attention, definitely. But what did Ben want from her exactly? So little, it seemed. The world made him happy, no matter whether she was in it.

And then, each afternoon, there it was: her cup held aloft, her name in the air—they had become a kind of clarion call. She was just beginning to understand that something was wrong about this, that something had to change. She'd wanted to be a stay-at-home mom who shared a snack with her son every day. But it was less about her son and more about the snack. She needed it, needed it all too much. The sermon at church that Sunday was about addiction, and that sealed it: she needed to change.

Did she need to go back to work? That was the first thing she considered. She hadn't told John, but right before they'd lost Ben, she'd sent a few emails to friends in PR and asked about freelance opportunities. She'd asked at the church about the price of day care there and was surprised by how affordable it was. The delicate filaments of her low-level ambition, her love of work, were just beginning to tingle in her again, and then, that final trip for her afternoon pick-me-up. The parking space just outside—*So lucky! How seldom that happened!*—followed by her luck turning on a lack of dime, quarter, nickel.

That awful night, after the search party had quit around midnight and Carrie and John had gone home, she'd taken out her Starbucks card and stomped it under the heel of her Converse, pounding it until it stretched and nearly cracked, like a sheet of dry, tensile dough. She'd vowed that night never to go back there again. If she hadn't gone there in the first place, if she hadn't stopped every day, if she had just brought a sippy cup and animal crackers and a bottle of water to the Y like everyone else, she would still have her son. She blamed the coffee. She blamed the hunger. She blamed herself. Of course she did.

Carrie opened the car door and stepped forward to get a better look at the storefront. Just one more look. She had no intention of going in. She'd made her promise; she'd made her deal with God. She would give it up, all of it. But when would God do his part? Her bargain seemed impossible, silly, remote. She stood outside and watched the people streaming out of the door with their matte white cups paired with deckled brown sleeves. Laughing, happier leaving than when they entered. A part of her wanted to be one of them again but knew she never could be. She wanted more.

She wanted a sign, she thought suddenly. *Give me a sign that I have been heard.* But the logo through the trees, mounted on wood—that couldn't be her sign anymore. Could it?

A horn tapped behind her. She startled, then turned. John's face behind the windshield of their car, filled with love and concern. How long had he sat there, still clutching the small Trader Joe's tote, watching her? His eyes stayed on her as she walked back to the car, and it struck her how often he managed to spot her, to find her, even in a crowd. He could follow her at a distance and always know where she was. She knew it was wrong—they both did—but it was an intoxicating dance, taking a terrible risk and knowing he was in the background, ready to save her, prove that he was strong. He looked so handsome inside that car, watching her walk.

Nothing had changed. And the next day, everything did.

The night of Ben's reappearance, Detective Nolan arrived at the house in minutes, as if he'd been hovering around the corner. Forrester came later, but not by much. John greeted each of them at the door, but Carrie sat in the kitchen with Ben. Her jaw was set firmly as she introduced Ben to each of them, watching these grown men crouch down and hold out one hand for a high five while guarding their holsters with the other. Now *they are here,* she thought. Now *they rush over?*

The Lower Merion police had certainly not rushed the day Ben had been taken. It was summer, vacation time, and there were a lot of empty houses and a rash of break-ins. That was what they had told her when they had finally arrived. *Stretched too thin.* They were being stretched when Carrie had stood in the street by her car, screaming for help, enlisting strangers, people coming out of Starbucks to search for him in every direction, *a blond boy in a blue nubby shirt with one blue sneaker and two yellow socks.* The sentence she kept saying and others kept repeating, over and over, stumbling over the word *nubby,* transposing the *one* and the *two,* like a whisper down the lane. Someone else calling 911, because she couldn't believe that it was happening, that they wouldn't find him, that he hadn't climbed down on his own and was hiding in the back of the car or near the toy store, which he always wanted to visit. A prank—it had to be a prank! Then the terrible length of time they waited after the call, before the police came—*twenty fucking minutes*, someone had said with disgust. Strangers giving her tissues, asking her over and over, *Who else can we call for you?* The words, the numbers, not forming in her mouth. The cold fear of going back into her purse to retrieve her phone. Her oversize, prosaic black purse, mother's salvation, mother's curse. She'd thrown it out a week later, stuffed it into a blue Dumpster in the back of a restaurant, still full of wadded tissue and brown Starbucks napkins and pennies, but no quarters.

Detectives Nolan and Forrester, both in her kitchen, were people again, not just phone numbers entered into her favorites. Lingering there, not called anymore. At first, yes, when there was hope. When she'd remember a scrap of something, like that time they were at Target and a male clerk had stayed too long near her son. Back when they all thought Ben could be saved and the crime could be solved. As time went on, the detectives believed only in the solving, not the saving. And then, after a year, they moved on. They believed he was dead. And now that Ben had returned, Carrie was beginning to think they were right.

Nolan looked gruff, with his porcupine hair and perpetual five o'clock shadow, but he had kindness in him too. At least, he had been kind at the beginning. Patient, even. But he'd grown rough edges. Carrie answered his clipped questions, knowing he wouldn't ask the right ones. More technicians arrived to sweep for new fingerprints in and around their house—doors, windows, crib—hoping to match them to one of the old unidentified partials from the car.

"So no forced entry," Nolan said.

"Doesn't look like it," Forrester replied, then turned to Carrie. "Did you lock the doors when you left?"

Carrie glanced at John, and he lowered his eyes. Aha. John must have told them she wasn't a door locker. As if she'd been asking for it, tempting fate. A woman who crossed herself every night before bed but didn't lock the doors of her house or her car.

"I don't remember if I locked them," she said defiantly.

"You don't remember?" Nolan's eyes widened.

"No."

"Were all the windows closed?"

"Yes."

"You're sure? Because—"

"Yes," she said.

Ben climbed down from his chair and went into the living room. Carrie watched him walk from the kitchen doorway, watched as he cocked his head toward the men dusting the window ledges, curious about their toolboxes and gloves and tools. Carrie smiled. It reminded her of how he used to love hammers and shovels and backhoes. She used to stop the car whenever she passed a construction site so he could look at real tools, not just play with plastic ones.

"How can you be sure about the windows if you're not sure about the door?" Nolan said as he scratched his chin with the end of a pen.

Carrie closed her eyes and took a deep breath. Why weren't they asking John any questions? Couldn't it just as easily have been him who found Ben, if she'd stopped for groceries before coming home? Why did she have to be the one to *both lose him and find him*?

"Mrs. Morgan?" Detective Nolan asked, bringing her back.

They'd known each other so long, it was ridiculous to keep using last names. But they did. The formality was important, John said. To keep them working, to never turn it into friendship.

"Yes, Detective?"

"Where exactly were you this afternoon?"

"At church."

"Doing what?"

She bit her lip to keep from saying: *Praying for your sins of gluttony*. "Putting clothes in boxes for the ann—"

"Did you go straight there? Make any…stops?"

She sighed. He didn't really want to know what she was doing, did he? Just wanted her GPS coordinates.

"No."

"You're sure? No gas, dry cleaning, milk?"

She winced at the way he said *milk*. As if accusing her of stopping and getting it for her son, of knowing. He saw her wince, took note.

"No," she said more firmly, angrily. "Why don't you just embed a chip under my skin?"

"Honey!"

"So you already had the milk," he said.

"We always have milk," she said. She felt her teeth gritting, her jaw locking up.

Detective Forrester stepped closer to his partner. Forrester was younger, leaner, and over the months, they'd watched him grow into his job—becoming more confident, more forthcoming, less remote. He'd been almost silent in the beginning, a rookie, still learning what to say. Back then, they'd actually liked him less, trusted him less. Now they knew better. He was the good one. Nolan was the bad one. John had said on more than one occasion that under other circumstances—if they'd been neighbors or coached a team together—he and Forrester could have been friends.

"Anyone know you were going? Know your plans?" Forrester asked.

"Well, yes, sure. The other ladies I volunteer with. And John, of course."

"I need their names and contact info."

"I have it," John said quickly, looking down at his phone.

"You don't know everyone there," Carrie said.

"I meant the church. I have that number."

Nolan breathed in sharply. Like a lot of portly men, it sounded like it hurt, like he needed more air and had to force it in.

"Also, we need to have Ben undergo a forensic examination. You'll need to bring him in."

"What do you mean?"

"Babe," John interjected, "I think you know what they mean."

"No," she whispered.

"I know it's upsetting, Mrs. Morgan," Forrester said gently, "but if there's DNA, hair, any evidence, we need to collect it. And we have to do it before he takes a bath or goes to the, uh, bathroom."

John nodded vigorously. He should have thought of that, of course. Of course. He thought of those precious moments while he let Carrie be alone with Ben, when he kept the secret. His face flushed with guilt. Had he knocked anything off his son's clothes by picking him up? And what about Carrie—had she wiped down his face, his hands, after she'd fed him that snack, sending evidence into the garbage? Why had he listened to her and not called right away? He looked at his wife. Her eyes met his, then darted away.

John didn't need to say anything to Carrie; she already chided herself for how badly she'd wanted to bathe Ben. She hadn't, but still, she'd come so close! Again, always, the wrong instinct. When had she become so careless, so unlike other people?

"Are you sure it can't wait till tomorrow? Can't we just have tonight and then—"

Nolan shook his head. "Don't you want to collect all the evidence? Don't you want to find this bastard?"

"Of course we do," John said quickly.

"Then why would you wait?"

John's breath caught in his throat. This was the second time Carrie had wanted to wait! What would Nolan and Forrester think if they knew that?

"I just…um…" Carrie struggled for words, and John, who sometimes felt that he had spent the entire last year defending his wife to his family and their friends, suddenly lost his ability to do so.

"Unless you're trying to…hide something?"

"No!"

"Well, I can't think of a single other reason why you would wait till tomorrow."

"Detective, no, no. She—" John stepped in but faltered, his argument unraveling inside his own mouth. She had acted the same way with him earlier—delaying, delaying. Why? Why did she need more time? For what?

"Well, Forrester will drive you down there since you're both obviously distraught."

He spat out the word, as if it were against the law to be upset.

"I can drive," John said. He walked the detectives to the door, took his keys from the peg.

"I'll follow you, John," Detective Forrester said.

"Okay," John said, glancing back at Carrie, who hadn't moved. She stood stick-straight between the kitchen doorway and the closet. Ben was on the couch, kicking his feet as he watched the men packing up their tools. Carrie was fixed on her son, but her eyes had a vacant look, as if she'd come into the room and suddenly, frighteningly, forgotten what she came there for.

"Honey?" John said softly.

"He needs a coat," she said. "Or a blanket."

"Give us a minute," John said to Forrester.

Forrester nodded and followed Nolan out the door. Carrie stood near the hallway, watched them all, not moving toward closet or door.

John said, "Babe, it's not that cold yet—"

"Are they gone?"

"Yes, of course they've—" He stopped midsentence. What was wrong with her? "Do you need me to get a blanket?"

"No." She opened the linen closet door, pulled out a quilted, zippered container on the floor. The containers that held extra towels and sheets. She unzipped the top, dug around, pulled out two diapers. John walked over to her and looked inside. Extra-large diapers, washcloths, towels with hoods. Baby shampoo.

John's brow furrowed. How had he missed them, all the times he'd swept through the house? Trying to take away all the things that made her cry. That made her crazy, absolutely wild, with grief. Hadn't he already looked in there? Had she been moving things around?

Carrie found her new purse in the kitchen, the smaller brown one she'd bought after the kidnapping, and shoved the diapers inside. They barely fit.

John glanced nervously out the window at the detectives. They stood talking at the end of the driveway, Forrester gesturing with his hands and Nolan looking down, scraping the sidewalk with one shoe, as if he'd stepped in something he wanted gone.

John looked back at his wife, the familiar set to her jaw that often preceded their fights as she verbally wrestled him to get her own way. He knew, as Carrie did, that something as simple as supplies in the closet could be construed as nothing or as something—like the milk. He was seized with a sudden regret. Should he have asked Libby to follow Carrie home? Was it not enough for Libby to check in with him to tell him when Carrie left—and his neighbor Ellen to tell him when she arrived home? It had worried him, in the beginning, that whoever took Ben had really been after Carrie, that Ben had been a pawn of some kind. His wife was beautiful, in her own simple, straightforward way. He'd seen the way men looked at her; ever since college, he'd worried that someone would follow her home, take her. And yes, maybe John tagging after her in the dark on her girls' nights out—to make sure she was safe—maybe that seemed possessive to some people. But the times Carrie had seen him, caught him? They'd had passionate, almost desperate sex immediately afterward, Carrie draping herself over him, insistent, forceful in a way that surprised them both. She liked being watched.

"Carrie, I—"

"What, John? Are you surprised to find something your search and seizure missions didn't unearth?"

"You know it's not that."

"There is no crime in a mother holding on to mementos," she said. "None." The word *milk* burned in her mind, the way Detective Nolan had spat it out. Like milk was evidence, a weapon!

John swallowed what he wanted to say. These weren't

mementos—they were groceries. It was like holding on to old wrapping paper because someone loved gifts!

Carrie went to the couch, leaned over, picked up Ben, and hoisted him onto her hip, where he still fit.

"We need to be together on this," she said.

"Of course," he said automatically. But he wasn't sure he ever could be. She had always been different from him in the way that women are different from men—or so he'd thought. She was full of contradictions. She needed to talk more than he did but shushed him when a great song came on the radio. She loved movies but could only watch them once. She cleaned her house but was lazy about her car. Her closets were organized by color, but she couldn't be bothered to lock her doors. But now, remembering how she looked, standing by the closet, her face like a painting of a person, he found himself feeling like an art patron staring at the colors, squinting at the expression, the blurred background, because he didn't fully understand its meaning.

As Carrie walked, Ben's legs bounced against her side, in the exact same place, just as she remembered. No longer, no heavier. They would measure and weigh him, surely, at the hospital. *Then* it would all become clear, not only to John, but also to the police.

Outside, a pair of bees dive-bombed her as she stepped off the front stoop, and she waved them away with one hand.

She opened the rear car door, then hesitated. When was the last time she'd opened that door? How long had it been? She stood frozen, the stale air from the car, wet leaves, oil. It suddenly smelled different from the front seat.

She looked back at John, who was battling the same bees, bobbing and weaving with his head and arm.

"There must be a hive somewhere. Happened yesterday too."

She nodded. It was late for bees, but it had been so warm, so lush. Only recently had the sun finally been muted and the clouds filled with gray, moving closer to Carrie's true mood. The metallic tang in the air was an anodyne for her loneliness; today had been the first day in a long time she felt aligned with the universe. Not sunny. Not rainy. Just the dark, endless in-between.

"John, will you…put him in the car seat?"

"Um, okay," he said.

Even after the detailing incident, she'd kept Ben's seat in her car, insisted. Fought John so bitterly over it that spit came flying out of her mouth. He'd said it was downright ghoulish—like keeping a sarcophagus in the backseat. And she'd been furious at his use of that word—when had he ever used it before? *He wasn't killed in his car seat!* she'd screamed. *He loved his car seat!* But winning that battle and having the seat—that didn't mean she could touch it. That didn't mean she trusted herself with this task.

John clipped in his son. Ben smiled at him, as if thanking him. He wasn't a boy of many words, but he had a million different smiles. Raising a child was like communicating with someone who spoke another language. It was all gestures, nuance, vibe. Almost like understanding a woman, John sometimes thought. He ruffled his son's hair, smiled back at him broadly, then got in the front seat.

It wasn't until they were at the bottom of their street, turning left onto Sugarland Road, that he realized, maybe, why Carrie had asked him to do it. Did she recognize that he was better at it? That she was simply too lackadaisical, too trusting? You would think that a latchkey kid would know the value of safety! But no, Carrie's childhood had made her tough, invincible. There was a shell to Carrie that other women didn't have, and she had relied on it too much. She had believed nothing would happen, and then it had. But this, oh, this signaled a change, he thought. That perhaps she had finally put him in charge of safety.

"You didn't have to adjust the straps," she whispered.

"What?"

"On the car seat. He's not taller," she said.

John swallowed, said nothing.

At the second intersection, idling at the long stoplight, a man approached the line of cars, selling flowers. John tapped the lock on their doors, and Carrie jumped.

"Better safe than sorry," he said. "That's why—"

She sighed. "John, I know how you feel about locking the doors. But…lightning doesn't strike twice."

"You know that reasoning doesn't wash with me, Carrie. I know too many guys who've broken both legs on the lacrosse field."

Carrie looked out the window. She was tired of arguing about this. It was the same way she had felt when her mother left her to go work, always saying the same words: *Lock up lock up lock up.* But locking up hadn't kept her father from leaving. Locking up hadn't kept their money safe from his gambling debts. Locking up hadn't kept out anything that had hurt her mother.

"But, John," she said softly but firmly, "you also have to know, to realize…if I had locked the house, Ben might not have been brought back."

John bit the inside of his lip. So she hadn't locked the door when she went to church, despite all his warnings. She hadn't forgotten *at all*, which meant she'd lied to the detectives! Was this the first time she'd done that? Or merely the most recent? He continued driving and didn't look over at Carrie, even though he felt her eyes on him, begging for him to engage. But he couldn't. He just couldn't. Especially with Ben in the backseat.

In front of him, the sky was gray and white, not a trace of blue. It had been like this for days, threatening rain, warning them that autumn was on its way.

It took every ounce of willpower John possessed not to say the words bursting through his pores: *If you had locked your car while you fed that goddamned meter, Ben never would have been taken in the first fucking place.*

John didn't forget things like locking doors. Just as he would never forget a million other details, like the day Ben was kidnapped. A woman he didn't know had called him on Carrie's phone and told him there had been an incident outside the Starbucks in Ardmore, and his wife needed him right away.

He'd been exiting a men's room in a sports bar along City Line Avenue, about to join a group of clients and another salesperson for lunch. He'd answered right away when he'd seen it was Carrie calling, but the call itself gave him serious pause.

"I'm sorry," he said, holding one hand over his ear to drown out the din of the ESPN announcer coupled with music, as if competing for attention. "Who are you exactly?"

"I'm a passerby," she said.

"Passerby?"

"Yes."

He frowned. It sounded like a hoax. Like something his mother would fall for on Facebook, although she wasn't asking for money or his credit card number. She was asking for him.

"Did you say 'accident' or 'incident'?"

"I don't know, but you need to—"

"Can I speak to my wife, please?"

"She's with the police now."

"The police?"

"You really need to get here," she said. "She's really upset, and—"

He cut her off by saying okay and ended the call. He left without truly explaining—because who could explain what had just happened, a random call from a stranger—and got into his car, thinking there must be a car accident and an injury. A reason Carrie couldn't call herself. He pictured a stretcher, a spent air bag, flashing lights.

When he arrived not even a half hour later, there was a circle of crime tape around his wife's car, three police cars blocking the intersection, and a crowd of at least twenty people gathered down the block, listening to a woman holding a sheaf of paper in her hands.

He put on his flashers and stepped outside. A uniformed police officer approached him, his hand raised.

"You can't park here," he said.

From behind him, a young man in a suit approached, tapped him on the shoulder.

"Excuse me. Are you Mr. Morgan? I'm Detective Forrester."

"Yes. Where's my wife?" John said, his voice rising, his neck craning. He searched the crowd for a flash of Carrie's shiny hair.

"She's in the squad car. I'll take you to her."

"Squad car? God, what's happened?"

"We're trying to sort that out."

"I mean…generally."

"Generally?"

"Has there been a car accident?"

Detective Forrester blinked, swallowed. He had been on the force for just a few years, had never handled anything but insurance fraud, a house fire, a stabbing between neighbors near the city. And here was the husband, a young guy who looked like they could have gone to school together, played soccer, who depended on him to make things right. And his boss, Nolan, standing like a wall behind him, just waiting to say it: *Find out where the hell the father was, to make sure his alibi was air-fucking-tight, and that these two's marriage was A-fucking-OK.* Because that was the way things went with these kinds of cases.

"John!" Carrie cried, emerging from the back of the squad car. "They've taken him! He's gone!"

And the looks the three men silently passed around spoke volumes. *Who's taken him? Gone where?* And *Whoa, wait a minute. She said "they."*

Later that night, after John had gathered all of Ben's photos for posters and called their families and helped search the woods below the Y and along the train tracks, as they had struggled to fall asleep despite being exhausted, John had asked Carrie what she'd meant when she'd said "they." Had she seen a group of people nearby? A gang of teenagers maybe?

"Maybe. I don't remember."

"Otherwise, why did you say that, Carrie?"

"I don't know. I don't remember what I was thinking, but I didn't see anybody. I guess I just…assumed. I mean, how could one person do that so quickly? It doesn't…make sense."

He had waited a long time before he'd nodded, agreed. There was something that clearly did not add up.

At the hospital, the female nurse who dealt with trauma victims wore bright, printed teddy bear scrubs. She picked up a large sterilized kit from the table and smiled at Ben. An acrylic, pastel plaid curtain trembled on a metal rod, separating them from someone on the other side. Carrie didn't want to see through the opening, but she could. She did. A girl. Sixteen or seventeen, alone, red-eyed, biting her nails, feet in stirrups. Carrie looked away, didn't want to think about sex and teenagers. *That girl should be doing her homework,* she thought. Should have a test to worry about, some innocent concern, not this.

They weren't there long. No crying, no fuss. Ben had always been good with doctors and nurses, fine with getting his temperature taken, getting shots. He got that from John's family, Carrie supposed, the ability to be both easygoing and stoic. Carrie held his hand but turned away, didn't watch. She stared at an aqua wall, wondering how they'd chosen that particular shade. She heard the sounds of plastic packaging being opened, metal tools sliding on a tray, the snap of a rubber glove tempered by its powdery interior. But no crying from Ben, who just listened to his father telling him he was a big boy and he was doing great, buddy, way to go.

An hour later, they were back in the car, driving to Ben's favorite place for dinner, a diner that had fifty flavors of milkshakes.

Carrie hadn't been there in over a year, partly because it was a place you only went with a child and partly because she hadn't allowed herself the pleasure of a milkshake, of a flavor, in a long time.

"John," Carrie said, "should we maybe go somewhere else?"

"What? Why? He'll love it."

"But...we went there every Thursday. They'll remember him. There will be...hoopla."

"Hoopla?"

She swallowed. It was a strange, old-fashioned word. Her grandmother's kind of word. She had been full of words other people didn't use anymore. *Hoopla. Rapscallion. Balderdash.* At her funeral, everyone had mentioned this singular tic kindly, with love.

"They'll ask questions. It will turn into... It could be too much."

"I guess you're right."

Why qualify it? she wanted to scream. Why couldn't she just be plain right, obviously right?

"They have another one out by the mall, don't they? We could go there instead."

She nodded. *Yes. Let's go where no one knows us, where we look vaguely familiar, but no one realizes who we are until the next day.* John eased the car onto a back road that cut across the township, heading the back way to the mall, hiding, slinking, she thought. Like a criminal. Would everyone make something of that too?

When Ben was a baby, they'd always taken turns putting him to bed. It was something a man could do at the end of a mother's long day: one last bottle, a fresh person attending, still patient, willing to rock, to sing, and to shush. But the truth was Ben always wanted John to do it. From the moment he could reach out his arms, form his words, if John was home, Ben wanted him, not Carrie. Oh, he was content with her during the day. He loved his mother; Carrie knew he did. She told herself that, over and over—*he loves me, he loves me, he loves me*—singing it like a lullaby, those nights when she rocked him and his eyes kept looking over her shoulder, searching for his father.

They put Ben to bed together, neither willing to miss out. John sat on the alphabet rug next to the green chair, holding his son's hand while Carrie rocked him. Later she would wish she could have a portrait painted of that moment, that synchronicity, her husband supplicant at her feet. She'd kept one of Ben's pale pacifiers on the changing table, but he didn't need it anymore; the world had weaned him of it.

Ben's eyes fluttered closed, and Carrie smiled, thinking of his happy dreams, the day he could relive when he fell asleep. She thought of Ben eating a cheeseburger, sipping a milkshake. His fat fingers dipping a french fry in ketchup. Ben standing in the leather booth at dinner, bouncing with happiness, and then, when John said something to Carrie, his hands on either side of John's face, turning his head toward him. They'd both laughed, but then she felt a tear forming. She'd forgotten, *forgotten entirely*, that he used to do that—not only reach for John, but also take him away, own him. How was that possible, after all her cataloging, that she'd forgotten this thing he did nearly every single day?

They stood over his crib a long time that night, watching his chest rise and fall beneath his fleece pajamas. Finally, John squeezed her hand and pulled her out of the room.

"Not yet," she said.

"Carrie," he said. "The windows and doors are locked. A car is patrolling the street, just in case."

She nodded; she knew. Forrester had taken every precaution. That was all it took for John to feel safe—these systems in place. She allowed John to guide her back to their room, two doors down. Ben's bedroom, guest room, master suite. In bed, he held her, knew better than to ask or to push for more, knew sex could ruin the purity of the moment, so he kept his pelvis tilted away from her. She knew he did this and appreciated it.

"Do you remember the day we brought him home?" she asked.

"Of course," he said, then immediately started gathering up details, in case she asked. How long it had taken the valet to bring the car while Carrie sat in the wheelchair, shivering. How he'd wished he'd brought her a sweater.

Carrie recounted how much trouble they'd had installing that first car seat. They'd both thought it would be simpler.

"Remember how I joked about how on earth you could possibly assemble our baby's tricycle on Christmas Eve if you couldn't put a car seat in a car?"

He smiled back at her. Yes, that he remembered. He also remembered how Carrie had ridden in the back because she was so disturbed by the idea of the baby facing backward, when they couldn't see him. They knew other moms who'd had mirrors installed to fix this problem and thought they were overreacting, nervous.

"I drove you two home like a chauffeur."

"Yes."

"And then you looked in the mirror and said, 'John, I just realized the baby could have been riding backward and upside down for nine months in my uterus too!'"

They both laughed, remembering this. For weeks, Carrie had fretted over Ben's head bending sideways in the enormous seat. *Why don't they make smaller seats?* she would ask over and over again, until they both saw, a month later, how quickly babies grew. How soon they filled the space provided. How much they outgrew, almost immediately. The difference between two years old and three years old? *Enormous*, she thought. It had to be enormous.

They talked for a couple of hours, or Carrie did. She talked and John listened, commenting here and there. He was used to this, her need to talk. He knew her old boyfriend had loved to talk; she'd mentioned this once with a kind of light in her eyes, as if she'd loved him, and John tried to do the best he could. To talk as much as he knew how.

She had been the most talkative in college, hopped up on coffee before exams, unable to wind down, and John, who could fall asleep anywhere, anytime, struggling to stay awake to listen to her as she cuddled into his side in his narrow dorm bed. Nothing had changed.

Carrie asked him what he wanted to do tomorrow, if he was taking the day off, and what would Ben want to do, what would Ben have missed most, and when John didn't respond, she knew he'd fallen asleep. She glanced at the clock—eleven thirty. She lay on her back for a long time, eyes too wide for sleep. A faint buzzing from the wall near Ben's room, a sound she always thought was electrical, related to the heating system. She wondered if it was something else.

She slid away from John's arm, got out of bed, took her pillow. She opened the linen closet quietly, grabbed a blanket. It wouldn't be the first time she'd curled up on that alphabet rug, her head on *C* and her feet on *T*. She'd done that whenever Ben had been sick. When she worried the baby monitor wouldn't be enough. That he could choke, gasp for air, and she wouldn't hear it. If she went to him, she could drink in everything, every breath, every time he turned over. The small sound of his wet lips opening to the air, to gobble more life.

She walked toward the opening of the door. Six inches, just as before. Just as she always left it, as if she'd measured it unconsciously with the width of her own hand.

Inside, squinting in the path of the green night-light that wasn't lighting up enough. Dark shapes, getting clearer. Then nothing. A flat plane. An empty crib.

She ran to the light switch, flooding it, no dimmer.

He was not in the crib. He was not in the room.

She screamed a scream she didn't think she was capable of anymore. She believed she'd used up her lung strength, damaged her organs. And then, suddenly, they regenerated.

John's feet in the hallway, Carrie on her knees in the room, too bright, too empty.

His rush to the window, testing the lock. His instincts, not hers.

Him throwing open the window and screaming into the night, "Where are you? Why are you fucking with us? Why?"

Running downstairs, testing all the locks, his fist slamming the kitchen table, jostling the sugar and creamer, as he dialed Nolan's number again.

Carrie curled up on the rug, crying, but not blaming herself for leaving Ben's room. No. She knew it wasn't her fault, that it was all she deserved, all she would be given. Knew it all along. *She'd made the wrong deal. She'd asked for the wrong thing. She'd made another mistake.*

TUESDAY

C arrie usually listened to her gut. She'd feel a kind of electric tingle she knew to pay attention to. When her father had come back to visit her mother that one time, she'd known it was the last. When her dog had been killed by a car, she'd known from the look on the motorist's face. And when she'd met John, she had known. Oh, how she had known. One buzzing brush of his hand against hers. And that was why she'd been so furious when Ben had been taken the first time: How had her radar failed her?

She'd met John at a fund-raiser at State. Her roommate, Chelsea, had pointed out the primary advantage of helping out the athletic association: *proximity to hot athletes*. But Carrie wondered, after dating a self-professed nerd like Ethan, if an athlete would be the right choice.

Carrie and Chelsea were given aprons and put in charge of grilling free hot dogs. They knew they'd be surrounded by boys. On some level, she knew before she even met John that she would. That he would be there.

And there he was, standing in line with a friend. Brushing his long bangs out of his eyes with a flick of his head that she found irresistible. A navy-blue lacrosse T-shirt stretched across his chest. Big hands, holding the white paper plate like it was nothing.

She feigned giving him a veggie dog, and he recoiled, and she laughed.

"I'm a carnivore," he said with a shrug.

"Maybe I'm a vegan," she said.

"Better not breathe too deeply," he said and smiled.

Then he asked, a little sheepishly, if he could have two hot dogs. His voice, burred and a little scratchy, different. So different from the practiced, mannerly, preppy voice she was expecting.

"You can have one now," she said, smiling, putting it on his outstretched plate. "And come back after practice for another."

"But what if you're not here? Or what if you run out? Maybe you better give me two now." The idiosyncratic way he spoke made certain words—like *two*—almost disappear. It made you pay closer attention, Carrie thought, made you listen harder.

"But if I give you two now, you won't come back."

"I will come back for thirds," he said, and when she nestled the second hot dog next to the first, she brushed his hand. It wasn't dry, no tinder of calluses striking hers. It was warm, soft, alive. His eyes were a color between green and brown she'd never seen before. And then they appeared in Ben. A miracle, twice.

They got to know each other quickly. In one night, she found out his voice had been damaged by a tackle that bruised his throat when he was thirteen. It went hoarse and never came back fully, and his teammates had started calling him Frog.

Carrie was more of an enigma to John—pretty but mysterious, downplaying her family and friends, not wanting him to know that she'd lived in a town his family considered the other side of the tracks. The only thing apparent, baldly apparent, was her unique combination of kindness and wit. Usually girls who loved words and irony and nuance were mean. Not Carrie. He was drawn to her empathy, her giving nature, her habits of going to church every Sunday and on long hikes every Friday afternoon. Other girls spent Fridays day drinking, putting on makeup, or choosing clothes for the parties ahead. Carrie always ended her week with a walk in the hills that ringed the campus. That was part of the allure to John—this separateness, this need to be alone.

But it also scared him. She was vulnerable, too trusting, not careful enough.

They became a couple instantly. They graduated, found jobs, settled into cities near each other. He worked at his father's insurance company; she worked in public relations. They commuted, saving, figuring it out, before they bought an affordable new house near Carrie's old hometown, a few towns away from John's family. It wasn't like they'd met and eloped and had an instant baby. But to Carrie, it had felt that immediate. She saw him in line and saw their future unspool in front of her. The difference between him and her other boyfriends, like Ethan, was immediately apparent. John was a man, and he would be a husband and a father. Not a frightened little high school boy who hid in his books and acted brave but wasn't. John was actually brave, brave to a fault. And loyal to a fault. He was different from other guys, and that was why he didn't trust them, why he occasionally followed Carrie—to make sure nothing happened to her.

And then she caught him. One night, walking back from a concert she'd gone to with Chelsea and Justin. There had been a rustling in the bushes, the dark green edges of the path oscillating more than a kicked-up night breeze could hope to move them. She stopped, took a step toward the movement. She heard his breathing, the ragged quality that presaged his raspy voice. The way she knew he was there, thinking of something to say.

"John," she said.

He took one step to the right, revealing himself, a half slice of his features. Everything she wanted to say, meant to say—the words bobbed in her mouth, drowning. She couldn't speak. The sight of his dark hair and eyes in the deep cobalt night. Even his tanned skin and his navy shirt looked of the woods, of the path; he was someone who belonged there, waiting only for her.

She had reached for him—for that was what he was waiting for, after all, evidence of her and her love. The smell of him, the dark wild taste of something that had turned, made her weak in the knees.

"I'll meet you later," she'd called out to her friends, as simply as if she'd seen another path, a better one, and taken it.

Remembering that now, she leaned into John's strong frame as they looked out the living room window, listening to Nolan berating his beat officer on their front walk, his hands slicing into the air for emphasis. *You had one job, one job, and failed! You don't go out for coffee, you don't leave for a sandwich, you don't fiddle on your fucking phone, you watch! When you're on twenty-four-hour watch, you watch, goddamn it!* The man's face, young, with a night's worth of blond beard appearing, was turning ever redder with shame and regret as he murmured something about how he didn't think he'd fallen asleep, but he supposed he might have checked his text messages. Would he lose his job?

Carrie disentangled herself from John, ran to the door, flung it open. "Stop it!"

The men turned to her in unison. Nolan's face, twisted with annoyance at this crazy woman interrupting him, and maybe, just maybe, pissed off because he was caught doing in public what usually happened in private: behaving cruelly toward another cop. Something he didn't want his wife or his children or anyone but another cop to know about him. And the uniformed cop, guilty and grateful at the same time, his chin quivering with the mixture.

"Stop?" Nolan repeated, as if dumbfounded that she'd said it and also, good Lord, that he'd obeyed. A woman trying to tell him how to do his job?

"Is this where the expression 'beat cop' came from? Because you beat up other cops?"

"Carrie!" John cried.

"Leave him alone, okay? It's not his fault," she said.

"Ma'am," the officer said quietly, "I'm afraid it might be my—"

"You don't have to apologize to me. To us. Or to him. You did the best you could. You're...human. You're human, for God's sake."

Nolan's eyes looked over her head, seeking John's, finding them, and then a slight raise of his brow.

70

"Please get a hold of your wife and go back inside, Mr. Morgan," Nolan said with a long exhale.

Carrie turned around. John's face was lined with concern. It was like seeing him older, projected into the future.

"Carrie, honey, you've got to let them work! They have their own ways of doing things, of getting results. They're the experts."

She shook her head, went into the kitchen. John paced in the living room behind her. She poured a glass of water, drank it.

"Their techniques are ridiculous. They're...pointless."

"What do you mean?"

"I knew he wouldn't say," she said quietly.

Her husband's footsteps, the rhythm of his worry, stopped. "I'm sorry. What the hell did you just say?"

"I said I knew. Knew that he would come and be gone again. That Ben would leave."

"Carrie, seriously, how could you possibly—"

He stopped, looked at her like she was another species entirely. The tiny hairs on her neck came alive, danced.

"You don't trust me?" she asked, eyes flashing.

"That's not what I'm saying."

"Isn't it?"

Wasn't that why he had done all the things he'd done over the years—not trusting, always trying to solve the mystery of Carrie?

"I don't understand," he said. "I mean, I've always been confused by everything that's happened, but now, now you say you *knew*?"

She started to tell him, tried to describe it, knew she had to: that Ben wasn't alive, returned by the kidnapper. That he was dead, returned by...God? The universe? The forces that governed them all? She struggled to explain the unexplainable. But how to outline the existence of something in between to a man who sold life insurance, who measured the distance between living and dying, brokered it, knew its dimensions by heart?

"See, this is why I wanted to stretch things out, to not rush things. Because I knew it wouldn't last. I knew because it's what I asked for," she cried. "What I prayed for."

"What?"

"One more day," she sobbed. "I just wanted him back for one more day. To hold him one more time, feed him one more time, bathe him. And that was all I got. I knew it, John," she cried. "I knew it."

She buried her head in her hands, but not before she saw his shoulders soften, his mouth loosen. He pulled her into his arms, forgiving her, erasing whatever terrible thoughts were there. They both felt his shame melting away with her tears.

"Honey, how about if I go call Dr. Kenney?" he whispered in her hair. The word *go* was swallowed by the crack in his voice. What was that like, to lose every fourth or fifth word, to not be understood? Was that all that was going on, that she didn't understand him, in addition to him not understanding her? "To help you," he added, as if reading her mind.

"Not now," she said. "Not today. Haven't I been through enough?"

He put her at arm's length and looked at her. Her dark blue eyes, when filled with tears, looked even darker, more unusual. Her hair, tumbling in shiny waves, still so beautiful even when it was mussed. Of course she had been through enough. Of course she was exhausted by it all. What was more exhausting than a roomful of questions and no answers? He folded her back into his arms. Her secrets would keep. Wasn't that what Dr. Kenney always said after John called and asked how it was going? It would take time, not to worry. Carrie's secrets, Carrie's problems, would keep until she was ready to tell them.

There's no right and wrong way to follow someone. Police do it all the time, but so do lovers. People form caravans, protecting one another. It's not always the bad thing people think it is.

I saw the way other people looked at that boy. They were jealous. You didn't have to be able to see the aura of green over their heads; you could see it in their narrow eyes and straightened lips. Jealous of his skin, smooth and golden, like buttery dough. His eyelashes so long you could see them a block away. And what is more beautiful than a tiny bottom slipping out of a slick red swimsuit? He was innocent, oblivious to it all, but the bigger problem was so was she.

She didn't hold him tight enough. She let him run, let him talk to strangers. She didn't stifle him, and he probably needed that. To be warned, to be put on alert. He was too innocent for his own good, and she let him be innocent, didn't try to toughen him up.

I'd seen this happen every week, sometimes twice, and something had to be done about it. But I didn't know when. And I didn't know who.

I don't know everything, but I try to. I look to the sky, I shut my eyes, and I try really, really hard to know. I wish I could know before, but it seems I'm only capable after.

O n the first anniversary of Ben's kidnapping, they had held another candlelight ceremony on the grounds of the Y. The director of the Y, Elizabeth Matthews, had suggested it and said she could arrange for a poet to give a reading and perhaps a priest to say a prayer. *Everyone here wants to help,* she'd said. *Balloons aren't healthy for the environment, but we could light candles again.* Carrie had been noncommittal until she'd talked to John. Of course, John thought it was a good idea; he thought publicity and people were always a good idea. Better to be outside, spreading the word, than inside, ruminating.

The swim moms were there again, and so were Libby and Anna and a lot of other folks from the congregation who Carrie didn't know. They were friends of John's family and circled around them in a tight knot. John's parents stood next to their son proudly, as if he were getting confirmed. Their chins were always up. Carrie's mother didn't fly in; Carrie had insisted she not come, but she had sent special candleholders for the occasion, as if the idea of her daughter and son-in-law getting burned by wax would be the ultimate salt in the wound.

It was a clear night, and though Elizabeth Matthews had promised the ceremony would be brief, one of the speakers—the poet—had chosen to read a long sonnet that lost focus, meandered. Under other circumstances, beneath the yoke of someone else's grief, Carrie and

John would have shared a look and a giggle over this woman and her tortured, dramatic delivery. But they kept their eyes lowered, focused on the candles. The last person to speak was a young rabbi, who offered a prayer related to the water, to swimming, and Carrie was grateful for its simple symbolism. Later she would recall its prescience and wish she could speak to the rabbi again, to see him at his temple, to know what he knew.

Afterward, after John thanked everyone for coming and then ran off toward a couple of his coworkers, whom he'd spotted in the crowd, Libby came up, put her arm around Carrie, and gripped the knob of her shoulder tightly.

"You'll find him, lovey," she said firmly, calmly.

"Will I?"

"We could do another collection at the church. Maybe it could pay for another billboard or increase the reward."

"Billboards." Carrie sighed. "His face was so large on the highway the first time I saw it, I nearly crashed."

"It *was* attention getting."

"That's for sure. You know, we got the Amber Alert on our cell phones that first night," she said suddenly. "Wouldn't you think they would take the parents off the list? Out of kindness?"

"When all this is over, that's the kind of thing you can fight for. The kind of thing that can be changed."

Carrie shrugged. It was hard to imagine it ever being over. Hard to imagine anything changing.

The crowd thinned out. A gibbous moon rose over the building, above the dark tops of trees. Carrie couldn't remember what the moon had been like that first night without her son. Why couldn't she remember?

John walked back toward her, smiling, with a young woman walking briskly behind him, almost catching up to his long gait. Her hair was bobbed and spiky at the ends, and she wore large black glasses that looked almost like a prop.

"Carrie," John said breathlessly, "this is—"

"Maya Mercer," the woman said, extending her hand.

Carrie shifted the candle to her left hand, shook with her right.

"From *24/7*," John added.

"The TV show?"

"The investigative program," Maya said with a half smile. A business smile.

"Oh," Carrie said.

"Maya's thinking about doing a story on Ben's disappearance, and she wants to interview you!"

"Me?"

"Yes."

"Not both of us?"

"Well, you were there, Mrs. Morgan," Maya said coolly. "Your husband wasn't."

"How do you know that?"

"Carrie!"

"I mean, if you're just thinking about doing a story and not actually doing one, how would you know?"

"You're a witness," Maya continued. "It's on record. Simple as that. We'd try to talk to anyone who was there—you, the detectives, other people on the street that day, at Starbucks, here at the—"

"No."

"No?" Maya Mercer looked genuinely perplexed.

John touched Carrie's arm. "Babe," he started to say.

"Don't 'babe' me!" Carrie said, yanking her arm away.

"Let your wife speak for herself, John," Maya said quietly.

Carrie's eyes met Maya's for a moment. For a second or two, they held, seeking refuge there.

"I'm sure she wants the publicity," Maya said. "I'm sure she has absolutely nothing to hide."

Carrie swallowed hard, lowered her eyes. She knew the detectives were in the parking lot, surveying the crowd. Looking for anything unusual, anything amiss. She knew strangling this woman would be considered slightly amiss.

76

"There's a difference between publicity and scrutiny," Carrie said, gritting her teeth.

Maya blinked at this, considering. "Maybe you need a few days to think about it. Discuss it."

"Just interview my husband. He's more photogenic."

As Carrie walked toward her car—parked a block away, pointed west, toward home—she saw Forrester standing on the sidewalk, staring across two lanes of traffic as if he were watching a movie projected on the other side.

She blew out her candle with an irritated huff. When she swung open the car door, wax sloshed onto her hand, burning her just enough to make her cry out.

The detectives swarming her house, taking it over like they owned it again, reminded Carrie of real estate open houses, of her mother trying to sell their house after her father left. Her childhood home had been more of a cottage, all windows and porch, but the real estate agent had called it a bungalow, trying to make it sound bigger, more exciting. When Carrie had read the ad written for her own house, she'd been surprised by how beautiful and expansive they'd made something small and sunlit and old seem. But "old" was part of the Main Line's charm; everyone wanted to live in a house that looked like it had always been there.

You weren't supposed to be home during the open houses, but Carrie hated studying at the library, so she'd stayed in her room with her dog, Jinx. He lay in a circle of sun, and she lay next to him, playing with his soft ear with one hand while she turned the pages of a textbook with the other. That was all there was: studying, working, and debate practice. There used to be soccer and tennis, but they couldn't afford it anymore: the cleats, the rackets, the lessons. She held on to cheerleading for a while, then stopped. She didn't care. Just thought about books, scholarships, college. No distractions between chapters but petting her dog. Her room was the smallest room, farthest from the bathroom, a room no one had any interest in anyway, with her posters and her mix tapes and the beads hanging in the doorway, beads her mother thought they should take down for the sake of the sale but allowed at the last minute. She stayed there and listened to people taking over downstairs, talking about the wainscoting and the ceiling height and whether the mantelpiece was original as if she wasn't there. She hated the intrusion but made a point of being pleasant and smiling, as her mother had coached her. She knew they had to sell the house, that they needed the money, that she had to do her part. Do her part and not say anything to them about the muddy footprints they'd left on the clean stair runner that she and her mother had scrubbed by hand with a brush, because they hadn't been able to afford to rent the shampooer at the grocery store.

Now, watching these men with their dirty shoes traipse through her and John's house, a house she had nothing to do with except keep clean, brought up those feelings all over again. *Be nice. Keep the peace. Stay on their good side.* She could almost hear her mother coaching her again. She stood at the kitchen island, sipping her tea, trying to stay out of the way. *Oh, what Dr. Kenney would do with this connection!* she thought. How he'd dig gently, picking at the scab of her mother and her childhood. How badly he wanted to know everything about her, as if that would explain. Sometimes Carrie thought he already knew everything and was just waiting for her to spill it all, to cry and to wail. To *caterwaul*, as her grandmother would have said. She'd allowed John to make her an appointment with Dr. Kenney for the following day, and she started to wish she'd indulged him and taken it today, just to get away from these people in her house.

John was talking to the fingerprint technicians with a fervor that made her cringe. Like he was interested in their line of work, of changing jobs. But that was how he was: he was just curious. He'd always been like that—his mother said it had been written all over his report cards. Curiosity. The last defense of someone who wasn't naturally sensitive, who wasn't tuned in. If he hadn't been curious, he would never know anything.

She was suddenly seized with the desire to go play tennis, to smash a ball. She wanted to tear up cardboard boxes at the church, break them down.

"John," she called up to him, her voice so sharp everyone looked, not just John. "I'm going for a walk."

"Okay," he said, looking at Nolan somewhat nervously. Nolan nodded his head slightly, and she wanted to murder them both. She didn't need permission to leave her own house!

John lowered his eyes with guilt. Did Carrie know that Nolan had been quizzing him again about her daily habits, asking him strange questions like whether she had friends over during the week, if he'd noticed extra dishes in the sink—wineglasses maybe? And mentioning again the presence of a pair of knitted gloves in her glove compartment. Did Carrie ever wear gloves to drive, even when it wasn't cold? *Jesus*, John had wanted to scream. *That's why they call it a glove compartment! So you can keep gloves in there in case your hands get cold!*

In the foyer, Carrie slipped into her low boots, pulled on a light quilted jacket. Still warm enough in Pennsylvania in early October, but you never knew. She walked down the stepping stones that led through the backyard and down to the walking path. They'd been laid to match a woman's gait or a child's; John took them two at a time. When they'd first looked at this house, the smallest model the developer had built, the curving dotted path from front to back had seemed strange to them. Carrie imagined that, if glimpsed from Google Earth, the gray swirl would look like punctuation, a question mark. The stones were only placed there because they had no back entrance, windows but no French doors, no patio. Those were upgrades, and Carrie and John had planned to make those changes someday. Carrie secretly thought that since John never took a walk around the community unless Carrie asked him to, access to the back simply wasn't a priority to him.

"Where you headed?" Forrester asked, and she jumped. Her hand went up to her throat.

"Sorry," she said. "I, uh—"

"You look like you've seen a ghost." He said it quietly, seriously. He stood beneath the living room window. She searched his eyes for the meaning behind those words, searched them as thoroughly as he was looking through her property for evidence. He was wearing latex gloves, had something in his hand, but of course he hadn't found anything important. She wished she could tell him, the one who was nice to her, not to bother. To give him a tip for a change. Still, they had to look. Of course they did; why wouldn't they look? His eyes were dark but large, kind. His skin after such a long, warm summer was a golden color that always looked more right on women than men. His hair was blond at the tips, and so was his trim goatee. Carrie supposed being pleasant-looking was also useful in his line of work. Especially against the gruffness of Nolan. The yin and yang.

She shrugged. "Just a walk."

"No destination, huh?"

She shook her head.

"Perambulating?"

She blinked. Maybe Forrester was like her grandmother—maybe he was the kind of guy who never said *home* when he could pull out *abode*. Maybe Forrester was more interesting too than Nolan. He definitely had a larger vocabulary.

"I guess you could call it that," she said. "But the path goes in a circle. You end up in the same place you began."

He nodded. "Well, I guess that keeps people from getting lost."

She smiled.

"Your husband ever walk on the path?"

She blinked. "Well, of course. We go sometimes, after dinner."

"I mean, ever just take off and go for a walk, clear his head, like guys do?"

"I don't know," she said, and he nodded as if he did know.

"You're more of the walker in the family, huh?"

"I suppose."

She wondered if they knew everything about her: the hikes she took in college, the ones she did with her family at Peterson Nature Preserve. Hell, they probably knew the size of her footprint and the pattern of her menstrual cycles.

"He just...watches you from a happy distance?"

She felt his words along her spine. She looked up, met his eyes for just a moment—brown, long-lashed, puppy-innocent. How on earth could he know about that? Had they tracked down Tracie or Chelsea and interviewed them? Or Dr. Kenney? Good God, had they talked to Dr. Kenney?

"I guess I'll see you later," she said awkwardly.

"Enjoy yourself," he said, a combination of words that could be an invitation or a kind of harbinger, a curse.

Was that why she didn't say "I will" before she turned and headed off toward the pond? She was unsettled by his questions about John—as if John had more secrets, as if he wasn't always where you expected him to be.

The community was built around the manufactured pond but designed to look as if it wasn't. You couldn't just plop a development in the middle of gentlemen farms and houses that had been built in the 1940s and expect the zoning to be passed. No, you had to be sneakier than that. You had to make things look accidental. The houses were all different, although some of the differences were slight—angles, colors, reversing of floor plans. The land was parceled in unusual shapes to look like it had been created over time, not all at once. Her mother, who had ended up getting her real estate license after she sold the bungalow, after she saw how easy it was and how bad other people were at it, had explained the whole theory behind Carrie's development when she'd visited. When she'd come up and tried to cover her own grief while tending to Carrie's. Losing a grandchild was hard too, Carrie knew. Growing older, missing your chances. Carrie could always have another baby, but her mother, at sixty-four, could drop dead. *Old people die every day*, she'd said wistfully to Carrie when she'd called her at school and told her Gran had died, as if she'd been preparing herself for it, a negative kind of pep talk.

Carrie headed down to the entrance of the walking path, the wood chips leading to the gravel that ringed the pond. One-point-two-mile circumference. They'd thought of that too, her mother had told her. One mile would be too perfect, too planned. When they'd closed on the house, the pond had looked like it had been cookie-cut out of the earth, too circular, its edges too sharp, the water too clear. When Ben first went missing, the police had set up down here with divers, circling the shallow water, which made no sense to Carrie or to John. He hadn't been taken at home; the man they'd seen at the Y wasn't connected to anyone who lived around the pond. Nolan had told John they were working "off a theory" but wouldn't tell him what it was, which drove John nuts. He'd pace the house, trying to come up with his own theories, then wonder aloud if Nolan had just said that to do this very thing: to make him angry, to rile him up.

With the passage of time, the pond had become murkier, loamy. The circle of water had fanned out, slowly swamping the sedges and rushes, carving a more irregular shape. Even the small birch trees around the perimeter had the first tendrils of moss at their base. Carrie walked slowly, listening to squirrels rustling in the tall, damp grass, water gurgling in the low cattails. It smelled like rain all the time, cold in her nostrils, but the rain didn't come, and the leaves didn't change.

A woman ahead of her on the path moved quickly, like she was power walking, even though she wasn't wearing the clothes for it. A dog ran toward her, and the woman froze, unsure of its intent. But it was wagging its tail, butt wiggling, like it was happy to see the woman. Carrie was seized again by how much she wanted a dog, how that was the next piece of the puzzle, to watch her son enjoy what she'd had, a loving pet. The dog stopped to sniff the woman, and Carrie watched with alarm as the woman kicked it away.

"Hey!" she yelled involuntarily. "He's just sniffing you!"

The woman turned back with a scowl, then broke into a run, heading off the path. Carrie watched as she passed through a small stand of lindens to the west, toward the trestle over the old turnpike. Where people ran alone. She wished she was closer, wished she could speak to her, educate her, or yes, tell her off. Who the hell kicked at a friendly dog?

The dog paused to watch the woman go, head slightly bowed, haunches lowering. Carrie could almost feel the outline of regret. Then it turned and trotted back toward the pond, tags jingling. It stopped and sniffed the air. Carrie couldn't tell the precise breed at this distance, but it looked like its fur had been rolled in the dirt—a pale dog, but a muddy one. It stood at the edge of the pond, then crouched, head down. Started barking frantically. As she grew closer, Carrie thought she heard the trill of a toad.

As she came around the curve, the dog glanced back at her, then lunged at a splash in the water. Ah, a frog. Or a fish? Did they stock the pond? She looked up at the metallic sky, unbroken by ducks or geese, clouds gradated from silver to granite. As she got closer, even the dog's coat looked cinereous—no hopeful tufts of yellow. He looked and barked. Barked and looked. As she came closer, something about the tilt of the dog's head made her pick up her pace. It seemed to be speaking to her directly, and she knew exactly what he wanted.

Yes, the silvery brown coat of mud and dust had thrown her off, but there it was—the telltale tinder of dry yellow under the chin.

"Jinx," she whispered.

She called his name louder, hurried to him, nearly galloping herself, and he ran to her, frenzied and leaping, licking her face.

"Oh, Jinxie," she cried, sobbing into his fur, not caring he was grimy. She sniffed his salty head, ran her hands across his velvety, wet ears, and he turned more golden, more himself, with each caress of her hands. The only comfort she had had for years, and it had been exactly enough. Exactly. She buried her face in the side of his coat and smelled something both sweet and woodsy, like moss.

She held him at arm's length, paused to wipe her eyes against her sleeve. She'd been sure, but she needed to be doubly sure. She put her hands under his jaw and lifted his strong, wide head, and there it was, carved into the yellow field clear as a crop circle: the scar where he'd tangled with a cat, the small scaly *V* where his fur never grew back. She ran her hands over him, rememorizing his contours. His expressive eyebrows, the rabbit-fast rhythm of his heartbeat, the thin, strong legs, the velvet pads of his paws.

She lifted her head. "Thank you," she whispered to the sky.

Jinx nudged her elbow when she glanced up, drawing her back, and she knew that signal.

"All right, all right," she said, smiling, and cast around for a decent stick. Everything she saw was light, a frond or cattail. Finally, she found a short stick hiding in a low tangle of weeds, solid and hefty enough to throw, and she did, laughing. Watching him run after it, knowing he'd come back. There was no friend like a dog, she thought. Even a dead dog.

The stick landed off the path, near the water, and Jinx retrieved it but didn't come back. He stood with it in his mouth, looking out at the pond again.

"It's just a frog," she cried out. "We can't play fetch with a frog, silly!"

But still, he didn't come back. She started toward him, and someone ran up from behind her.

"There you are!" a man's voice said, panting.

"What?" She turned, expecting to see Forrester or Nolan or even John, not a stranger.

"Here, Jack!" A young man, ignoring her, called to the dog, waggling an unbuckled collar at him. "Come here, you bad boy."

The dog dropped the stick, as if in defiance, and ran toward the water.

"Jack!" He sighed. "Wiggled out of his electronic collar. Thank God I keep the tags on the other one."

"I think you're mistaken," she said.

"Mistaken?"

He was a few years older than her, dressed in plaid and corduroy, his feet testing the contours of his brown cotton TOMS shoes. Wayfarers perched on his head, as if he still held out hope the day could turn sunny. He smiled at her, bemused. "Mistaken how, exactly?"

"Well," she began, her confidence only faltering slightly, "I think this dog is actually my—"

The dog ran toward them, stick gone, replaced by something stringy and wet hanging from his mouth.

"Jackie boy," the man said as the dog came closer. "Now you're listening." He wrapped the second collar around his neck and petted his head roughly, too roughly, Carrie thought. She'd never liked seeing men tossing children, wrestling with dogs. It made her nervous, nervous that they couldn't control their strength. But the dog half jumped on him with delight.

Carrie blinked. No, she'd been certain. His scar. His smell.

"What do you have there, huh? Can you drop it?"

"Tickle him under the chin," Carrie said.

"Excuse me?"

"Tickle him under the chin and he'll drop it."

"Hey, whoa," he said suddenly, looking at her with his head cocked a little, like the dog. "Aren't you the lady who—"

He didn't finish his sentence. As he spoke, he tickled the dog's chin, and the animal released his sodden quarry, tumbling in what seemed slow motion, dripping, ruined.

Carrie fell to her knees, her face pale as paper.

A small sneaker that used to be blue.

A child who used to be here.

The shoes had been purchased at Target. Would they make something of that too, that her son's feet could be anyone's feet? Carrie had loved buying him clothes, dressing him in colors that suited him, like blue and green, yellow and pale orange. John never went with them; Ben sat in the cart while Carrie picked things out. She'd always bought him a small toy, something with moving parts, something he could bang or work with his thumbs, to hold at the register, a reward for being good. He never begged for anything, never whined. Always happy with what he had. Not like the rest of the family: not ambitious like John at work or Carrie's mother or even Carrie when she was young, always striving. It was as though Ben had been cast from something different.

She stared at the shoe on the ground, its color almost gray, the moldy green around the eyelets, the laces muddy and dark. She couldn't bear to touch it, and she was glad; that was, finally, the right instinct. This shoe wasn't Target's, wasn't hers, wasn't her son's. This shoe belonged to the police.

John, Nolan, Forrester, and the other technicians came in a group, racing down the path, Nolan well behind the others, panting. They'd heard the screams, the frantic barks. They hadn't seen Carrie rise from her crouch on the ground and run flat out into the water, shrieking her son's name over and over, splashing, kicking, until the man with the dog waded in next to her and persuaded her to come back out, to calm down, to pet the dog, that it was going to be okay.

Neil McGibbon, he said his name was. Half soaked after going in after her, wringing out the tail of his shirt. He gave a statement, told them exactly what had happened, but he left out the parts that were dangling, the parts that made no sense: that Carrie thought the dog wasn't his, that she seemed to know the dog, to know what he liked. Those weren't things he could explain; they were things he felt. And how seldom did anyone in law enforcement ask you how you felt? *They wanted what you knew. What you saw. What you heard.* The dog was muddy. The dog loved the pond. The woman loved dogs. Neil McGibbon had stumbled upon something that had seemed simple, then turned into more.

Neil was ready to go, having done his civic duty, but the dog and Carrie seemed to have other plans. Carrie sat shivering in her soaking pants, clinging to the dog as Neil clipped on the leash, breathing her good-bye into his flank.

"You, uh, can come visit him any time," he said gently. "I live right over there." He pointed across the field to the back of a house that looked just like Carrie and John's, with pale yellow siding and green trim instead of red. "If you squint, you can probably see him watching out the window, his paws on the sliding glass door. Some days he scans the pond all afternoon, looking for birds."

She shook her head, wiped her face. "No, I don't think that would be a good idea."

"It would...help me, really. You could walk him; he needs that."

She gave the dog one last squeeze and said she was sorry, but that would be too hard.

"She loves dogs," John offered.

"Yeah, I get it. I really do." Neil pulled gently on the leash. "Say good-bye, Jackie," he said, and the dog barked, offered his paw.

The cops smiled—such a nice respite in the grinding routine of police work to deal with a dog, something alive that didn't talk back—but Carrie's mouth was pulled small, grim. She took the dog's paw and shook it, holding back more tears. She didn't dare say what she wanted to say. She turned away, couldn't bear to watch the dog's rolling gait as they walked off.

Carrie sat in the grass, folded her arms against her knees, and hung her head. The exhaustion of it all, the weight of these tilting, circling questions, the heavy, damp breath of these men around her, asking the same thing over and over. Combing through old places, looking for one new thing. Everything always coming back to her. Everything always her fault. Couldn't someone else find something important for a change? Why did every clue form a mantle over her head?

"What happens now?" John asked.

"Forensics on the shoe. Dredge the pond again tomorrow at first light."

"What about the dog guy?"

"What about him?"

"You don't think he's a suspect?"

"Him? God no. Wrong place, wrong time."

"But...he can see our house from his. And his dog—"

"Smelled something in a public place. He wasn't even here, according to your wife. It's not like we found the shoe at his house."

"But what if it smelled of the guy? If that's why the dog went into the pond and fished it out in the first place? You're not going to go look at his car, at his—"

"John," Nolan said with a sigh. "We looked at everybody's car in this complex already. Every. Single. Car. As well as hundreds of sedans around the Main Line that people thought might be the one."

"So look again!"

"The guy drives a light green SUV. You can see it in his driveway from here."

"He had messy hair though, like the guy at the Y, right? Tousled, didn't you think, honey?"

Carrie looked at her husband. "I...didn't notice."

"You didn't?"

"John," Nolan said, pulling him to the side, lowering his voice. "What we need to do is talk more with your wife. As soon as... well, as soon as possible. Soon as she's up to it."

"What are you saying over there? Why are you whispering?"

"I guess she's up to it." Nolan sighed. "We are saying, Mrs. Morgan, that we'd like you to come down to the station tonight to talk more. Since you were here first, before the shoe was found and all."

"What are you suggesting?" she said, lifting up her head, suddenly alert.

"It's just procedure. Just following the book."

"You think I planted that shoe? That I knew it was there?"

"Hang on, babe," John said. "Nobody said anything remotely like that!"

"Well, of course they're not going to say it, John!"

John looked at Nolan, who gave a slight shrug. The five of them standing on one side of the path, her seated on the other.

"That's it," she said, standing up. She brushed the front of her yoga pants. Wet and full of dog hair. She worked a tuft of hair downward, curled it into a tiny pile, then slipped it into the pocket of her jacket. "I'm not saying anything more to you without a lawyer."

"Carrie." John said it like a warning, like she was being ridiculous, even though he'd been thinking the same thing, ever since Ben had come back. The gloves in the glove compartment, the milk, the box of diapers. How long did it take to find a quarter? Who was so ditzy they could miss a child being taken from their own backseat? And his own parents, who'd been doubting ever since he'd told them he was getting engaged to the girl from State: *Who is she? Her mother lives where? How well do you really know her?*

"You heard me," Carrie said.

The girl who loved to talk in the car and when they were tucked in at night and about to fall asleep was done talking. Just like the day when Maya Mercer had come to interview her—the camera crews, the producers, all of them hanging on her every word.

And no one believing a single syllable she said.

The day of the television interview, the day that was supposed to break the case wide open, John and Carrie had stood in her small, well-organized, walk-in closet, discussing her clothes in a way they never had throughout their marriage. It was shortly after the one-year anniversary of Ben's disappearance, and John and his parents had convinced her that publicity might help the case. Publicity might bring Ben back.

Carrie didn't know what to wear; she only knew what not to wear. She didn't own anything wildly inappropriate, nothing tight or low-cut, which had always been a relief to John. But knowing she was about to go on camera, she found herself rethinking everything.

She had on a gray sweater dress that was almost black, and John thought she should wear something brighter, more hopeful. He'd always liked her in blue and green and coral.

"The producer said no small patterns. Anything else is fine," Carrie said.

"What about this?" John pulled a coral tunic, edged in white, off the bottom rung.

"That's a swimsuit cover-up."

"Oh," he said. "Would anyone know that?"

"Just every woman in America."

"What about the green shirt?"

"It's just as dark as what I have on."

"No, it's…prettier."

"Is it?"

"It makes your eyes look green. The gray makes them look gray."

She changed into the green blouse, added a necklace, put on a pair of black pants and boots.

She applied her own makeup in the bathroom while the camera crew set up in the living room. John watched them from the landing, occasionally coming back and filling her in on something innocuous, like how many people were there, how half of them were doing absolutely nothing, and that Maya was still in her trailer, parked on the street along with the lighting truck.

"I still can't believe they don't want to talk to us together," Carrie said.

"The producer said that you make a better story angle."

"Angle," Carrie repeated, and John nodded at her in the mirror. "That's an awful word."

"It is kind of pointy."

"And aimed. It has trajectory."

John swallowed hard at the sound of *trajectory*, which made him think of bullets. If Maya Mercer questioned them both at that very minute, they would confess they were on edge. The same edge.

They went downstairs together and stood awkwardly in their own living room, trying not to get in the way of all the people moving a cord here, a light there, a sandbag over there. Two young men, casually dressed, sat on the sofa, turned slightly toward each other.

The female producer gestured for Carrie to come closer. "He's just standing in for lighting. Just go ahead and—"

"But he's sitting," Carrie said.

"And now he's standing because you're here. So just sit like he was, please."

She sat down. A young makeup artist wearing absolutely no makeup came over and dabbed a little powder on her nose. "You look fab," she said. "Seriously. And the earrings will read just enough."

Carrie instinctively touched the small turquoise drops in her ears. "I'm not sure what that means, but thank you."

"They'll read just enough *as earrings.*"

"Oh." She nodded. As opposed to...spears? Play-Doh caught in her hair?

John walked around so he could be in Carrie's eyeline and gave her a thumbs-up. A female technician gave her a microphone to thread up the back of her shirt and clip on her collar. Then she moved her arms around a bit, drying the dampness that was starting to creep in.

The man next to her on the sofa smiled, and she smiled back.

"If she takes any longer in her trailer, I guess you'll have to interview me."

"Oh, it takes forever to light Maya, because, you know."

"Because she's more important than I am?"

"No, she's not as pretty as you are. Good thing I'm not miked, huh?"

Just then Maya came in, trailed by another makeup artist and a man holding a comb and a canister of hair spray.

Maya waited for her stand-in to leave without saying hello or acknowledging his existence, then sat down next to Carrie and asked her if she was ready. Carrie nodded.

"I'll do the intros and cutaways separately. We're just doing the interview today, maybe get some wild sound afterward, understand?"

Carrie nodded, although she didn't fully understand the terminology.

Maya gave a nod to her producer, and someone clapped a slate in front of them, started to count down, then said, "Action." When the camera turned toward her, Maya leaned in and cocked her head. Her eyes squinted ever so slightly, like she was focused only on Carrie and struggling to understand her, to know her, before any words were even exchanged. That softness in her eyes reminded her briefly of Dr. Kenney.

"You grew up in the same place you raised your son."

"Yes. Just a few towns away."

"What kind of place do you think this is, here in the heart of Pennsylvania?"

"Safe. Quiet. Good schools."

"You thought you were safe here. You and your husband and son."

"Yes."

"You had no reason to think otherwise?"

"No."

"When you were a young girl, you spent a lot of time home alone here, isn't that right, Carrie?"

"Yes."

"Your father was gone, and your mother worked a lot of nights."

Carrie shifted in her seat, swallowed. "Yes."

"You grew up alone. Is that why you felt it was somehow okay to leave your son alone?"

Carrie glanced over at John, who shook his head.

"I...did not leave my son alone."

"I mean in the car? That day, outside Starbucks?"

Sweat beaded on Carrie's upper lip.

"I was putting money in the meter. Obeying the law."

Maya nodded, as if agreeing with her. "So you say," she said softly.

"Yes," Carrie said, glancing at John again, who was nodding. "Because it's true. I say it because it's...true."

"Isn't it also true that, when you were a child, your father was treated for psychosis at the VA hospital?"

Carrie's mouth hung open in surprise. "I have no memory of that. My mother never—"

"My producer has his records, if you'd like to see them. I know it must be a shock—I can see it in your eyes—but it's true."

The heat of the lights bore into Carrie. She felt a droplet of sweat beading up on her nose.

"My father was in the war, so he—"

"Yes. And we thank him for his service. But I have to ask—is there any other history of mental illness in your family, Carrie?"

"No, no, there isn't, and my father was—he was fine, just unhappy."

"'Unhappy' can be another word for 'depressed,' can't it?"

Carrie blinked. John licked his lips, looked around for the producer. Where was she?

"Were you depressed too, Carrie, back in high school?"

"No."

"Really? Because a friend of your high school boyfriend led us to believe—"

"A friend of Ethan's?"

"Yes, one of his friends had quite a bit to say—"

"I don't even know his friends—"

"Well, they made some troubling statements about your senior year of high school."

"Turn off the camera," Carrie said.

"I beg your pardon?"

"Turn it off!" she said, gritting her teeth.

Carrie pulled the microphone off, nearly ripping her blouse, and threw it on the floor. She stood up, surveying the obstacle course to every path of escape. This was her house, and she was trapped. Then John was at her elbow.

"I can't breathe," she whispered. "I can't breathe with all these people here."

Maya stood up and took Carrie's hand. Her eyes again, soft like the doctor's, as if they were friends. "What's wrong, Carrie?" she whispered. "If you won't tell me on camera, tell me now, for background."

"Nothing's wrong," John said. "You don't need to attack her like that!"

"I wasn't attacking, John. I was asking simple questions. If she's not hiding anything, she can answer. If she's innocent, there's no reason—"

John said, "She's just...private. About her family. Aren't you, babe?"

Maya winced at the word *babe*. But Carrie nodded her head so vigorously as John led her away that the droplets of sweat clinging to her lip and hairline flew off her.

When Ben first went missing, John had researched criminal lawyers for Carrie, just in case. Everyone had told him to do this, from his parents to his boss to his friends. And Carrie had been incredulous. *How is it possible*, she had asked, *that they could ever suspect me? What motive could I possibly have? There was no life insurance policy, no chronic illness to save him from, no desire to not be a mother anymore, to dance on top of tables at night clubs. What evidence suggests I wanted to get rid of my son?* And people had said, *Well, the terrible twos. It happens.* And she'd think about Ben's miniature rebellions—a few tears because he wanted a second cookie, throwing a sippy cup once when it was empty—so small you couldn't call them tantrums. Potty training, they'd say. Most people who beat their children do it over potty training. Ben hadn't been ready for that at two, so she didn't know from experience. But still, she'd think, really? When they'd been changing diapers for years, people suddenly balk at doing more of the same?

But even though Forrester and Nolan had questioned her vigorously then and perhaps doubted her abilities as a mother, she had believed the focus of the investigation was always on the man at the Y. There were too many witnesses who corroborated Carrie's statement—they saw her and Ben at the Y, and Carrie again outside Starbucks. The time frame was short—minutes. And no one the police had interviewed, driving the same route at the same time, saw a woman giving a child to someone else or taking a baby out of a car. No one. But John had kept the lawyers' names in his phone, and Carrie was incredibly glad he had.

When they got back to their house from the pond, Carrie shivering and John holding her tightly, John said he'd call them all and see who was available. He said they should interview them, meet with them to see which one Carrie liked best, and make a decision quickly.

"Like speed dating for criminals," she said.

"Yes," he said and smiled. She sounded like herself.

She went upstairs to change clothes. Her yoga pants and socks were still sodden from the knees down; a blade of silvery spartina stuck to the bottom of her short leather boot. She unzipped her boots, pulled them off, then swapped her yoga pants for dry jeans. She looked at her feet in her green socks and started to cry, thinking of Ben's feet without shoes. She sat down on the corner of the bed and tried not to look through the half-open closet door. *I have all my shoes*, she thought, *and he has none now.* She cried harder, letting the waves travel through her. *He has nothing, nothing anymore. And we don't have him.* She would never be able to wear sneakers again. Just thinking of the delicacy of canvas and laces, their cheap impermanence, broke her heart.

Finally, she stood up and grabbed a tissue, blew her nose. She threw it away and gathered up her jacket from the floor. She reached inside the front pocket, taking out the swatch of the dog's hair, lifting it to her nose. The salty, sugary smell that was so hard to explain to people who have never loved a dog. She opened her top bureau drawer and buried the small bundle in the corner, wishing she had a lock of Ben's hair too. But he had been too young; he'd never even had a haircut.

She blew her nose again and went downstairs.

John sat in the living room, his arm dangling off the edge of the sofa, his phone in the suspended hand. His eyes were focused on something far away.

"Are you sure," he said slowly, "there's nothing more I need to know?"

"Know?"

"Something else you haven't told me, maybe?"

"John, what are you saying? God, I just can't believe—"

"Were you having an affair?" He blurted it out, this set of words he'd never spoken before, despite his worries, his flashes of jealous concern. A nice way of putting it, not "Were you fucking some guy at the Y?" That was the way another man would say it. Another man who wasn't careful about what he said to his wife.

"Affair?"

"That guy at the Y who no one can pinpoint," he said slowly, struggling to swallow. "A couple of the women the police interviewed said he was handsome. Young. That's what they remember: not the color of his hair, or how tall he was, but that he was good looking."

"John, don't start thinking like this again," she said slowly. "Please don't believe that every guy on every street is after me."

"I don't."

"Good. Because the last time a man chased me down a street, it was to tell me I had toilet paper on my shoe."

He managed a small smile for his wife. His pretty wife who didn't even need makeup or highlights, with her long lashes and hair that boasted golden threads every summer.

"You didn't answer my question."

"John," she said, grabbing the hand that didn't hold the phone. "No."

"That guy was kind of good looking. In a hipster way. That Neil guy."

"No. No, no, no, no. Please don't think such a thing."

"He lives right around the corner too, and he has a dog, and he—"

"John, no. Please don't worry about this. Not now."

"I know in the grand scheme of things, it seems…small, but—"

"No, no, it's not small. And it's not true, all right?"

"Okay."

She stood up. "I'm going to take a drive."

"A drive? Babe, you shouldn't be driving. This has been a terrible day—"

"I'm fine. I need to clear my head."

"Let me drive you then. We'll go together."

She shook her head. "I want… I need…I need to go to Saint David's. Alone."

"Alone?"

"Yes. To the…cemetery."

He blinked. "How will that look?"

"*Look?*" she said, screwing up her face. "To whom?"

John didn't say "to the police," who were likely following her. Didn't say "to the community," who might be watching. "To him" would have been the correct response. It didn't look good *to him.*

When he opened his mouth to try to explain, nothing came out at first. His half-ruined voice failed him, and he struggled to clear his throat.

"So I guess maybe you, um, miss your dad? Ben being gone kind of reminds you of that?"

"I guess," she answered. "My grandmother used to say that all loss was the same."

"I don't know if I believe that."

She sighed. "Well, I'm going to stop to get flowers."

He nodded. The idea of the flowers soothed him; it was so like her to think of that errand, to remember the niceties. It proved to him that she was actually better, that she was stronger than he ever gave her credit for. And part of him liked the thought of Nolan watching her from a car parked on a distant hill and feeling guilty as she laid the flowers down and dabbed at her eyes with a tissue. *Let them see that. Let them see the good in the things she did and not the bad.*

Carrie didn't drive the long way this time. She stopped at the grocery store for a mix of lilies and roses and headed east on the main drag. She parked her car in the corner of the lot, away from the cluster of cars. As she walked to the small, square cemetery, the old sycamores edging the driveway barely moved in the breeze. Their knotted silver trunks bulged like the calves of old athletic giants, looking vulnerable and sturdy at the same time. A leaf fell into her hair, and she brushed it out with her hand. Green leaves, gray sky. Only a few gravestones dotted with colorful exclamations of flowers. She opened the gate.

She'd been surprised when her mother had buried her father here instead of at their own parish. As it turned out, her father had been christened at Saint David's, had attended services off and on as a child, and had inherited a plot from his grandfather's estate. But he and Danielle had raised Carrie a few towns to the west, rarely returning. When she'd first met John's parents, she had mentioned her father's connection to their church, thinking perhaps someone might remember her last name—Griffiths—from their years there. But they hadn't. Carrie visited the grave perhaps once a month. And though she hadn't felt close to her father for many years— she'd been almost as angry at him as her mother was—she didn't feel quite that way when she was at his grave.

She arranged the buds in the small opening near the modest headstone, then stood up and looked around, inhaled deeply. Wet earth, some of it ancient, some of it recently turned. The loam of decomposed flowers, bodies, leaves. Was that what she had smelled on Ben and again on Jinx at the pond? No. Maybe. She didn't know. But she also knew that wasn't the question she needed to ask. That wasn't why she came.

"Dad," she whispered.

She tried to picture him, not sick like the last time she saw him, not angry and drunk, always drunk, like the last few years with her mother, but an earlier version, the one in her childhood photos. He'd been happy then, surely. Thin but strong, a ready smile. He'd taught her to play soccer; he'd driven her to gymnastics. Once, she'd had a normal father just like everyone else, someone who earned money and put it away and slept next to his wife at night.

She closed her eyes. She didn't know how to meditate, how to chant, how to breathe. How many times had Dr. Kenney suggested yoga to her? And how many times had she tried to explain that she was a mover, a doer, not a sitter and a breather? But she knew this much—she knew how to pray. She thought if she could pray for her father, he might appear. And if she could see him, then she'd know. Then she'd know. And then she could ask.

She opened the small prayer book she kept in her purse and looked up the verse she remembered vaguely from funerals, from Easter services.

> *Your soul is in the hands of God, and no torment will ever*
> *touch you.*
> *God tested you and found you worthy of Him.*
> *Mercy and grace are upon you, watching over you now.*

"Dad," she whispered. "Is Ben there with you? Is he…" She stopped, her breath caught in her throat, and she started to cry. "Is he safe?"

She opened her eyes. The light had changed; a few rays of sun broke through the cluster of clouds, bathing the gravestone in a thicker, brighter light. The flowers were there, the close-cropped grass. But that was all. No person. No entity. She looked around her, as if he could still surprise her, find another way in. She sighed. No revisionist history. Her father wasn't going to bring her a present from one of his "business trips," change his mind about the divorce, win the lottery, or be summoned from death on command.

She lowered her head and prayed an ordinary Sunday prayer. She stayed half an hour, hands folded, going through the mental list she used whenever she bowed her head. She started with Ben, then went to John, then to whomever she knew, whomever she'd said hello to, a random person on the street who'd looked sad. She called those faces to mind and prayed for them, and for good measure, she prayed for all the dead people she'd known too.

Behind her, the church bells rang, car doors closed, engines turned. The clouds covered the last hopeful finger of sun, and she shivered.

Finally, she looked up to the heavens. "Well, Dad," she said, "you never showed up when we needed you before. I don't know why I expected it to be any different now."

She left one last space in the air for an answer, but there was none. She stood there a while longer, thought of all the questions Dr. Kenney had asked her about her father. Questions she had trouble answering, more questions than she had ever had when he was alive. And how, at the next appointment, he had moved on to John. Why John drove her to the office. Why John made her appointments.

"I've noticed that John likes to be involved in your life," he'd said.

"He's protective of me."

"Well, those are two different things, Carrie." He hesitated a moment. "Is he ever what you would call overprotective?"

"Sometimes," she said softly, then told him. Told him what she shouldn't have told him. He'd asked her to describe the first time John had followed her. The time of day, what she wore, what he said. She struggled, coming up with details, squirmed.

"It's hard to remember?"

"Yes."

"Because there were so many times?"

She shrugged.

"How did that make you feel, Carrie? When John followed you."

"I felt angry at first. Not trusted."

"And then?"

"Then...I felt love."

"Love?" he'd repeated, cocking his head and frowning a little, as if he'd heard her wrong.

Carrie left the cemetery to walk back to her car. No other people, no other cars left in the lot. It had to be a coincidence, what Forrester had said about John watching her. Surely the doctor wouldn't tell the detective—or Maya Mercer. Surely there were ethics about that, laws.

She turned the key in the ignition and drove home. She instinctively looked in her mirror every so often, only half expecting to see her husband trailing behind her.

O nly two of the five lawyers John called said they were available—one being Jeb Harris, who had been in the news for successfully defending two Philadelphia rap stars in a drive-by shooting despite an overwhelming amount of circumstantial evidence. John didn't like Harris's attitude on the phone; it was as if he'd interrupted him. John felt like a nuisance rather than a client who would be paying him an extraordinarily high hourly rate, money he'd have to borrow from his parents.

The other was a young woman named Susan Clark, a former prosecutor who had "seen the light" and who told John she was fascinated by Ben's case, that she'd been following the story all year. The decision was easy. John arranged a short call between her and Carrie when Carrie got home from the cemetery, then searched for other high-profile names he could call in New Jersey and New York, just in case Carrie hated her.

Within seconds of introducing herself on the phone, Susan told Carrie she thought she should agree to a police interview right away, as proof that "we have nothing to hide." She said *we* like they were a team. They spent a few minutes exchanging information, but everything Carrie offered, Susan already seemed to know. She put her on hold and a few seconds later came back on to tell her she had cleared her calendar and arranged for the detectives to meet them at the precinct at eight o'clock the next morning.

Carrie hung up the phone in the kitchen. She felt queasy, exhausted, empty. She opened the refrigerator, took out a can of Diet Coke, and poured it over ice. John was upstairs changing his clothes. She swallowed the caffeine gratefully, felt the rush of bubbles as she heard the drawers above her open and close slowly, the clinking of a belt buckle, a clatter of change going in and out of a new pocket. Finally, he came down and sat across from her, his face pale.

"What's wrong?" she said.

"Carrie, I—"

"What, John?"

He opened his hand and held out the dog hair from the bureau. "Are you sure you're not in love with that guy?"

Carrie closed her eyes, took a deep breath. "You went through my drawers, John? What's next, a cavity search?"

"I don't understand," he said.

"John," she said, "you have to stop doing this. I am not having an affair with that dog guy, okay?"

He looked down at his hands, suddenly ashamed. The same look he had the night she'd caught him on the path at college. Hiding behind the bushes. Strong but weak, vulnerable as a boy. She reached up, kissed him hard, and held him.

"I love you, John," she said.

"I love you too."

"Then stop going through the closets and drawers."

They slept with the windows open most of the year. There was something comforting to them both about the piney air, the wind moving the soft, low branches, the small splashes made by birds or frogs on the man-made pond. And yes, occasionally, a sound that wasn't restful broke through—a rustling that woke only Carrie.

This time, it was one a.m. She sat straight up, clutching her chest. She looked over at John, his eyes closed, his mouth slightly open, sleeping soundly as he always did. *Did he not just hear that? That...cry?* She got out of bed and went to the window overlooking the pond, cranked it open wider. A few lights here and there across the way, on timers. No flashlights, no footfalls she could discern. No animal rustling in the brush. The breeze picked up again, and she smelled something that reminded her of manure. Grassy, sharp, but just an undercurrent of sweet.

She ran downstairs, put on her coat and clogs, and took a flashlight from the kitchen drawer. In the garage, she pulled a folding beach chair off the pegboard. As she hit the electronic button to close the garage door, she did not immediately recognize this as a mistake. John could sleep through anything—that was what she believed.

But he didn't. He heard the familiar clanging outside, woke up, and rubbed his eyes. He patted the empty side of the bed, then stood and looked out the window. He watched the bobbing polka-dot trail of her flashlight as she made her way to the path. One of his instincts was to call out to her, to demand an answer, but another, deeper one, was to be quiet. To slip into the dark, become one with it. He pulled on a sweater and slippers and moved gently through the house and onto the lawn, stepping lightly on the balls of his feet, staying well behind her as she walked down near the water's edge, testing the swampy grass for firmness, deciding where to set up her chair. She sat down.

John stood behind her on the path, trying to calm his breathing. She didn't look like she was waiting for anyone. She didn't turn around toward the other houses, crane her neck. He stood in one spot for fifteen minutes, twenty, his heart pounding, hands curled into fists, preparing for Neil McGibbon to arrive. Prepared to finally be right. But Carrie didn't look at her watch or her phone. Finally, he saw her dig into her pocket and pull out a tissue, dab at her eyes. And that was when he made his move.

He came to her unquietly this time, not hiding, calling her name when he got close enough for her to hear.

"What are you doing out here, babe?" he asked. "It's not safe."

"John," she said through her tears, "I couldn't leave him out here alone."

He felt his face drain of color; his hands and limbs, every inch of him, went suddenly numb.

"Carrie, what are you saying? What do you—"

"What if he's in there, John?" she said, sobbing. "What if he's in there?"

"Honey, we don't know—"

"We can't just leave him here alone at night."

He blinked back at his wife, then crouched down to sit beside her, taking her hand, watching the water and the outline of the squat trees. Every so often, a leaf would detach, and they followed the shadow as it fell into the water. How long before that familiar shape soaked up the brackish surface and broke down? Until it was nothing but veins and spine? He shivered and pushed the thought aside.

He leaned into Carrie and dozed until the first glimmers of sun arrived, illuminating the silver dew on the long grass. John woke his wife gently, rubbing her arms and hands to warm her, and told her it was time to get ready to go to the precinct. She didn't protest. She followed him, and she didn't say good-bye, because it was morning, and it was safe, and because she was still so unsure of everything she sensed—what she saw, what she heard, what she smelled when the breeze switched direction.

WEDNESDAY

S usan Clark had stick-straight red hair, pale freckles, and wore no makeup that Carrie could discern, only lip gloss. She shook hands with Carrie and John in the corridor and told Carrie to just stick to the plan and not answer any questions that weren't the ones they had discussed.

"We'll meet you back in here in maybe half an hour," she said to John.

"I can't go with her?"

"I'm afraid not."

"What if they, you know, turn bad cop or something? They know me. I don't think they'll behave badly if I'm—"

"Mr. Morgan," she said, "you cannot accompany your wife."

"But if something happens, you'll text me, right? I can wait right outside."

"It will be fine, I assure you."

He nodded, then pulled Carrie in close and kissed her on the forehead.

Nolan led Susan and Carrie to a room with a long, nicked table, and all of the former warmth Carrie occasionally saw in his face or Forrester's was gone. Now that there was a lawyer in the room, there would be no more buddy-buddy inside scoop for her or John. No more feeling like those two were looking out for them.

No more patrol cars on their street, no more kindly glances. The detectives were not on their side anymore; there was only room for the lawyer.

"Okay, now, Mrs. Morgan, I'm sure you'd like to clear your name."

"Clear my name?"

"Yes. Remove any doubts or suspicions. And the best way to do that would be to submit to a polygraph."

"Ask a question, please," Susan said with a sigh. "We are not interested in a polygraph."

Her phone pinged, and she looked down at the text.

"Mrs. Morgan, would you like to comment on why your Google search history included looking for adoption agencies?"

The blood drained from Carrie's face.

"Excuse me, Detective," Susan said, looking up from her phone. "Before we go any further, is there any new information you'd like to share?"

He blinked twice.

"Such as?"

"Such as the result of dredging the pond."

"Still in progress."

"My boots on the ground say the divers are gone and there's crime tape up."

"Boots on the ground? Please, the area is sealed."

"There's a news crew at the scene now reporting otherwise."

Carrie's arms began to tingle. She felt herself shrinking in the chair, melting, as if she were about to no longer exist. The sticky-sweet coffee smell of the room began to sour, like old milk. *Here it comes*, she thought. *This is the feeling of being right all along.*

"I'm not going to comment on the media, couns—"

"Did you or did you not find a child's body in the pond, sir?"

"Until we're ready to release that infor—"

"Surely you're not saying that you refuse to release that information to the mother of the victim?"

"As I said, until we're ready—"

"Are you prepared to charge Mrs. Morgan with a crime right now, at this moment?"

"No."

"Then my client has nothing to say."

Carrie looked up suddenly. "I do have something to say."

"Carrie, no, we—"

She looked at Nolan and Forrester. "Shame on you," she whispered. "Shame on you both for leaving him there in the dark."

Susan turned to Carrie and lifted her by the elbow. Carrie felt what she'd expected to feel at the cemetery and didn't—a weightlessness as she rose, light, as if floating, as if in a dream.

———————◇———————

Their baby was dead, but he was *found*. They had their closure, that horrible, zip-up-the-body-bag word.

John made the phone calls to their families, pacing, jingling the change in his pocket, yet talking calmly, occasionally clearing his always raspy throat. Not pale like Carrie. Not shaking like Carrie. This was how he operated. When Ben first went missing, John still slept, still ate. He still played squash with his friends once a week. He didn't let it take over the way other people would, did. Shouldn't that alone make *him* a suspect, not Carrie? If they subpoenaed Carrie's records from Dr. Kenney and found out how callous Carrie thought her husband could be and how controlling the doctor thought he was, what would they think then? Who would they be after then? Still, it was useful, John's buoyancy. They had a service to throw, a million people to call, a defense strategy to build, and a search warrant to deal with—for their house, their cars, and Saint David's Church.

Carrie sat and listened as John spoke into his phone, as he insisted his parents not return from their trip to Italy, as he told his brother and sister to wait and come for the memorial service the following week. She breathed a small sigh of relief that on top of everything else, they didn't also have out-of-town company. It would be too much, and it was already too, too much.

Ben had been found near the middle of the pond, not far from where the dog had been barking. He'd had a concrete block tied around his waist with rope and was faceup in the silty bottom. They knew these things because Forrester had surreptitiously told John. Risked his job to whisper it to him from a pay phone near the mall. Because Forrester was convinced of Carrie's innocence, even if Nolan was not. Because Forrester felt sorry for them, John said.

"Faceup," she repeated. An image of her son at the Y the very day he went missing, floating on his back in the pool, kicking his feet. His long, wet eyelashes like the points of stars. She smiled, then stopped, knowing she shouldn't smile. It wasn't right to smile, even at the good things, even with John. But her reserves of sadness were dwindling. The tears were going to dry up eventually. She'd been sad for so long, there was just so little left.

"That's what he said."

"Facedown would have been more heartbreaking, don't you think?"

"It's all heartbreaking," he said.

The word *heartbreaking* came out without a catch in his voice, not a snag or dip. How was that possible, with his stretched, vulnerable voice, not to break in the right places too, not just the wrong ones?

John had been the one who had gone down to the morgue and offered to identify the body. They'd told him it was too gruesome, that it wasn't necessary. They had the dental records, so they sent him away. But he'd been the one brave enough to offer, who could imagine himself looking at Ben's muddy, swollen face and choking out the words "That's him." How could he not feel worse than Carrie, just picturing that? How could he speak at all, stand up, function?

"What did you say to him?" she said suddenly.

"What? To who?"

Carrie saw it in his eyes: John feared she meant Ben. He didn't want to confess the flat prosaic words he'd choked out in the corridor when he'd seen the drawers, the body bags. That he'd said not only *Good-bye* and *I love you, buddy* but *I'm sorry. I'm so, so sorry.* No poetry, no monologue, no prayer.

"Forrester. When he told you the details. What did you say?"

"I don't know. I don't remember. I felt queasy. I—"

"John, listen to me. This is important. I think...I think he's playing you."

"Playing me?" He screwed up his face so tight it hurt.

"Feeding you details, telling you he's on our side, when he's actually investigating you. All this stuff about me, it's just to, you know, throw us off. Make you do something or...tell him what he wants to know."

"Jesus, Carrie," he said. "Why would you say that? He's trying to help—"

"No. No. It doesn't work like that. No one tries to help that way. He wants you to think it, but it's not true. He asked me questions about you the other day, weird questions, about you following and watching and going out in the middle of the night."

His face drained of color. "What? I don't believe it. You have to be wrong."

"Well, we need to keep our eyes open. Both of us. About both of them. Okay?"

"Okay."

"Promise me, Frog," she said.

He smiled the smallest smile he dared. It had been a long time since she'd called him that. "I promise."

He held her tightly, rubbing his hands up and down her back in a way that she sometimes liked and sometimes didn't, depending on her mood. She didn't stop him. She leaned into him, accepting his touch, his closeness.

"Carrie," he said suddenly, "did you know...the minute you saw the shoe?"

She pulled out of the embrace as if she needed air. "No," she said softly.

"I just thought, you know, because that guy, Neil, said you fell when you saw it. That you collapsed. And then...well, running into the water. Screaming."

John looked at his hands. He had fought back tears when Neil told the detectives that. He shouldn't have let Carrie go walking alone without someone to catch her when she fell.

"No." She shook her head, put her hands against her mouth. "I knew when I saw him here."

"What? Who, Neil? Neil was here? What do you mean?"

"Ben. I mean, he was dead then."

"Jesus, Carrie!"

"I'm right, and you know I am. That's why he was the same size. That's why he still fit in the car seat. That's why he hadn't aged, couldn't talk in sentences."

"He was underfed! He could have been...kept in a box or something, confined. Carrie, good God!"

"No, I'm sure."

"Please tell me you didn't utter a single word like that to Susan Clark!"

"No."

"Well, promise me you won't!"

John ran his hands through his hair, trying to keep it out of his eyes. He wished he knew exactly what to tell Carrie to say, instead of what not to say. If only there were a script he could hand her.

"They come back to give us what we need," she said suddenly.

"What?"

"The dog, John," she said softly. She reached for his arm, searched his eyes, this man who knew her better than anyone, who had to know that she had never spoken a false word to him, ever. When he'd asked her if she'd cheated on her biology test, she'd said yes. When he'd asked her if she'd surreptitiously found out the baby's sex after the ultrasound, she'd said yes. Whenever she could have lied, she told the truth. Everyone knew that about her, all the way back. Ethan, her mother, Chelsea, Tracie. Didn't he remember that? All the church and Sunday school had carved her into an open book. She might not tell everything unprompted, but if asked? It was all over. Dr. Kenney, foolishly waiting for her to offer, hadn't figured it out yet. But John—didn't John know that, even though he didn't know everything about her, all he had to do was formulate the questions and open his mouth?

"At the pond? That was my dog. From when I was a little girl. He came back and led us to the shoe, to put our minds at rest finally. Don't you see? That's why I kept the dog hair. That's why."

John swallowed hard and took a step back from his wife.

"Carrie, you are talking like someone…like someone who is… seriously confused."

"I'm not confused."

"I'm calling Dr. Kenney as soon as—"

"I don't need Dr. Kenney, John!"

"Carrie! Listen to me! Your life is at stake. Our life! We've lost our son, but what's ahead could be worse. And you have got to get your head screwed on straight and stop talking like you're hallucinating, like you're seeing ghosts!"

"You don't get it."

"You're damn right I don't get it," he said, heading toward the stairs. "I don't get it at all. And neither would your lawyer, the detectives, or a jury."

"What about a priest, John? What about Reverend Carson or the priest who confirmed you?"

"Carrie, just because, you know, Christ was resurrected, doesn't mean—"

"Doesn't it? Did you actually read the Bible while you were sitting in chur—"

"Carrie! Look around you. We are not in heaven! This is not… None of this—"

"What, John?"

"We need to call Dr. Kenney," he said, "and get this fixed."

This, she thought, stunned. *He called me a* this.

When Carrie heard John whispering on his phone in the bathroom, she wondered, not for the first time, if he was hiding something too. Was that why he'd asked if she was having an affair? Was that why he had been so jealous at college—because he was cheating on her? Because he was, as Dr. Kenney would say, projecting? After all, except for one summer he'd spent in Europe during which they'd agreed to see other people if they wanted to, they'd been together since their freshman year of college. Was that normal? It was for a woman, maybe, but not a man. His friends had teased him, told him he needed two bachelor parties before he got married, just to deepen his experience. And the only other couple they knew who had met in college—Courtney and Justin—were divorcing over infidelity.

So she stood outside the bathroom door, listening to him running the bathwater to cover up his conversation. *Please*, she thought, *you can do better than this! When was the last time you took a bath, John?* Then her heart sank with the answer. *With Ben.* The two of them, covered in bubbles, laughing. Ben, who always laughed at everything John said or did. Ben, who on bath nights waited by the door at six o'clock like a puppy, watching for John's car. Ben, who used his hands to turn John's head back to him whenever it turned toward Carrie. Ben, who always wanted

John after a long day with Carrie. *Dada*, learned months and months before *Mama*.

She could pick up only every second or third word, but a few of them were clear: *Funeral. Flowers. Danielle.* She sighed. He was only talking to Carrie's mother, but it still annoyed her, as he'd known it would. They'd already called Florida the day before and told Carrie's mother everything they knew. John had dialed the phone, then had put Carrie on. Carrie had told her mother she could stay in the guest room if she wanted and that John was arranging a hotel room nearby for his parents, even though they lived just twenty-five minutes away. Had told her yes, she could be in charge of flowers and food, because organizing things like that was Danielle's strong suit. If her mother hadn't been a real estate agent, she could have been a wedding planner, Carrie always thought. And now, a funeral planner. But she hadn't had the heart to mention to her mother, who always offered to do, to go, to fix, that it was all done. The photo boards, the menu, the playlists. She'd done it all, months ago, to keep herself busy. She'd figured she would fall apart the day she found out he was dead and be grateful she'd done it when she was feeling stronger. When she was celebrating, remembering Ben, full of hope, that was the time to pull it all together. It had all made sense. And her mother, her organized mother? She would understand. She would understand and promptly find something else to do. Picking weeds. Sweeping floors. Filling flower boxes.

But John had clearly called to tell Carrie's mother something else—something that he didn't want his wife to hear. Like that Carrie was seeing things. Communing with the dead. Or worse: lying about it all. Pretending, to throw off the trail. And the next step, she knew: If she could lie about this, couldn't she lie about everything?

She pulled on skinny white corduroys and an old blue sweater. She hadn't eaten much, and the pants slid down her hips, so she added the needlepoint belt that Libby had given her, knowing it would make her happy.

More police would be there soon enough, doing a more thorough search, combing through their house. Poking around in their bureaus, turning up their noses at their knickknacks, sniffing their soaps, making something out of nothing. She wasn't about to stick around and watch.

She went downstairs and grabbed her light, quilted coat, tiptoed out, didn't leave a note.

John wasn't the only person who could be secretive.

I don't know what I want to do with my life, and neither does she. She loved her son, but she was bored, I could tell. That's why she let him talk to other people. She was just a little tired of him talking to only her all day. Babbling, really; that's what the look on her face said. Did she even know she was lucky?

My father works so hard he has to lie down at the end of the day in a dark room, alone, no sound. And my mother works two jobs that pay the same as one. So I don't know what I want to do. I just know I don't want to do what they do.

But that woman? She didn't have to do what they do. She just had to read, play, sing, and stop for snacks along the way.

And I wonder: Does she regret that now, the snack, more than anything? That they stopped at Starbucks when they could have kept going, if she'd just had a little more willpower, a kind of firmness in her voice that allowed her to say no? Did the boy really need a cake pop that day, in the afternoon?

What kind of mom doesn't know when to say no to her child?

U pstairs, candles burned and light streamed in, dancing in color, but downstairs, in the northwest corner of Saint David's Church, it was as dark and damp as any prison. Libby, walking backward, dragging a trash bag of donations too heavy to lift, backed right into Carrie as she reached for the light switch.

Libby shrieked with surprise. "Mercy," she said, smoothing her blouse. "You scared me half to death."

"I'm sorry, but I thought you heard me walking down."

"I wasn't expecting anyone, so I didn't hear anyone."

"But...it's Wednesday," Carrie said slowly. "I'm always here on Monday and Wednesday."

"Carrie," Libby said, grasping her hand, "no one expected you to come, today of all days."

The police had clearly made a statement for the morning news. It was as if that video were reflected in Libby's eyes, illuminating them both.

"Libby, I—"

"I know, I know, you poor thing. You need to stay busy, of course. And not be alone. And what better place than here, where you can also seek comfort?"

Carrie nodded, bit her lip, and Libby wrapped her in a hug, squeezing her twice before holding her at arm's length and looking at her tenderly. Libby's face, with her slightly furrowed brow, her high pink cheekbones, and her concerned blue eyes, was like a palette of pious motherhood. A good churchgoing woman who believed.

"Libby…"

"Yes, lovey? What is it?"

"I believe Ben has been… He's been dead for a long time."

The bag of clothes next to Libby fell over, releasing a small puff of air. Was this what John was alluding to when he'd called her and told her about Ben's death? That Carrie wasn't herself, that she seemed like she was losing her grip? Carrie looked normal enough in her simple sweater and corduroys. Libby saw the edge of the needlepoint belt beneath the sweater, calling to her with its turquoise waves and coral crabs and smiling whales. It was either a belt that went with everything or Carrie always wore Mary's belt when she was seeing Libby.

Carrie's face became streaked with tears, but she didn't look crazy or confused or manic. No, Carrie looked exactly like Carrie, just with wet cheeks.

Libby took a deep breath. Was it possible John had just misunderstood? Didn't men have trouble understanding women all the time? When she'd started going through early menopause and she'd come home one day to find dishes in the sink, papers strewn on the floor, and the dog's water bowl completely dry, she had catapulted her purse across the kitchen with a warrior's rage, screaming that no one did anything at home but her. Albert had stared at her blankly and, the next day, had called the family physician and asked for the name of a psychiatrist. That was how uncharacteristically women could act sometimes. That was how ridiculously men could respond. Was that, after all was said and done, what was going on here?

"Lovey, do you mean he's been gone so long that you gave up hope of him being alive long ago?"

Carrie breathed in the damp air. Cold and wet, it sat in her lungs, weighing on her.

"Yes," she said finally, thinking of press conferences and judge's chambers and hands raised over Bibles. She couldn't tell anyone, apparently. No one would understand, not even Libby. "That's exactly what I meant."

Libby pulled her back into a hug, told her the clothes could wait, and asked her if she'd like a cup of tea. She'd found out the hard way that Carrie didn't drink coffee anymore after she ran out of a church reception, sobbing at the sight of people gathered around the big silver percolator.

"Yes, I guess tea would be nice," she said.

"Does John know you're here?"

She shook her head.

Libby went into the small kitchen to make the tea and texted John to tell him his wife was fine, safe. At least for now.

———◦———

John's parents had thought he and Carrie were marrying too soon. They'd made that clear. They'd kept saying they should wait until they had more money, were more settled. And Carrie simply hadn't understood what they were talking about. How much more settled could people who'd been dating for four years be? They both had job, owned cars, had clean credit histories. Wait for more money? To a girl who had eaten ramen for an entire month when her father had left them with nothing and her mother had been unable to sell the cracked and peeling house, they had plenty of money. When Carrie started getting paychecks that covered more than her needs, she would stare at the bank statements and raise her eyes to the sky and just thank God for her good fortune. And Carrie's mother and grandmother? They probably would have been in favor of the marriage even earlier, in college. They'd loved John unconditionally, in a way John's parents couldn't quite reciprocate, and Carrie was afraid it had something to do with her more humble upbringing.

His parents had said the same thing about having a baby—that they should wait. *You haven't traveled to Europe yet. You don't own a house.* But Carrie was twenty-eight, nearly twenty-nine, and she'd been with John for ten years! If that wasn't long enough, how long was? Occasionally they'd return from a family holiday party and

Carrie would grouse that his parents didn't love her. When he asked her why she felt that way, all she could cite was one word: *cautious*. They were so cautious and polite around her. So happy in photos, so happy with other people. All those teeth! Where was that unbridled enthusiasm for Carrie? John said she was describing how dogs acted, not people. Then she asked if he was saying his parents were cats, and he laughed and said, yes, maybe. Maybe that was all it was.

After Ben was born, John's parents pressured them to move closer, to buy something in their town, not Carrie's. They even remembered that Carrie's father was buried in their church and that Carrie herself had insisted on joining that parish.

"You're here every Sunday anyway," John's mother said. "If you lived even closer, we could pick you up on the way to services. Or if you found a carriage house on one of these charming little lanes, you could walk to church!" Her eyes shone at this possibility, as if Carrie and John could ever afford anything nearby. Carrie's mother was a Realtor: she'd taught her daughter that *charming* was just another word for *overpriced*.

John had held them at bay until Ben had gone missing, and then he'd brought it up again himself. *It's safer there. There are people all around. No one locks their doors!* But they were John's people, not Carrie's.

As she drove home from church, anticipating their arrival and how tentative they'd be, her stomach gurgled. She turned off River Road and went home the long way. This route changed her approach, bringing her to her street from the opposite end. She drove past the larger homes, the ones closer to the pond. Was one of those the house of the man with the dog? She'd thought the one he'd pointed to was smaller, like theirs. A dusty car sat in one of the driveways, a bucket nearby. Maybe that was the one. Or maybe she remembered wrong.

She turned onto her street. Three news vans littered the right-hand side of the road, their loud logos and splashy graphics assaulting her like graffiti in the quiet neighborhood. *Action News. Eyewitness News. News Now.*

She drove past her house slowly, looking but trying not to look like she was looking. John's car was gone. A black sedan she didn't recognize was parked in the driveway. Great, just great. *Instead of people following me discreetly, they are doing it blatantly now! No,* she thought. *It must have to do with the search warrant.* Yes, that was it—the fingerprint technician or the DNA person, that was whose car it was. They were probably waiting for her with the warrant. At the other end of the street, she considered going farther, driving to the Marriott, staying away as long as she could. *No,* she thought, making a U-turn. *I've done nothing wrong, and I'm not going to act as if I have.* That was what Susan Clark had said: *You have nothing to hide; let them search till the cows come home. All they have now are gloves in the glove compartment and milk in the refrigerator.*

She doubled back and pulled in next to the black sedan, and as she opened her door, she heard the sliding of van doors, footfalls of running feet. *Like deer,* she thought as she walked as quickly as she could up to her own door. *Just ignore them, like you ignore the animals.*

"Excuse me," they called to her. "Mrs. Morgan? Do you have any comment?" "Did you kill your son, Mrs. Morgan?" "Do you know who did?" "Would you like to tell your side of the story?" But she didn't turn. If she saw Maya Mercer near her driveway, with her big glasses and her phony empathy, it would be too much. She walked up to her front door, opened it, put one foot in, then realized, with a sharp intake of air, that she'd been holding her breath. As if she couldn't bear to inhale what they flung into the air.

She stepped into the foyer and half jumped when a man stood up in the living room.

"Dr. Kenney!" she said, her hand against her chest. "What are you doing here?"

"John called me. You had an appointment later, remember? He thought you'd need help navigating this gauntlet," he said quietly, "and he had to go to a meeting. So I cleared my schedule. We can meet right here instead."

"Okay, but…did he let you in? Or the officers? Are they still here, searching—?"

"No, I let him in," a voice said from the kitchen, softened with splashes of water from the sink. Carrie thought she must be hearing things; she wiggled her finger in one ear.

The woman stepped into the living room. Motes of dust sparkled above her head in the light. Her bobbed hair, streaked with gray. Eyes that squinted down to nothing when she smiled. Carrie's lip trembled with the weight of memory. The candy hidden in Mason jars in the narrow kitchen closet. The poems decoupaged to the coffee table. The tap shoes, old and worn and used on any wooden surface she could find.

"I tried to keep him in the vestibule," she said, smiling, "but he snake-charmed his way inside."

She wiped her hands on two dish towels knotted together around her small waist. *Who needs an apron?* she used to say. *An apron is just a towel with strings!* How long had it been—eleven years? No. Thirteen.

"Yes," Dr. Kenney said, "your neighbor was kind enough to answer the door."

"My neighbor?" Carrie's quivering lip broke into a smile. "Yes, the neighbors around here are always so…helpful. They just, um, appear out of thin air whenever you need them."

"It's good to have support."

"Yes, so you see, I, uh, don't need you here, Doctor, truly."

"Carrie, John told me you've been having some issues, and—"

"Doctor," the woman said suddenly, "I'll stay right here with her. Not that she needs much mollycoddling."

"Well…let's make another appointment then. For later today or first thing in the morning?"

"She'll check her calendar and give you a jingle, won't you, Care Bear?"

Carrie closed her eyes for a long second. No one else had ever called her that.

"Yes," Carrie said. "I will."

"You must promise me, Carrie," Dr. Kenney said solemnly.

He stood up, and Carrie nodded. He'd heard this before, she knew. John saying one thing, Carrie saying another. Neither of them making complete sense.

"I'll see myself out," he said. "No sense getting the natives restless. Nice meeting you, Mrs.—"

"Oh, just call me Gran," she said. "Everybody else does."

Carrie bolted the door behind him, then turned to her grandmother.

"Care Bear," Gran said and reached out her arms.

Carrie leaned her head against her shoulder, and the memories came flooding back. Birthday parties, Thanksgivings, Christmases, and just plain Saturday mornings. She'd come over with something she'd baked, still warm from the oven, and listen to Carrie talk about her week while she swept the floor and did the dishes and let Carrie's mother sleep in.

Carrie leaned in close, inhaled her earthy, cinnamon scent. How was it possible for someone dead to smell so much like cookie crumbs?

C arrie used to pretend her mother had been adopted by her grandmother. Found in a basket, dropped on the doorstep. How else to explain the difference between the two women? Her mother, thin and almost brittle, angled and sharp from a lifetime of determination. Always working or cleaning, barely sleeping. And her grandmother, slight but soft, even her hair feathery. How could cancer even take hold in a body like that? Gran moved almost silently, a perfect body for secrets and surprises. Carrie wouldn't hear her matches strike as she lit the candles on her birthday cake or sense her moving toward her with that circle of light; she just heard a dozen party balloons squeaking softly against the wall in the room behind her. Gran would set down the cake, illuminating herself and her granddaughter, with Carrie's mother still in the dark. All of Carrie's birthday photos had Gran's arms in them—placing the cake, distributing the presents. Gran would go through her photo album with Carrie and say, "I really should have invested in more bracelets."

And here she was, with her smile too wide for her small face and her blue eyes lighting a way out of her laugh lines. Her colorful words always surprised, coming out of that soft little body.

Tears ran down Carrie's cheeks onto her grandmother's sleeves. She felt so solid, so real. And Dr. Kenney had met her! Now John would surely believe her. If she told him at the right time in the right way, even Dr. Kenney would have to back her up! *She was there. She was real.*

"I suppose you're wondering why I'm here," Gran said finally, giving her a big squeeze before releasing her.

"No."

"No? Poppycock! It's not like I'm here every day."

"I wish you were."

"I wish I could have been here Monday," she said with a sigh. "So I could have met your little boy."

Carrie's tears flowed again, and she wiped her eyes with one hand.

"The first thing I said when I gave birth was 'I wish Gran could be here. I wish Gran could see this.' Okay, that was the second thing. The first thing was 'I want a glass of wine and a cheeseburger.'"

Gran laughed and patted Carrie's hand. "Well, I did see it, of course. I was there with you the whole time. But seeing him is not quite the same as meeting him."

"So…it doesn't work like that? You won't meet him…up there?"

"It's not the country club everyone thinks it is, Carrie. Everyone you love together, having a big party. No. I'm mostly in transit."

"Why? Because people here need you?"

"No, dear," she said and smiled. "Because I need them." She looked around the living room with satisfaction, ran her hands across the velvety throw on the back of the herringbone couch. "I miss things," she said. "Isn't that horrible to say? But you don't just miss people, it turns out."

"I think I would miss hot showers," Carrie said.

"I miss mohair," Gran said. "There is really nothing in the world, known or unknown, like mohair."

"Dogs. Kittens in a box," Carrie said.

"Tumbleweed. Queen Anne's lace. The curls at a baby's neck."

Carrie sucked in her breath, holding it in, thinking of Ben's curls, his hair so slippery and soft, it wasn't even capable of tangling.

"You have your mother's gift for decorating houses, I see. But thank God you didn't have her taste in men."

"Don't speak ill of the dead, Gran," she said.

Gran burst out laughing, so loud it sounded like it might break her, if she'd been breakable. If she'd ever been just human, flesh and bone only. Maybe that was the difference: some people are indestructible and others are ephemeral. Only a few were built to last forever. Maybe it wasn't heaven and hell at all; maybe it was just venerable versus vulnerable. Some people simply *stay*.

"Well, *him* I haven't run into yet. I suspect your father is probably avoiding me."

"Yes," Carrie said. Her father had never forgiven her grandmother for uncovering his infidelity. Maybe that was why he didn't come to her yesterday—he knew Gran was nearby and simply didn't want to see her, to deal with her again. Carrie smiled at the illogical logic of that.

"Well, what should we do before John gets back? A game of Scrabble?"

"I don't have a board."

"What? Well, I'll tell your mother to get you one for Christmas."

"Wait, you see Mom?"

"Not really. But she talks to me every night."

"My mother? Seriously?"

"She wasn't born a stick-in-the-mud, Carrie. Life made her a perfectionist. As if that would fix her marriage, her finances, her unhappiness. That's why she pushed you so hard too. Why she expected so much. She believed in the power of doing. But I don't think she believes anymore. You ought to give her another chance."

"To do what? Love Dad?"

"God, no."

"Parent me?"

"Well, sort of. To comfort you. It's kind of nice having someone living to hug."

"I hug her," Carrie said defensively.

"You know what I mean."

"Well, I also have John to hug."

"Yeah, that's not exactly working like gangbusters, is it?"

"I have friends."

"Really? All those muckety-mucks you went to high school with who wouldn't give you the time of day? And when was the last time you saw your college roommates anyway?"

"I'm not alone, Gran."

"Carrie, you need your mother. And did it ever occur to you that maybe your mother needs you?"

"She doesn't need anyone," Carrie said. Wasn't that what her mother had told her friends on the phone night after night when she dialed them instead of dialing Carrie's father? That she could do it on her own, that she didn't need anyone?

"Balderdash. Now, what about a game of cards? Double Solitaire maybe?"

Carrie smiled. "Would it be okay if we just made cookies like we used to when I was little?"

"Thumbprints with jam?"

"Yes!"

Together they assembled flour, sugar, butter. Carrie brought out raspberry jam and a new jar of strawberry. They worked side by side, taking turns sifting and stirring, while Carrie told Gran all about Ben. The details, like his long lashes and wide platypus feet. The way he looked mostly like John but a little, Carrie was certain, like her grandfather. If you laid the baby pictures side by side, you could see it. And she told her grandmother about seeing Jinx and finding the shoe. Gran nodded, just letting her talk. Carrie would realize later she'd already known everything she'd told her. Like she'd been watching everything, everywhere, all along.

They dropped the cookies onto baking sheets, and Carrie pressed her thumbs in while Gran dropped in the jam.

"Fix that one, will you?" Gran pointed to the second row. "It's gone all catawampus."

Finally, the cookies were in the oven, and the house smelled like home again. When the first batch came out, Gran held them aloft, inhaling the buttery scent.

"Too many for just you and John," she said. "Are you thinking what I'm thinking?"

"That I should freeze some for the funeral?"

"No, Care Bear. That you should bring some out to the reporters."

"Feed them? And talk to them? No, thank you."

"They've been out there all day."

"I don't think we should reward them for invading my privacy."

"Carrie, really. They're doing their jobs."

"That's the problem, Gran. They only care about their jobs, about ratings. And one of them, well…one of them knows too much about me already. I don't want to give them any new material."

"Just take out a plate. If you don't do it, I will, and I'll tell them I'm your dead grandmother, resurrected. How's that for juicy material? Now giddyap."

Gran watched Carrie walk outside. She held the plate in front of her like a shield, and miraculously, the reporters put down their microphones and cameras. She did one nice thing, and no one recorded it. But if she started throwing things or screaming, that would be captured for posterity.

"I'm sure you're hungry," Carrie said to them evenly, not smiling, not frowning. She had trouble holding her face that way. It hurt to keep it still; that felt like lying, that stillness. "And I'm sure you're hungry for answers too, but I don't have anything to say right now, okay?"

"Okay," one cameraman said as he took the plate. "Thank you!"

"You're welcome," she said over her shoulder as she walked back up the driveway.

"That's my girl," Gran said, putting another tray in the oven.

While subsequent batches baked, Carrie walked Gran through the house, showing it to her as if she'd never seen it. In Ben's room, Carrie stood at the crib, gripping the sides. She bit her lip and looked up, trying to keep the tears from starting again.

"You knew, didn't you?" Gran asked.

"Knew what?"

"Knew that Ben was dead?"

Carrie nodded but added that John didn't know. Didn't believe it. And didn't believe her about the dog either.

"But he'll believe it if he sees you," she said.

Gran shook her head slowly. "I can't stay that long, Care Bear. And it wouldn't be right."

"But what about the funeral? Mom will be here, and I—"

"That's not why I'm here, dear heart. Remember I said we come because we need to, not because you need us?"

"So you…missed me?"

"Every day," she said and sighed. "Of course. But I came to tell you, even if you don't listen to me about being kinder to your mother, that you have to tell John now, sweetheart. You have to tell him what happened."

"What? Grandma, no. No."

All those years ago, when she'd confessed to her grandmother, it had almost seemed redundant, as if she'd already known.

"Yes."

"No, don't you see? I'm a suspect! They think I had something to do with this!"

"Did I say tell the detectives? No. But John is confused, darling. He's hurt. He doesn't understand why it's all so much harder for you. Harder than it is for him. You need to explain to him that, well, you're sort of grieving, in a way, exponentially."

"No."

"You have to trust me on this, Care Bear. He needs to know. Someone else besides me needs to know."

"Ethan knows," she said softly. "Father Paul knows."

"That won't help, and you know it. Now, look at me. Promise me."

"Stay," Carrie said suddenly, gripping her grandmother tightly. "You can tell him. He'll believe me then, about everything. And you can explain what it was like. What she was like. What I was like. And the church, how I always went to church, and I was sure if I—"

Gran shook her head slowly. "John doesn't have to believe in me to believe in you, Care Bear. Now, wipe those tears. I have to skedaddle soon."

"I can't do it," she sobbed. "I can't bear to watch you leave."

"I'm always with you, Carrie. Always. Now, close your eyes," she said, pulling her into the rocking chair. "Close your eyes, and I'll sing you a song." She started in with a slow rendition of "Amazing Grace," then stopped.

"Hell's bells." She sighed. "What are we doing up here for my last five minutes when there are cookies to eat downstairs?"

———————⬦———————

Carrie didn't understand how it worked; all she knew was that her grandmother had said not to think of it as good-bye, just see you later. Gran had walked to the door, holding a cookie, and told Carrie to close her eyes. Carrie heard the door close heavily, and she jumped up for one last glimpse of Gran in the driveway, but she wasn't there. And neither were the reporters; they'd given up after the last batch of cookies.

Carrie grabbed her car keys and circled around the block. Where would Gran go next? To the park? Or would she travel to their old house, to remember Carrie as a baby? Carrie drove out to Ludbury Avenue and turned left, the route she knew by heart, to the neighborhood one street from the trolley tracks.

She hadn't seen her childhood home in years, and she almost didn't recognize it. The street wasn't littered with bikes and skateboards anymore; it was tidy, with a bright, new, almost-white sidewalk, but no people or cars except for what looked like a young man sitting in a dark car idling down the block. Probably a boy texting a teenage girl, telling her to come out. Nobody went up to the door anymore.

The new owners had painted the exterior a dove gray, almost blue, and trimmed it with maroon shutters. *Awfully colorful for Pennsylvania,* Carrie thought, *but still pretty.* Small houses should either be light or bright, her mother used to say. Not dark. These people had chosen bright. On the porch, two yellow rocking chairs moved slightly in the wind. No car in the driveway or tucked up against the curb. Carrie went up to the porch and looked through the mullioned windows of the front door. No Gran inside. No one home. She circled around the back. The patio stones were neatly edged with grass, and planters flanked the back door. A woodpecker tapped on an upper eave, making her jump. She realized how terrible this would look if someone came home—the infamous mother of a murdered child lurking in someone else's backyard, as if she were looking for someone she didn't dare to name. The thought deflated her, and she headed back to her car.

On the sidewalk, a few doors down, a young blond woman stood watching her. Perhaps this was the girl the boy had been waiting for? But no, she was too far away from that car. She continued to stare.

Yes, Carrie wanted to say. *I'm the woman on the news. I'm the one they don't believe. Go ahead and call the police.* But something in her easy girlish stance, hand on one hip, head cocked, made her think that wasn't what she was thinking at all. Carrie lingered for a moment before she opened the car door, then returned her gaze.

"I like your belt," she called out to Carrie.

"Thank you," Carrie said instinctively. And then thought, *That was random. That was odd.*

Carrie blinked, got in her car. She drove toward the girl, but she was moving faster and disappeared into the gated garden of one of the houses. Blond and tiny, like a bird. Something familiar in the set of her jaw and the feathery lines of her hair, and yet old-fashioned, like she'd been lifted from another era. And wearing, she saw, a needlepoint belt too. In the same colors.

She put her hand up to her mouth. Could this be Libby's daughter? Was this Mary, who recognized her belt?

The other car on the street pulled out behind her, and when Carrie glanced back in her rearview mirror, she didn't see anyone in the passenger seat. Just the boy. Just a boy with long hair who seemed to be waiting for something or someone.

Ben's shoe swung beneath the mirror as she turned to go home.

J ohn had had a completely different upbringing than Carrie
except for one thing: they both attended Episcopal churches.
When Carrie agreed to be married in John's church, it was one of
the few things that gave John's parents comfort—they had home
court advantage. It had made the wedding run a little smoother
and made everyone feel better about how their grandchildren
would be raised. Of course, as far as Carrie could tell, John had
never dated anyone too far afield of his mother's tastes. Carrie,
with no country club affiliation, no father to walk her down the
aisle, and a mother who worked harder than any man, was about
as rebellious as John had ever gotten. And if anyone was looking
for blame, it could clearly be placed on his grades—if he'd had
better test scores, he wouldn't have been at a state college, and
he would have met a larger cross-section of the same girls he'd
known at boarding school. And they wouldn't have been quite
like Carrie.

Over the years, Carrie had felt a kind of softening, an accep-
tance, as if they were tallying her best features: she was bright,
honey-blond, and had provided a grandson, an heir to continue
the family name. How bad could this pairing be?

But now, sitting alone in her son's bedroom, remembering her
visit from her grandmother, Carrie questioned whether she and

John even had their faith in common after all. John rarely went to church; was it possible he didn't believe? Maybe Reverend Carson would talk to him if Carrie asked. Talk to him about heaven, about resurrection, about the afterlife. Had John ever known anyone, other than Ben, who had died? If he had, would he be doubting her, doubting Ben? He would be more experienced about conjuring love. Pure love. Well, if John didn't believe her, maybe Libby would. Maybe she would try talking to Libby again. She looked up at the ceiling. *See Gran*, she thought. *I'm not alone in this. I'm not.*

Carrie stood and looked out the window in her son's room. The dark orange of sunset through the trees. Beautiful down by the pond. Neil and his dog. The jogger. Couples on their nightly walk. Living their lives, getting on with it. Nature painting a gloss over anything that was wrong. But it didn't always work like that, did it? Sometimes clearing your head, breathing in the world, only made things worse. Like going to the path. Like visiting her old house, running into no one except someone who was likely dead. It hadn't made her feel any better.

A car in the driveway. Keys in the door. She wiped her eyes and headed downstairs.

"Smells good in here," John said, glancing into the kitchen. "You made cookies?"

"Yes." *I, not we.* She knew he wasn't ready. Not after the dog. After Ben. She would have to find a new way to convince him.

He fiddled with his phone. "I haven't gotten any alerts. Did Dr. Kenney help you draft a statement? Or Susan Clark maybe? Did she call?"

"A statement?" she asked dumbly. *And then—wait—alerts? He has a Google alert on me, on Ben?*

"For the reporters. They're gone, so I assumed you spoke to them."

"No. No, no."

"You have to say something, Carrie. They'll come back every day until you do."

"I gave them cookies."

"Cookies? What?"

"You shouldn't have called him, John."

"Wha—who?"

"Dr. Kenney."

"Oh, for God's sake, Carrie. I had to leave, and when the vans started showing up—jeez, one guy got so close to me, I could smell his cologne! And what if Maya Mercer comes over again, upsetting you? I asked the doctor to come over so you wouldn't be alone."

"I'm not alone!" she said.

John blinked, ran his hand across his eyes. "Honey, I—"

He stopped; he didn't need to say more. His face had fallen; he looked older, tired, pale. His hair had grown long in the back, over his ears.

Carrie knew she had to be more careful; she had to choose her words before she spoke them.

"How can I be alone with a million reporters outside?"

John looked at his hands. She was trying to lighten the mood, but sometimes he believed the mood shouldn't budge.

Husbands didn't have to testify against their wives. They both knew John would never have to get up in front of a courtroom and tell them his wife was delusional, hallucinating. That her story had never made sense to him: How could a man sneak into a car and unbuckle a child in the space of time it took for a woman to dig for a linty quarter in a dark-bottomed purse? How? He'd never asked that question of Carrie, but she'd seen it in his eyes and wanted to scream: *People crash when they change the channel on a radio! People are struck by lightning before they even see the flash! The dangerous world moves fast, John! Faster than careful mortals can keep up!* If he knew what it was like to care for a baby all day, he'd know that it wasn't easy! That sometimes people had to make choices. Sometimes people made mistakes.

And she knew that whether he had to say it or not, that every television camera, every reporter, would read it on his face. They could look at a man and know if he believed in his own wife or if he thought, as Gran would say, that she was full of *bunkum*.

Carrie sat on the edge of the sofa, fiddling with the fringe of the throw. John stood in the middle of the room like it wasn't his house.

"When they come back, I'm just going to say no comment," she said. "Or nothing. I'll say nothing."

"No," John said. "That will make you seem too cold."

He looked cold when he said this, and he never looked cold. His eyes looked darker, more brown than green. His jaw locked, like it did when he was concentrating on writing a report for work. Was that what she was now? A spreadsheet, a task?

"Well, what then?"

"That's why I sent for Dr. Kenney, to help you figure that out."

Carrie sighed. "John, that is not why you sent for him. Susan Clark said I could say no comment, and I'll just add something warm to that, okay?"

"Like what?"

"Like 'Thank you, but I have no comment.'"

"As long as you don't just go adding...other things."

"Like what, John? Like cookies? Am I not allowed to give them cookies?"

"No—"

"Like the things that make you doubt my sanity?"

"I didn't say that."

"You didn't have to."

Still standing, as if he were her superior. She stood up too.

"How is it possible, John, that you went to church every Sunday your entire life and you don't believe in heaven?"

"Carrie, really, I—"

"Really what, John?"

"There's a difference between an afterlife and...ghosts."

"So you don't believe in ghosts? Or resurrection? How about Easter, John? Do you believe in Easter? Or just in chocolate eggs?"

"I didn't say that. I—"

"You don't." She sighed. "You don't believe. That's what this comes down to."

"Carrie, come on. We're not…clergy. We're not nuns. Nobody buys into everything wholesale. There's…a scale of belief."

She blinked. A Chinese menu? Just pick and choose?

"Does that scale include not believing your wife? Calling your wife a liar?"

"Carrie," he said with a sigh.

"How is this different from when you used to accuse me of not telling you where I was going? I'd say 'book club,' but you'd hear 'club.'"

"It's not the same!"

"It's exactly the same," she said through gritted teeth. "Just admit it, John. It would be so much easier if you would just admit it."

But he had no answer for her, no gesture of support or defeat. She walked upstairs and went into the guest room, and for the first time since they'd been married, she prepared to spend the night in a separate bed in the same house.

She brushed her teeth and put on a T-shirt and flannel pajama bottoms. In the corner of the guest room, on the small desk, sat a crystal perfume atomizer that had been her grandmother's. She picked it up and held it to her nose. Barely there, the notes of amber, jasmine. In a few months, it might be gone altogether. She put it down next to a small calendar she'd gotten in the mail. When she was a girl, she'd crossed out every day as it ended, as if she was relieved.

She looked at the week that had passed, the numbers, the empty boxes, no *x*'s through them. Wednesday, she'd seen her grandmother. Tuesday, it had been Jinx. And Monday, it had been Ben. She swallowed hard, a lump in her throat. Would there be someone else tomorrow?

John stood at the window, staring out at the small backyard. Still green, the grass. Soft enough to slide in, to fall, to roughhouse. It was almost dark, and the floodlights came on automatically, illuminating the leaves that were starting to turn. Only a few fell as he watched. He'd never stood in that spot before; he'd been out back a million times, of course, playing with his son, looking at the sunset with his wife, or grilling on the Weber balanced on the edge of the lawn. His path was practically worn on the carpet runner beneath his feet. But stand there, like a piece of sculpture, like a new piece of furniture in the room? Never.

That was why Carrie, who'd come down to the kitchen for a glass of water, approached him slowly, calling his name, then coming around and searching his eyes as if they could tell her what he was looking at. And they did, to some degree, when she saw the tears hovering.

"John?" she said.

"Look at that," he said and sniffed.

Her eyes followed his gaze. Even from up there, above the path, in the waning twilight, she could make out bits of color and shine—blue ribbons flapping parade-happy in the breeze, red Mylar balloons, darker shapes on the ground.

"I've seen them on the highway a million times," he said.

Carrie nodded.

"But the teddy bears," he said. "All those little stuffed animals. What good does it do? Why do they keep bringing them?"

"Well—"

"I keep imagining them…wet. With him, you know? Because he died without any toys," he said, almost choking on the words.

Carrie blinked, tried to focus. These were the kinds of things she'd said to John in the early weeks, months. *He doesn't have his toys. He doesn't have his juice. He doesn't have his crib mobile.* Was it more sad or less to picture a teddy bear on the silty bottom with Ben, plush paw clasped in his hand, its button eyes as flat and expressionless as fish?

She squeezed his hand. "We should donate them," Carrie said. "To the church day care center."

"Yes," he said.

"We'll do it together."

She got her coat and grabbed a roll of white garbage bags from under the kitchen sink. As they walked down to the path, the wind picked up, and the plastic edge of the bags lifted, flapping behind her. She didn't try to stop it. A year ago, she would have rerolled it, tucked it under her arm.

The shrine grew larger and shinier as they approached. So much silver. So much blue.

"They didn't know him," he said.

"What?"

"None of these people. If they'd known him, they would have left baseballs and bats and hockey sticks."

"Yes," she said. She reached for his hand, but he pulled it away. "John—"

"Let's just fill the bags, okay?"

They worked side by side until it was done. The bags were full but light. They carried them back by twos in each fist. John was about to put the bags in Carrie's trunk, then thought better of it. He let them down gently in the foyer to sit overnight. The tops of the bags, ungrasped, fell open a little as he started to walk away, releasing a small plastic sigh. John turned back. He leaned down and spread each bag open further, as if offering them some air.

I tried to tell them what I'd seen. Those two men, one mean, one kind.

They came door to door, looking like they had something to sell or something to hide. They were really looking for a camera, a machine that doesn't make mistakes, doesn't lie, doesn't get confused—not a witness. Didn't expect to find a person recording events in her memory. Sorry to have disappointed you both.

They looked at my Raina outfit—my costume, I call it—and sniffed with distaste. "You used to wear a uniform," I wanted to scream. "What's the difference? You wear what needs to be worn, what makes people feel respect or comfort. You do what needs to be done, and so do I."

They talked to all of us, and I told them what I knew, but they didn't listen. The mean one's eyes kept growing wider, which meant I was becoming a story he would tell later to his friends.

I knew when he thought about it more, when it settled, the doubt would sink in. How did someone like me know so much? And slowly, in the middle of the night, I would cross the line between witness and suspect. I knew that the same way I know all kinds of things.

But the young one gave me his card and told me to call him if I remembered anything else. Not saw, but remembered, he said.

And as they were leaving, I gave him one of my little cards too. My mother had a real card, but I made mine on the computer at the library and cut them up carefully, lining up the edges on the paper cutter just so.

He held it in his hand for a second and smiled.

I knew he wouldn't throw it away. The other one would, but not him.

THURSDAY

I t was hard to believe, looking out the window at the news vans assembling on the street in the early morning light, the people standing around them laughing and gripping cups of coffee as if they were at some kind of festive breakfast picnic, that Carrie had once considered broadcast journalism as a career.

It had been her mother's choice, based on her having good grades in English and writing, a strong, low voice, and a face that was pretty but not overly expressive. That was what she had said anyway, but Carrie knew it had been about money. It was about Katie Couric; it was about Kelly Ripa. She'd obviously never seen how ruthless these women could be. Her mother admired anyone whose cuteness hid the edges, the ambition.

But Carrie discovered in college that she didn't like the scrutiny of the camera, the effort required to hold the planes of her face a certain way, hair perfect, a certain kind of clothes worn. She was more comfortable behind the scenes, writing, producing. So she'd majored in print journalism instead but ended up working in public relations, which her mother considered a huge comedown and Carrie considered a lifeline, since all the journalism jobs were drying up. She always thought that after Ben went into kindergarten, she could work part-time in PR, have a few clients, keep a toe in, work from home, still juggle her volunteer duties. It was a good job for a mother. But she'd never gotten that far.

And now she was sure, as she pulled the linen curtain back, she would not have liked this aspect of broadcast journalism: stalking people who'd lost their children just in case they felt like confessing to the crime. No, she would not be very good at that at all.

She hadn't heard John showering or making coffee, but he was already gone, his cup and spoon in the sink. These last few months, she'd envied him his work, that automatic focus. Always a client to take out to lunch or dinner. Sales meetings to go to, and always in sunny places. Off-site meetings that took up two days and two nights. But he used it as an excuse—to turn off, to turn away. He'd gone back to work three days after Ben was kidnapped. *Three days!* As soon as the flyers were distributed, bam, he was out the door. *Robotic*, she thought, and then, sickeningly, *like my mother.* Maybe John was actually not cool and calm and strong but detached and mechanical, in the same, precise way. Cold enough to let her sleep in the guest room, to not come in and get her, to not run after her. Didn't John of all people know that women want a man to run after them, to reel them back in?

Carrie pondered her options—staying inside, making food for when the family arrived next week. But staying home would just make her think of her son, her grandmother. She could call the school and see if they needed her to take over a shift at the library. But oh, the looks on their faces. They'd be like Libby, wondering what on earth was wrong with her, how she could go out when her son, her baby, was dead. They didn't understand that she was ready. That she had known all along and been mourning every single day. That she was prepared, and now that it was here, there was nothing left to do. Maybe her friend Chelsea, who left her Facebook messages every couple of days, wondering how she was, could meet her for lunch? She couldn't stay home. She couldn't putter around the house, listening to that swarm of people outside. No. They wanted her to leave? She'd leave.

She grabbed her purse and a cardigan sweater, took a deep

breath, and opened the door. As the group ran toward her, heels clicking, equipment jangling, she looked over their heads, like she'd learned to do during presentations, and said, "Thank you, but I have no comment." Calmly. With neither smile nor grimace. Not of one world or the other.

"Carrie, do you know what happened to your son?"

"Mrs. Morgan, do you want to share your side of the story?"

"What about the allegation that you already had planned his funeral?"

She froze in her tracks and turned back to the person who said that. A short, fit man, his hair so lacquered it glistened.

"What did you say?" she asked. The cops had probably found everything relating to the funeral—but the media?

"Did you know he was dead, Mrs. Morgan?"

Her spine tingled with electricity, a conduit moving in both directions, rooting her to the spot. Was it visible on her? A second-sight halo around her head? The others moved around her with their cameras and their microphones and their expensive heels, capturing her confusion and her silence, her shock from the current buzzing in her ears, adding them together to form fury. The man had oddly colored green eyes, like marbles, and they bore into her as if he could excavate something with them. No, he didn't know what he was saying. He meant it completely differently, like a detective. He was just digging.

She opened her car door, and a pair of bees buzzed around her suddenly, then bounced across the windshield, sounding hard and soft at the same time.

"No comment," she said, giving them a last chance to get out of her way. As she was about to close the door, someone grabbed the handle from outside.

Maya Mercer leaned in next to the door.

"Carrie," she said with a smile. When she put her mind to smil-ing, it was as wide as someone on a parade float. Everything else about her was calculated to look no-nonsense and smart, from the stylish black glasses to the spiky bob. But that smile gave her away: she'd been beautiful her whole life. She wasn't used to people saying no to her.

"I don't have anything to say," Carrie said. "In case you don't know the meaning of the words *no comment*."

"But if you don't speak to me," Maya replied, "your old friends will do plenty of talking on your behalf. Is that what you want?"

"What do you mean?"

"I'm tempted to say no comment," Maya said.

Carrie's hands shook as she tried to insert the car key. She turned it too hard, and the engine scraped sickeningly. She turned it off, closed her eyes, took two deep breaths, and started again.

The passenger door opened, and Maya, on the other side of the car, slid inside.

"What are you doing?"

"Just drive around the corner. I need to say something to you in private, Carrie."

Carrie backed out too quickly, nearly hitting one of the vans. She drove around the corner onto a neighboring cul-de-sac, then pulled to the curb. She turned to Maya, her eyes narrowing.

"What?"

"Look, people make mistakes when they're young. Everyone does. Even me."

"Just stop. Please stop. I had nothing to do with my son's disappearance! Nothing!"

"I believe you."

"You're just saying that so I'll talk to you."

"No." Maya sighed and took off her glasses, cleaned them on the hem of her tailored coat. "I'm saying that because I'm observant. And because I'm observant, I want to ask you, completely off the record, if you...if you are okay."

"Okay?"

The list of people who did not think Carrie was okay was growing every day. She had almost begun believing it herself.

"If your husband has ever…hurt you."

"What?"

"He answers your questions for you, and he tells you what to wear. When he calls you babe, it makes my—"

"Get out of the car, Maya."

"That's how it starts, Carrie."

"You don't know what you're talking about."

"Don't I?" she said. She leaned over and lifted up the edge of her hair. A long thin scar snaked around the side and back of her neck. "I know exactly what I'm talking about."

Carrie shook her head. "It's not like that. I mean, I'm sorry for whatever happened to you, but—"

Maya nodded, then opened the door. "All right, Carrie. Have it your way. But if you decide it's time to stand up for yourself, well, you have my phone number."

Maya got out of Carrie's car and headed back to her own, parked with the other reporters. Carrie pulled out and headed for Sugarland Road. She turned left and drove too fast in the only direction she could bear to go: Away from the media. Away from her husband. Away from the pond.

The long southbound on-ramp to the interstate curved like a question mark. Carrie leaned into it, wondering how far she could drive until she could bear to go back. One exit? Two? Three? She could find a new town she'd never been to before, where they wouldn't automatically know her name and all the details of Ben's face—his long lashes, his tiny even teeth—as they loomed on stilts above the town exits. Where no one would ask where she was or why she'd done what she'd done, combing over the smallest things. Surely she could find a place where simple acts didn't mean anything, other than that a person was bored, sad, and organized to a fault.

The sun warmed the interior of the car, and she turned off the heat. She listened to a few songs on a classical station, but when the signal flagged, she turned it off. No reception toward the middle of the state, even now. Even after all these years. After forty miles or so, she passed a sign for Peterson Nature Preserve and tried to remember the last time she'd been there. As a child, she and her parents had gone there frequently, and when she and John had first met, they'd marveled over the fact that they both might have been in the same place, picnicking as children, at the same time. Could she have seen him, throwing a Frisbee to his brother and father? Might he have passed by her and her parents, eating on a cloth spread out on the lawn, and seen her father once before he left for good?

After they'd been dating a few months and it had gotten serious, they'd exchanged grade-school wallet photos, and though his had been sweet, it hadn't been familiar. She was sure that if she'd seen John and his family even once, she'd have remembered them. Their big white teeth, their strong jaws. Why did the very people who couldn't bear discussing things always seem to be all mouth?

She turned on her signal to exit the lane, and a lone dark car behind her did the same. *Couldn't be the same car. It's just a car.*

Nature, that was what she needed to heal. Ben loved to be outside—it was a way of honoring him, she thought. And if it reminded her of those happy days with her parents, would that be so wrong? She stopped at the log cabin at the entrance and paid the five-dollar fee. She must be getting old—it used to be two dollars. The man perched in the entry offered her a map, but she waved it away. She could recite the name of every trail from memory.

She parked near Greenback Trail, which was short and flat and circled back to the lot. She got out of her car and headed toward the Martin Overlook. She passed a handful of cars and a group of senior citizens who looked like they were power walking. A few students from the nearby community college laughed as they scrambled down the rocks. Not many moms and kids; some of the trails were steep. She'd never brought Ben here. He'd been too young, too apt to run off. She felt another pang of regret. All the things he'd missed out on, all the places he hadn't gone.

A few leaves floated down onto her shoulders as she walked toward the overlook. How Ben had loved autumn leaves, chasing them in the wind, clutching them in his small hand. She'd bought him his own small rake and plastic wheelbarrow, and he would gather them up, throw them back in the air, crying, "Again! Again!" as if he could propel them back into the trees.

Tears tumbled down her cheeks. She wished Nolan, wished everyone, could understand what she understood. Ben wouldn't come back for one more day to the person who'd hurt him! He would only come back to the person who'd loved him, who'd loved him more than anyone! She wished they could have seen how she had sobbed as she'd assembled all the playlists and photos. Lingering over each memory, embracing it before she picked up her computer mouse and made the collage. If they'd seen her, they would know!

She looked out over the gorge, the emerald trees framing the silver rocks, the gray-green column of river. She let her tears fall over the whole scene, muting its beauty. She didn't wipe them away. Some things were too beautiful to bear; they had to be softened with sadness. The rush of the river swam in her ears, mixing with hot tears. She didn't hear her name at first. He had to say it a second time.

"Carrie. *Carrie.*"

A statement, one word ironed flat. He'd always hated that lilt that signaled a question, railed against Valley girl up-talking taking over the world. Those were the kinds of things they had talked about. Global crises or verbal tics. Macro or micro. Everything had mattered to him. The teenagers around them who acted like children. Companies who still polluted the earth. The loss of vinyl records. He'd gone on for months about that. She smiled, thinking of his turntable, the wall of albums, his futon on the floor.

"Ethan." She gasped, smiling, and then the horror, before she turned around, of what this could mean. That he was here now. The last she'd heard, he'd moved to Canada when George W. Bush was reelected. But she smelled something thicker than crushed leaves or wet earth. Mud pies—it reminded her of mud pies.

"Oh my God, Ethan," she cried. "What happened?"

"Well, that depends. What period of time are we discussing?"

He leaned back against a wide tree, stretched his arms, and smiled his crooked smile. He'd grown into himself so nicely, she thought. His strawberry-blond hair cut to almost corporate length. A few wrinkles around his eyes. Corduroys and a soft shirt that was almost what a grown-up would wear. Almost. She ran to him, knocking him against the tree, leaning into his narrow chest, hugging him hard. He smelled like lemonade and mud, like spring. Like earth. Like...the others. Just a little bit of dirt. *Oh God, Ethan. So young.*

"Did it just happen? How...how old were you?"

"So...you know."

"Yes. My grandmother and Jinxie kind of tipped me off. This seems to be a popular week for"—she swallowed hard, searching for the right word that wouldn't cause her to burst into tears—"for...communicating."

He cocked his head and smiled at the tear in her eye, like he was glad she still cared about him. Then he sighed and gestured broadly, as if wiping the emotion away.

"Yeah, it's the leaves."

"The leaves?"

"Leaf peepers. We miss the glorious colors of fall. What can I say?" He swept his hand across the expansive view. "Timed it a bit too early though, I'd say."

"And here I thought it was because I was in trouble."

"Have you lost your sarcasm detection radar?"

"I guess." She smiled.

"Well, still, you can't beat a leaf."

"You always said fall reminded you of—"

"Death, yeah. Well, not so much now. Now it reminds me of beauty. Of love. And I like spring now too."

"You've lost your wintry cynicism."

"Not quite." He smiled. "Damn, Jinxie. Jinxie! How the hell is Jinxie?"

"The same," she said softly. "Exactly the same."

"It's kind of nice, not growing old. Twenty-six, to answer your earlier question. Would have been more interesting to put it off till twenty-seven and join the Jim Morrison club, but alas, I just couldn't wait."

Only a few years ago, but she hadn't heard anything about it.

Ethan's parents had moved away long ago, and of course Ethan—cynical, nonjoining Ethan—would never deign to be on Facebook and had probably included the phrase "whatever you do, don't give the alumni association the satisfaction of knowing I'm gone" in his will.

"How did it happen? I hope…it wasn't painful."

She'd seen her grandmother go through the ravages of cancer, her face sinking in those last days, her soft skin almost gray. And she'd never forget Jinxie panting too quickly after being hit by a car.

"Not one teeny bit," he said. "And my parents, they kept every detail private, just like I wanted. Last wishes and all."

She nodded. Of course Ethan wouldn't want a spectacle. Wouldn't want to give any assholes a chance to say anything he didn't want them to say.

"God, Carrie, remember the hours—the days—we used to spend doing absolutely nothing? Just talking, listening to music, staring at the sun? People don't do that anymore. It's appalling. At dinner parties, they check their phones to see who else they could be talking to. I think I had to die just to get away from all these fucking idiots."

She laughed. That was vintage Ethan. He wasn't meant to be a teenager; he could have gone straight to adulthood in fifth grade.

They hadn't kept in touch when they'd gone to college—Carrie to State and Ethan to Brown, where he, of course, had hated everyone. They had run into each other once over Christmas, just after Carrie had met John, and Ethan had not been able to stop talking about what fools he was surrounded by. Worse than high school, he'd said. Worse because they didn't have the excuse of being in high school. *You think the Pepsi Generation is bad? The Pepsi Progeny is ten times worse.*

"You changed the subject," she said.

"I said it wasn't painful."

"Sins of omission, Ethan. And how ironic, considering why you're here."

"Why am I here, Carrie? Illuminate me."

"I'm guessing the same reason my grandmother was. Because you want me to confide in someone. As if that would help. I don't know if you know, but the situation I'm in right now, it's—"

"I'm aware," he said softly. He sat down at the base of the tree and leaned back against it. "I'm also aware that your husband is worried about you. I think that's the real point, explaining to him."

"You really have to stop hanging out with my grandmother."

"Not that many options, kiddo. There're a lot of assholes everywhere, not just on earth."

She laughed. Ethan had always made her laugh, even when things were darkest. That night, when she'd been shivering so hard her teeth had chattered, when she'd thought she couldn't go on, he'd said, "Someday, we'll look back on this and laugh," and she'd burst out laughing at the sheer absurdity of it.

"Ethan, I—it's too late."

"No, Carrie. It's too late for me, but it's not too late for you."

"My mother will never forgive me."

"I think you need to give your mother a little more credit."

She shook her head. Ethan had always defended her mother, but the answer was no. No, no, no. Especially now. How could you tell a woman who'd lost one grandson that she'd also lost another one?

"Ethan, I—"

"Carrie, you were young, and you were frightened, and you had no money. You were this perfect girl who got straight A's and always did her chores and went to church every Sunday and got a job after school to help out. You hid your pregnancy from your mother because you were afraid she wouldn't love you if you weren't perfect, and I'm here to tell you, Carrie, that it's a lie. We believed it then, but we were wrong, both of us."

"No, you remember how she was! How her face fell if I got an A minus because she was so afraid I wouldn't get a scholarship! You understood! You knew I couldn't tell her!"

"No, Carrie. Your mother is the ultimate survivor. She was a warrior. She would have made it work because that's what people like her do. I only agreed with you because I was chickenshit. I bought into your excuse because it dovetailed with my own."

"No! It's too late, Ethan. Too much has happened. Even if they weren't questioning me in Ben's disappearance, it's—it's…"

"It's what, Carrie?"

"She'll want me to get in touch with Safe Cradle, to find out who adopted him, to try to see him. She'll push me, hammer me, until I agree to do it. And then what? Will it replace Ben? No. And it will mess up his life too! Don't you see that? That poor couple who adopted him and have probably loved him to pieces… It's hopeless. I always thought I'd find him one day. I did, really, Ethan. But now—now I just can't. It's too much. It's too much. I can't do it."

"That won't happen, Carrie," he said softly.

"You're right," she said. "Because I wouldn't let it happen. I'm stronger now; she can't push me around."

"No," he said slowly, standing up, stretching his legs. He leaned back against the tree again, as if appreciating its breadth, the safe strength of its bark. He ran his hand across a wide, mossy expanse. He took a long inhale of air. "That's not why."

"Then why?"

"Because no one adopted him at Safe Cradle."

"What? What do you mean? How do—"

"Because I didn't take him there when I left you that night."

She suddenly couldn't feel her feet. Both went numb, threatened to not hold her up any longer. Was this how it felt when the earth was about to open up? When lightning prepared to strike?

"What?"

"I brought him here," he said slowly.

"No," she said, backing away. "My God, no, Ethan."

"Yes. I chickened out. For years afterward, I told myself it was because I thought they'd ask too many questions. I thought we'd be caught, and you'd lose your scholarship, and I'd lose my chance to finally get away fr—"

"No!"

Carrie's mind went back to that night, how strange he'd been when he returned. How long it had taken—an hour and a half. His pale lips. Not talkative, like he usually was. She'd put it down to the events of the day, the stress of helping his girlfriend give birth in the basement with nothing more than a few towels and a pair of scissors and a how-to book on home birthing. She'd never thought; she'd never questioned. Why would she? *There could have been a line at Safe Cradle. There could have been paperwork.* They'd had a plan! He'd agreed to the plan!

She waited for him to turn it all around, make it into some kind of joke. "Oh, my mistake; it was the towels I threw out!" But there was no laughter, no smile. His face looked like someone else's.

"But the truth is I was just punishing you."

"Me?"

"Yes. For refusing to have an abortion."

"Ethan, that's—"

"Crazy? Evil? Yeah, yeah, it is. So you asked me if it was painful, my death? No. When I jumped off that bridge in Canada in the middle of the night? It didn't hurt at all. My life was what hurt, from the guilt and the stupidity and the cowardice. When I floated through the air, and when I hit the pure, clean water, I didn't feel a thing. But after all these years, I just needed to know. I needed to know if it hurt him. I needed to feel everything he felt. And what's really crazy? For years and years, I convinced myself that you knew all along what I did. That you were glad I did it."

"Good God, Ethan—"

"There was a look on your face when I came back—"

"No!"

"A look of pure steel, like we'd crossed it off the list together."

"I'm going to be sick," Carrie said, leaning over at the waist. "I'm going to be very sick."

"No, you're not, Carrie," he said. "You're going to be well. Happy and well and loved your whole life. And forgiven. *You are going to be forgiven.* But not me. Never."

Bile rose in her throat. He had done what no one could conceive of, and yet, here he was. Talking to her. Moving through the universe, seeing her, seeing her grandmother.

"But wait, Ethan," she said, raising her head. "If you're with my grandmother, surely you've already been forgiv—"

"If you believe that crap, Carrie, then I have seriously misjudged you. I always thought you were smarter than the rest."

Smarter? To have not seen what had unspooled that night before her very eyes? She retched into the edge of the path leading down to the trail's head. Behind her, she heard a small child say, "Ew!" and a mother shushing him, telling him that everyone gets sick sometimes.

When she turned around, she caught a glimpse of that little boy, his red hair, his blue pants, still staring at her.

But Ethan? The tree stood in the same place, moss crawling up the bark. Carrie walked over and brushed her hand against it, pressing her palm to where Ethan's had been, inhaling the green tang, more alive than the tree. But Ethan was nowhere to be found.

C arrie's hands gripped the wheel tightly. She headed home, but there was nowhere she wanted to go. There were reporters lining her street, detectives following her every move, a husband watching her like a hawk. And did any of that matter after what she'd just found out? Tears spilled from her eyes, trailing down her neck, evaporating down to nothing against her collarbone. All these years, she'd wondered why she hadn't felt more of a pull to locate that baby. Yes, she'd occasionally looked on the Internet, wondered what the process would be. But she'd never taken the next step. Why hadn't she wondered more about what he looked like, how he'd turned out? A few fleeting thoughts, when Ben was born: *Do they look alike?* But not the driving force that other people feel. Now she knew why. *He'd been gone.*

She couldn't change the past; she couldn't look forward to the future. She couldn't even experience the full satisfaction of being angry at Ethan, to pound him with her fists, to show up at his door furious all over again. He was a true coward. He waited until he was dead and untouchable, floating in the air, to tell her the truth.

All she could do was drive home. Taking the curves along Vestry Road, winding past properties whose stone walls only hinted at their beauty, she didn't think, as her mother would have, about the people living in those houses—whether they were happy, if their families were growing, if they needed more space or light, if they felt a kind of wanderlust that might bring them to a Realtor's door. No. She thought instead of the work that went into the facades, how long it would take to carry the stones from quarry to truck to rolling green hill. How, depending on who you were, a stone or log was merely a weight and a building block, not a color or ornament or exclamation point. She had a worker-bee mentality. That was what her PR boss had told her in her first review, and the way she'd said it, with a taut, smug smile, Carrie had thought that, even though it had been stated as an attribute, it was definitely a flaw. That was why it was so easy for her to stay home with Ben at first. She knew she would never be fully appreciated in the workplace, but perhaps she could be in a home.

She understood that a million small acts kept the world spinning. She supported unions even when they went on strike, believed teachers and police were the highest callings. Sometimes at a cocktail party or even a coffee-cake gathering at church, Carrie would be caught up in a clutch of Republicans, trying valiantly to defend her position, and John would see her hands gesturing from across the room, a telltale sign she was debating someone, and come over to rescue her. He'd pretend to support her positions just so she wouldn't feel so alone. She always said the same thing: *you didn't have to do that.* But she said it while squeezing his hand, her eyes damp with gratitude.

And that was why, when Carrie finally got home and got out of her car and barreled toward John as he stood next to the Orkin truck, her hands balled into fists, her stride half running, like the cheerleader she used to be, about to launch into something fiery and spectacular, vaulted and soaring with a twist, his first thought was that there was something wrong with choosing that company. That they'd been unfair to their workers, that their policies or practices outraged her.

"Stop!" she screamed. But her eyes weren't on John. She ran past him toward the backyard, heading for the man in uniform crouched at the back corner of her house. John wasn't fast enough to save her this time. Carrie grabbed the hose out of the gray-uniformed man's hand, twisting it loose from its backpack, and John imagined all the chemicals spraying across her, across the yard, instead of pointed at the base of the house, measured and remote.

The exterminator, apparently envisioning the same thing, fought Carrie for control of the hose, his protests muffled by the mask over his face. They tussled over it for a few long seconds before John reached Carrie, wrapped his arms beneath her, and pulled her away, the hose falling to the ground while she kicked and karate-chopped the air like a feral child.

"Shh," John said. "It's okay."

"It's not okay!"

"Let's go in the house."

"No! No! He has to stop!"

"Fine, all right. We'll get someone else. We'll—"

"No! No more killing! No more death!"

John set Carrie down on the pavement in front of their yellow garage door. Her eyes were red, and a long piece of her hair was still stuck stubbornly across her lip. He pulled it away gently, tucking it behind her ear, as if the errant lock were part of the problem, blocking her true reasoning from being communicated clearly the first time.

"All right," he said softly, sheepishly. *He should have known. Of course he should have known.*

She nodded, then swallowed. Along the side of the garage, the man walked tentatively toward them, gripping his equipment tightly.

"I'll go ahead and cancel the contract then," he said, and John nodded. He hesitated for a moment before opening the door to his truck, as if waiting for an apology, but none came.

They went inside, and John wrapped Carrie in his arms. "No more death in this house," he whispered. "I get it."

She hugged him back and apologized. "It's just…the thought of it. It's too creepy, John. I can't…I can't imagine."

"The…carcasses," he said. "Carapaces, whatever they're called. The idea of that under the house, buried in their hive—I understand."

"No," she said.

"No?"

He lifted his face from her hair.

"I mean, what if they all came back too, angry, buzzing, stronger than they were before?"

"What?" He held her at arm's length, searching her face like a dictionary. If he paid more attention, looked carefully, wouldn't it all be simple to understand?

"Murdered bees," she said. "If they come back to haunt us, wouldn't they be the angriest, the most dangerous souls of them all?"

His mouth started to form a familiar sentence. That she was not making sense. That she needed to see Dr. Kenney. That something larger, and more profound, was wrong with her and needed to be addressed.

But he didn't. He closed his lips and didn't say anything more. He just hugged her as if he feared what she feared, as if they had, at last, another fear in common. They held each other for a long time until she pulled away and looked at him quizzically.

"Why are you here, John?"

He surveyed her eyes. Was it a trick question? His life's meaning being called on the carpet?

"Home," she said. "Why did you come home in the middle of the day? And where—where are the news vans and all of their stuff: their trash, their—"

"I, uh, I have good news," he said.

"Good news?" She screwed up her face as she said it, the opposite of how anyone else would have reacted. So unexpected and so wrong. Not today. He had good news. She had bad news. They canceled each other out.

"Come on," he said, pulling her into the kitchen. He poured her a glass of wine, told her to drink it.

"Why? Why do I need to drink it?"

"Carrie," he said breathlessly, "they're interviewing a person of interest."

"What?"

"Forrester told me about it all, in confidence, of course, after the news con—"

"Not the dog guy. Oh my God! I stood next to him, side by side at that pond, and I never—"

"No. The parking lot guy."

Carrie had almost stopped believing in him. He'd become a myth, a vague dark shape, like Big Foot.

"No."

"Yeah."

"The guy from the Y? How did they find him?"

"New info from one of the witnesses."

"Who? What witness? From someone around here, or someone from the past?"

"The past?" He screwed up his face. "What do you mean?"

"I mean, is it a new witness or new information, someone who remembered something different?" She thought of the moms at the Y, how desperately they'd wanted to help. And all the footage from the surrounding businesses, the cameras tilted at exactly the wrong angle at precisely the wrong time. What had changed?

"Sounds like Forrester followed up on something. I sensed a big disconnect between him and Nolan."

"Imagine the disconnect if he knew his partner was feeding you information."

"No, sounds like Nolan didn't believe the person and Forrester did. So he followed up."

"A hero," she said quietly.

"Not really. Just a man trying to be heard, I think."

"So they're interviewing someone else," she repeated, chewing nervously on her thumb.

"Yes."

"Well, it should be interesting to see what…details he even remembers," she said softly. "After all this time. It's probably hazy, or—or—"

"Well, it's huge," John said, smiling. "He was there."

"Do you think they'll believe him?" she said suddenly. "Believe every last little thing he says, even though they don't know him?"

"Uh…I don't know, Carrie. All I know is it's good news. Extremely good news."

"Does Susan Clark know this?"

He nodded. "I called her right away. Forrester said Nolan is being a prick, trying to undercut the significance, saying he's still investigating other leads, which probably means you. But Forrester says he never lost faith."

"Well, that would make him the only one, wouldn't it, John?"

John paused, wounded. He'd told her; he'd shared. And hadn't he pretended to understand what the hell she was talking about with the Orkin man? *This was his doing! It was his buddy-buddy relationship that brought them the inside scoop. Wasn't he the true hero? Didn't Carrie want to cheer him now?* But he swallowed it; she wasn't herself. Hadn't Danielle warned him to give Carrie lots of rope, lots of slack? To leave her alone, to let things slide a bit? Hadn't she told him that stress could undo a person, make anything happen?

"No, honey, of course not. It's just—the stress. The stress of everything is getting to you, that's all. And all that time you've been spending at church. It's…putting ideas in your head."

Her lip quivered. Ideas in her head? She knew. She *saw.* She was more observant than anyone! If she hadn't had her face buried in her purse, this all would have been solved long ago! Because she remembered *everything.* She remembered how her grandmother looked before she'd gotten sick. She remembered the flat way Ethan ended his sentences. She remembered the contour of a bald divot under a dog's snout. She remembered the tiny head of a newborn baby with its pale blue veins. She could pick up the details of the dead, their shadings, their timbre and lilt and loamy potpourri, after years had passed. She remembered—only her.

Detective Nolan's stance at the press conference—feet wide, hands grasped in front over his wide belly, jaw locked, eyes straight ahead—conveyed confidence. As if he'd been the one to figure it all out. As if he were the smartest man up there, and not just the oldest. As if he were the one at the podium, flashing the stripes of the chief, charming the female reporters. Forrester, standing off to his right, was a collection of slack limbs, lowered shoulders, cocked head, soft knees. He looked like he was lying down even when he was standing up. Was that his trick? He relaxed people, made them trust, even when they shouldn't?

"We're pleased to announce a major development in the Benjamin Morgan case," the chief said, his eyes working the room as though he was already the politician some assumed he would someday become. If he handled cases like this right, maybe. Not that he wished for more crimes, more homicides, but still. The spotlight. The challenge.

Microphones raised, cameras poised. Not just the local affiliates anymore—not after all this time, and all the strangeness of this case. The woman from *24/7* was there, right up front, in a row of her contemporaries from CNN, *60 Minutes*, and others.

The boy's reappearance had reignited the imagination of everyone who had heard about it. And they didn't even know the half of it.

"We have a person of interest in custody at this time," he continued. "Thanks to the tireless efforts of the Lower Merion Police Department, who don't believe in cold cases. They only believe in cases that need perseverance, judgment, and close, careful attention." He used a hand gesture to separate each word, clear as commas. "Now, we have time for just a few of your questions before we get back to it."

"Has the suspect been charged?"

"Person of interest. Not a suspect."

"But—"

"Not at this time."

"Do you anticipate—"

"No comment. See, I anticipated what you were going to say."

A few titters of laughter from the room, a rueful smile from Forrester. Nothing from Nolan.

"Is this a new suspect or someone you already interviewed?"

"New."

"Was the suspect apprehended as the result of a citizen's tip or a witness?"

"Not a suspect, as I said before. And it was a witness who came forward with new information."

"Not a new witness, but someone you interviewed before?"

"We are not prepared to discuss the witness at this time. Thank you all for helping us shine a spotlight on this important case and the hard work of our police officers. Good day."

He turned and led the way, followed by Nolan, then Forrester. If any of the reporters saw John standing quietly at the back of the room, upright behind all the people leaning forward with the weight of their microphones, notebooks, and cameras, they didn't acknowledge him. Nor did John try to do anything more than blend in. He didn't even make eye contact with Forrester, not daring to. All he knew for sure was that his wife was not the suspect in custody, because his neighbor had already texted him and told him she was at home, safe at home.

And later, when he got the next phone call from Forrester and they arranged a place to meet for a beer, he would find out for sure that his wife was not the witness either. After he finished his beer and felt the relief of the last swallow going down, that small consolation would spread across his head and heart. He could not bear the thought of Carrie suddenly recalling a perfect, incriminating piece of information. Something that floated up and shimmered, proud of its shape, the missing, interlocking piece. The guilt, the shame Carrie would feel, of her memory burying it for so long, too long to be helpful. It was too late for that. It was just too late for anything but justice.

C arrie took a bath, just as John had suggested. She ducked her head under the water and didn't think about the dying bees, the buzzing she sometimes heard at night when she couldn't sleep, the honey-sweet smell of a dead one soaring back, aiming at her heart. And she tried not to think of Ben or of Ethan or the baby, the baby she hadn't thought about in so many years, the baby she would get around to, get back to, someday, when the time was right. All that time she'd wasted, thinking she had plenty. When she had had nothing—nothing—all along. She tried to just focus on the water, on getting clean.

As she went downstairs into the kitchen, the smell of garlic wafted up. The room had been erased of her grandmother. Gone were the cinnamon notes of cookies and vanilla tea. Now the smell was savory, dark, meaty. She was still queasy; the last thing she wanted to do was eat.

John stood over the chopping board, wrestling with an onion and winning. His strong capable way of doing everything he did. She used to love the way he peeled it in one go, then stacked up the rings as he cut them, in quick, even piles.

"What are you making?"

"Steak surprise."

His pet name for fajitas, which was the only thing John really knew how to make. Cut things up, grill them, put them on a tortilla. A *grilled* tortilla. She supposed men liked to grill because they were impatient. No stirring or simmering. Flame, color, branding. Evidence they had made their mark.

Her face was on the verge of a frown. John put down his tongs. "What's wrong?"

"It just seems odd to celebrate," she said softly. Her throat was still sore from screaming at him, her breath sour from throwing up earlier. Didn't she look as terrible as she felt?

"It's not a celebration. It's just..." He shrugged his shoulders. "Well, it's been so long since we had anything good happen, right?"

"Right."

"And it *is* good news for you, for us."

She wanted to nod but couldn't. How could they have good news when their son could not?

John added the onion to the griddle, turned up the overhead fan. He'd already grilled the meat and the peppers, which lay curled on a platter. He did it in a logical order, according to the way his brain worked, but Carrie believed he'd done it backward. Weren't you supposed to caramelize the onions first?

He left the onions sizzling and folded Carrie into a hug. His wide chest, his big heart. She'd always thought they correlated. Now he felt almost too big, twice as wide as Ethan's narrow hug.

"Carrie, I have to tell you something, honey," he whispered.

"What?"

"What you said, about Forrester playing me, suspecting me?"

Her tongue throbbed inside her mouth, and her answer came out cottony, cloaked. "Yes?"

"Before I met you, you remember me telling you about Lyndsey?"

"Your old girlfriend? The one who transferred?"

"Yes."

"I remember."

"Well, I don't know if I ever told you, but...she was really a reckless girl."

"Reckless?" That was a word of someone else's generation. She'd never heard anyone their age say it.

"Wild, you know. Loved to party and loved to argue. A real drama queen."

Carrie winced. She'd always hated that phrase. It always seemed it was a way for men to dismiss women who wanted to talk, to say their piece.

"I could never...trust her to do the right thing. And she didn't understand me, you know, like you did."

"Why are you telling me this, John? Did you look her up on Instagram and then go visit her, fall in love a—"

"No! No. I would never want to see her again. She...she got me arrested one summer."

"Arrested? For what?"

"For stalking."

Carrie felt queasy, her knees threatening to give out.

"I didn't do anything except, you know—"

"Follow her?"

"She basically needed a bodyguard, Carrie! She did! If you had seen her... I—I saved her on a few occasions. Three guys, four, on the path by the river, you know? God knows what would have happened. But she didn't get it. She just didn't get it."

"Do Forrester and Nolan know? God, they must know."

She thought back to Nolan. Working off a theory, following up on a lead. They were playing him! Was this the theory?

"That's just it—it was a week before I turned eighteen. So the records were sealed."

"But couldn't they still find out, John? Is that why you never told me? Why you're telling me now? Before you get caught?"

"No! I just, well, I wanted you to know. The police could always talk to her or her parents, I guess. But I don't think they will now."

"So you must feel relieved," she said.

His hands on her shoulders, sliding down to her waist, pulling her in tighter, like they were dancing. Swaying side to side in that dark expanse of a hug. Safe, but also enveloped. Hidden. And sometimes smothered.

"Yes."

"So we're celebrating your relief. Is that it?"

"Carrie," he said. "Seriously. I do feel like it's a good thing, finally. And maybe the beginning of a fresh start, a clean slate. It's like our mothers say," he whispered into the hair he loved so well. Golden and shiny, always clean looking. Even when she was at her lowest points, she always took care of herself. She smelled a little dusty now, like old fruit, but he didn't care. "We have to remember we're still young. We can go on. We can try again. Start all over. We can."

Bile bubbled and burned in her throat. She elbowed her way out of the cage of his embrace, ran to the sink, tried not to gag.

"What? What's wrong?"

"John, I—I don't know if I can."

"Well, not...now, honey. I didn't mean now. Oh, geez, I mean... you misunderstood."

"No, John, that's not—"

"I meant not now, but soon. Eventually. We'll get past this and then, you know, later—"

"I said I don't know if I can!" she cried.

"Okay, okay. I just thought... I... Oh crap, Carrie, I don't know what I was thinking. I just was looking for something...happy. And feeling bad that I didn't tell you about Lyndsey a long time ago."

The onions sputtered, demanding attention. He picked up a spatula and started to stir.

"John," she said in a voice she didn't recognize, "I have to—I have to tell you something too."

"What? Did you remember more? Should I call Forrester? They're still building the case, so—"

"No, I—John—I...I've kept a secret from you as well."

"A secret?"

He smiled initially, but it faltered a little on the edges, like he didn't know how long he could hold on to happy. A secret sounded like it could be good or bad or anywhere in between, kind of like his. John was hoping for good. He really needed good. But the look on her face! He steeled himself; he'd already asked if she was having an affair—could she have lied to him?

"I...had a baby in high school."

"What?"

"With my boyfriend."

He dropped his spatula. "What did you say?"

"I had a baby. Before. Before you, before Ben."

He blinked, ran his hand across his face. "And you, what, you gave it up for adoption?"

"Yes." She was on shaky ground still, she knew. Didn't dare tell him the rest. No. Dear God, *no*. "The detectives, they, um, they found the word *adoption* in my search history, so they found that suspicious. Like I wanted to..." Her breath caught in her throat.

"Wait a minute," John said, running his hands through his hair. "A boy or a girl?"

She swallowed slowly, took a deep breath. Why on earth would he ask that particular question? She looked up at him and saw the pain in his eyes. He realized too what a stupid, inane question it was. He was simply buying time, and they both knew it.

"A boy," she said quietly.

"A boy. You had another boy, before Ben." He recited it back to her, but she didn't correct him.

"And that's why, you see, that's why it's been so hard for me. Psychologically. Because I—I've been grieving twice. Reliving the first loss."

He nodded slowly. "That's what Dr. Kenney said?"

John's hands tingled. Had Dr. Kenney known this but not been able to tell John, because of client privilege? He was probably trying to convince Carrie to tell him, to choose the right time. But this—how on earth could this be the right time? What was wrong with her? Or had the police found out? Is that why?

Did Susan Clark tell her to tell him, before he found out some other way?

"Not...exactly. It's...that's just—what is. What's true."

"So—but you just—decided not to tell me or my family this? Like, ever? Even though our son had a brother out there in the world?"

"Half brother."

"Doesn't matter, Carrie."

"I suppose you're right. I should have told you. I know I should have told you."

"This is...this is huge." Unspoken: *This is bigger than my secret. This is worse.* "And Danielle was okay with this...this...deception?"

"John, I didn't even know you back then!"

"I can't believe your mother wouldn't understand how *my* mother would feel, how my family—how we all would feel. That she'd let you do this? Keep a brother from a brother?"

Carrie thought of John's younger brother Luke, their wrestling hugs, their bunk beds. She didn't have a sibling. She didn't understand. She searched his eyes, as if she could locate the source of his connection.

"John," she said with a sigh. "My mother didn't allow it. Because she didn't know."

"What?"

"You heard me."

"How could she not know?"

"We were struggling. I needed a scholarship. I couldn't afford to lose that, so I—I hid it all from her."

"Wait," he said, contorting his face. "So you were one of those girls who give birth in, like, their garage? Or a public bathroom? And just...clean it up and don't tell anyone, even their family and closest friends?"

The look on his face, the sound of his voice, the words he chose, chilled her. She was one of *those girls*? The girls you read about in other towns? She was a grainy photo in a tabloid newspaper? He said it as if she were less than human. Hadn't he ever read a newspaper, learned about the backgrounds behind the headlines? Didn't John know anything about people other than himself? How dare he!

"Yeah, and you were one of those stalkers who ends up beating his girlfriends to a pulp?"

"I didn't beat her up! I didn't do anything to her."

"John, I was sixteen years old! I was terrified. I was—"

"Carrie," he said slowly, "that was only two years before we met."

"Two years is a long time when you're a teenager."

"Maybe," he said. He took the onions and piled them on top of the food. He put down the tongs and walked into the foyer, picked up his car keys, his briefcase, his coat.

"John!" she called.

"Have some steak," he said. "Or do you still like steak, Carrie? Do you even eat meat these days? Because I have to say, I feel like I don't know anything about you anymore. Anything."

And then he was gone.

She leaned into the nearest chair. The arrivals and departures of the living were as abrupt as the dead. How was she supposed to know who was coming, who was going, what was real anymore? All she knew was she was alone. Completely, utterly alone.

She put her hands up to her face. It didn't feel any different than her grandmother's had. Flesh, bone, curves, lashes. *It never goes away*, she thought. The essence of a person is the same as the outline, the form. She held her hands over her eyes a long, long time, trying to decide who she was angrier with—her husband or her dead ex-boyfriend.

FRIDAY

B efore she went to kindergarten, Carrie used to wait every day for the mailman to arrive. As soon as she'd hear the sound of his Jeep coming up one side of the street, she'd run out to stand by the end of their short driveway, right where Danielle could see her. She'd wait as he made his rounds, up one side of the street and down the other, until he'd reach their bungalow.

Danielle had always thought it was because Carrie was an only child, lonely in this neighborhood of mostly empty nesters and bored with her mother by the middle of each day, glad to see someone new. The mailman seemed to understand his role; if he didn't have any promising-looking mail to deliver—a magazine or package, for instance, or a card or letter addressed to Carrie—he always included a lollipop or Hershey's kiss on top of the stack of letters. Later, when she was older, Carrie was surprised to learn from other people that their mailmen did not deliver candy. Surprised, but not disappointed. It was the others who were disappointed, not her.

The day the creamy envelope came in the mail from State, she'd heard the sound of the Jeep rounding the corner. Heard it right through the din of her earphones. She lifted her head off her bed, then shushed Jinx, who always startled when he heard a car.

Ethan had already been accepted to Brown, but he waited to

celebrate, insisting that it was all or nothing. Both of them happy, her with her scholarship too, or neither of them.

When the mailman handed her the envelope, smiling, and she felt its heft, she knew it was a good sign. The rejections were always thin, the other kids had told her. *No* is a smaller word, much smaller, than *yes*.

When she opened it, not on the phone with Ethan, as he'd told her to, but alone, in the heat of her stuffy room, she had not felt joy. She had not felt pride, or righteousness, or belief that it had all been worth it.

She had felt something larger, and if she'd had to name it, she would have said relief.

What had Carrie done during two years' worth of nap times in her house? She cleaned, she baked, she looked at home decorating websites. She cooked dinners and froze them in containers so John would have something to eat after he put Ben to bed on those evenings when she had book club, a tennis match, a charity event at church. She binge-watched TV, read a book, planted peonies. Nap time in her house represented the domestic life she thought she'd always wanted, but now, without a husband or a child, she felt as empty as she'd felt at college without Ethan. *What is my agenda without their agenda?*

As she sat in her pajamas with her lukewarm coffee, contemplating another empty day, she understood better the words John had spat at her. She didn't recognize herself anymore either. After the grieving, after the knowing, after the defending, what is left? *Less, far less than you envision. The weight lifts off, and you miss the pressure of it, sitting on your chest.* The same way she'd felt after she got her scholarship.

Dr. Kenney had said she would know when it was time to move on—to look for a job, to have another baby. That she would feel a seismic shift. Was that what she felt when she'd been with Ethan on Thursday? A sign that it was over, that her old life was cleaved in half, with Ethan on the other side?

She woke up, and her first thought was, *Only one other living person knows*. She had thought telling John part of the story would make it less lonely on her side, but she'd been wrong. So maybe moving on meant moving past John. She had to face that possibility. Mentally, he was already there, wasn't he? He proved that by walking away last night. Proved that he could leave her, start over, if he had to. And all those times, following her, looking through her things, worried there was someone else—maybe he wanted there to be someone else.

She took off her pajamas and pulled on jeans and a T-shirt and an old green V-neck sweater. She went into the spare room, opened the closet. She slid the ceiling board away from the crawl space entry and pulled the large cloth box down. The lid was askew, and she knew she hadn't left it that way. Only a man would leave it that way—a policeman, not John. She lifted the crooked lid. The photo boards, with flannel baby fabric, moon- and star-shaped pins holding the photos chronologically.

There they all were in the hospital. There were Ben's tiny fists, his little feet, his first steps. She had taken care to include photos of everyone in their families, knowing they'd want their memories documented too. She'd searched *funeral photo boards* on Pinterest and copied ideas. She believed choosing the fabric and making all the boards would take up some of the empty days. But it had been too easy; it had taken only two days, maybe two and a half. Ben's life hadn't been long enough to fill more time.

She fingered the lists of songs she'd written out first by hand, jotting them down as she thought of them before she'd sat down at the computer and downloaded everything, created a playlist. The menu from the caterer, with all the dishes she wanted circled and the price they'd quoted, their business card stapled on the front. A DVD of a video she'd created on her MacBook, a montage of photos and videos. She pulled everything out, propped the boards up in the bedroom. *Let John think I did them last night*, she thought. *That I did it to keep myself busy while he was gone.*

The church was already locked in; she and John had made that phone call together. She called the caterer and ordered the foods she'd circled. She went to the florist's website and ordered the bouquets she'd already chosen. She did what needed to be done, without apology. Just as she'd done the legwork, the research, a long time before.

As she finished, she heard something metallic downstairs. *John's keys on the countertop. Home to apologize?* She walked downstairs, but the kitchen and living room were empty. She looked out the divided window of the front door, expecting another news van. Nothing. Not a car, not a truck, not even a bicycle. She imagined the vans were parked outside the suspect's house now. Had they charged him? Had he confessed? Over the months, he'd grown blurry in her mind, this person other people who seemed to remember him more clearly talked about. A guy at the Y with a white iPhone, hanging around. Couldn't picture his face, just his long, swinging hair. Everyone had an idea of what he looked like except her. Still, whoever he was, he belonged to someone. Someone who did or didn't believe in him. Who worried about him. John had wanted to celebrate this man's terrible news. She felt a momentary sense of empathy for his family. Not him, but them. The innocents around him.

She went into the kitchen and starting cleaning up John's mess from the night before.

The brass knocker on her door rapped lightly, as if the wind had picked up and caught it. Or as if someone didn't really want to be there. She walked toward the door.

Detective Nolan stared at her through the mullions of the window. His weathered face cut into four planes—four ways of looking at her and doubting her. No Forrester with him. No lawyer with her.

"What do you want, Detective?" she called through the door.

"I want to talk," he said evenly.

"My lawyer wouldn't think that was a very good idea."

"Well, your lawyer's not here, Mrs. Morgan, is she? But you can bet if you call her, she'll bill you two hours for that three-minute call. You think she's on your side? The only side she's on is money's. That's what being a lawyer means."

"I don't have anything to say to you, Detective."

"Oh, I think you do."

His bristly head, his shoulders beneath his coat, rougher and larger than other people's, a mastiff of a man. She was aware of the sound traveling, the thinness of glass, the modest protection of a hollow wooden door. She felt the nap of her pajamas brush against her vulnerable skin, scratching a little.

He coughed, bent over, clutched at his side as if coughing hurt. Not so tough, was he? He looked paler, grayer than the last time she'd seen him—probably because he'd been working the case. He was rumpled because he'd put in too many hours, but he still counted on his size, and the person he used to be, to intimidate. He came because he thought she was weaker than he was. *But where was his car? Where was his partner?*

"I'm calling your precinct," she said, "and telling your boss you're harassing me."

He cleared his throat. "You do that. And then remind him that I'm here to ask you what he asked me—why the hell you planned Ben's funeral early. And also to explain why a handsome young man we interviewed has photos of you on his phone. Did you two lovers think up some kind of adoption scheme together, huh? A twisted way to get rid of your own kid?"

"What?" she asked, then regretted it. Didn't want to let him have an inch—not an increment of surprise, disgust, anything. A man like him could take the purest sentence, the most innocent response or tidbit, and ruin it.

"You heard me. Dozens of them, taken at all times of day. Some of them with you looking right into the camera. How is that possible, do you suppose? Oh, I know. You were sleeping with him. Your husband's worried about the guy who owns the dog now?"

He clicked his teeth. "Way to throw him off the trail. Well played, Mrs. Morgan. Well played."

"You need to go," she said. She could walk away, but he could move to another window. He could circle the house. He could get to her one way or another.

"Is that what women like you do? Cheat on anyone who loves you or cares about you? Is that why your high school boyfriend killed himself? Is that why all the girls on your cheerleading squad called you—and I quote—a *stone-cold bitch*?"

"Get out of here!"

"Is this why you went all the way out to Peterson Nature Preserve? To talk to a tree like a crazy person, sob about your disgusting life, then vomit over all the terrible things you've done?"

"I wasn't talking to a—" She stopped. She remembered the dark car on the highway. Perhaps it had been parked in the lot too, behind the wide tree sheltering Ethan.

"So you're—you're following me?"

"Is that why you keep a list of everywhere you've ever volunteered your whole life, to trick yourself into believing you're a good person when you're actually a monster who would kill her own child?"

"Stop it! Stop it!"

"What, are you going to call 911? Explain that the police are already here but you want the whole squad over here, maybe? Mrs. Morgan, this looks bad. Real bad. I mean, we can explain away you nearly killing the Orkin man for doing his job, but y'know, this—this is different. And the only one who can make it better is you." He coughed again, and when he stopped, his voice was broken, weaker. "So yeah, I'm here for a reason. Just like you're home, right now, alone, for a reason."

A prick of heat at the base of her spine. His face was almost gray. His right hand clutched his side oddly. The coughing bent him in two. Two partners always. One backing the other up. But what had happened today? Was today the day when one of them couldn't protect the other one anymore? Friday. It was Friday.

Her nose was so close to the thin glass she was almost on the other side. The air smelled vaguely of smoke, of earth. *Tobacco, maybe? No—gunpowder*, she thought suddenly.

"Have you been shot?"

He blinked at her, and the sharp, smoky scent barreled into her nostrils.

"Oh my God," she whispered. "You're—you're dead too."

The weight of her words pulled her down, and she disappeared from the frame of the glass. She lay on the floor and felt her eyes flutter before they closed, as if in slow motion, as if wishing she could just take a minute to sort things out, to think, to finally, finally, at last, get some rest.

When her eyes opened again, everything was white around the edges. Under other circumstances, she might have thought she'd died too and landed in a gauzy version of heaven, but when she squinted and recognized Dr. Kenney standing over her, she knew exactly where she was and precisely how he came to be there. Regret flooded her brain. She blinked a few times, as if she could brush her memory clean, start over.

"Carrie," Dr. Kenney said and smiled. "Thank goodness. Are you feeling better now?"

"Yes," she said, forcing a small smile. But she did not feel better. She felt worse; she'd made a stupid, completely avoidable mistake, and it was going to cost her. She hated this combination of wisdom and naïveté. What was she supposed to do with what she knew, what she sensed? Something had to be wrong with Nolan—she felt it in her bones, her muscle and tissue. She just didn't know what.

She tried to sit up, prop herself with one arm, but a firm hand behind her guided her back down.

"Don't sit up too soon," the other man said. She tried to twist her neck to see him, but his hands guided her away from that motion too. He fluttered a light above her eyes, checking her pupils, and she saw him upside down, but even upside down, she could tell: he was young and in uniform.

"Just take it easy," he said. "Deep breaths."

In the corner, near the table in the foyer, a stretcher was propped up against the wall. Of course. A paramedic. The wood frame of the door splintered and jagged where someone had kicked it in.

"Where is..." She hesitated, reluctant to limit her question. She wasn't sure if she wanted to know where her husband was. But she needed to know where Nolan was and why Forrester hadn't come with him. Was it possible Forrester was with John? Could her husband be that disloyal?

"The detective?" Dr. Kenney asked, as if she'd forgotten her own husband's name.

"Yes."

"He stayed here till I arrived, but then he had a call from his partner."

Carrie tried to swallow, and it hurt, like something was caught. "Did it seem urgent?"

"Somewhat, yes."

"And John?"

"He's on his way, with the others."

"Others?" Her voice filled with panic and possibility, all contained in one short word.

Dr. Kenney glanced at the paramedic, who waved his penlight over Carrie's eyes again.

"Your family," he said, overpronouncing every syllable.

"My family?" The word sounded foreign coming out of her mouth. How long had it been since she'd said or thought that? It was always simply her mother. Even when Ben was alive and she'd created her own family, she'd never grown accustomed to the idea, to the word.

"He's at the airport picking them up."

She blinked. Surely Dr. Kenney meant John's family, not her mother, but no one was due in for at least three days. But she didn't want to say anything; she couldn't blurt things out anymore. She really, really had to be more careful.

"Who called you?"

"John called me."

"No, I know that. I mean the paramedic."

"Detective called 911," the paramedic answered.

"So...you kicked the door in?"

"Nope. Already like that."

Carrie frowned, trying to imagine Nolan being able to accomplish that feat in his condition. Wondering if he even cared where the door fell, if it hit her or not.

"Don't worry about all this now, Carrie," Dr. Kenney said. "You need rest. I know you've been under a great deal of strain."

She wanted to ask him what he knew. What had John told him, exactly? And if John had told Nolan about the guy with the dog, what other secrets had he shared? And who—who on earth had called John?

"Dr. Kenney, can you call the precinct and find out if the detectives on Ben's case are—"

"Carrie, as I said, you need to rest."

"No, I need to know if those detectives are—"

"Are what?"

"If they're both...okay. Hurt or anything."

Dr. Kenney's eyes were kind, so kind. It was as if they radiated a different energy than other people's; they almost warmed the whole room. Was that how all his patients felt? Did he know he had that quality, that it would make people trust him automatically?

"Have you been...sensing things again, Carrie? Or seeing confusing images?"

"No," she said, but her lip quaked, and she had to bite it to stop it.

"We've always been honest with each other, Carrie."

"He was here, all right? Detective Nolan was here."

Dr. Kenney glanced toward the paramedic, then back at her.

"Yes, he was outside and witnessed you fainting—"

"Oh, you know that then."

"Of course we do, Carrie. That's why we're here."

"Oh, so he's okay."

"What do you mean?"

"I mean he seemed unwell. Injured."

"Is that why you asked him if he was dead?"

All the sound went out of the room. The metronome of the heart monitor. The buzz of the clock in the kitchen. All of it swallowed by an oceanic fuzz, like being inside a shell.

"He looked like death warmed over," she said quietly.

"Are you saying he misunderstood you?"

"Yes," she said. "That's what I'm saying. Of course, maybe he was twisting my words. Since he's always had it in for me."

She swallowed hard and nodded for emphasis, and Dr. Kenney did a slow rocking nod in return. He always did that when he was processing something, when he was halfway toward believing. She wrapped her hands up inside her sweater sleeves. She didn't feel guilty—sometimes you had to lie to save yourself. She'd learned that lesson the hard way—like when she told her mother she stayed in bed all day because she had cramps and not because she was bleeding postpartum.

There needed to be another term besides *white lies* for lies that weren't innocent but weren't dark as much as they were self-preserving. Gray lies. Sometimes you needed to tell a gray lie.

Dr. Kenney stayed another hour or more, stayed as the paramedic packed up, discussing their need for more appointments if Carrie didn't feel up to talking. Always that word: *talk, talk, talk.* She liked to talk, always had; that was why she'd been drawn to Ethan. He was the kind of boy you could nudge awake with a question, the kind of person who would sit around a campfire until it dwindled to embers, discussing an idea. But that was a different kind of talking. Dr. Kenney wanted more: he wanted answers.

Finally, after Carrie's vitals returned to normal and she declined the offer to go to the hospital, Dr. Kenney left shortly after the paramedic did. He called John to verify that he was on his way back from the airport, then fingered the ragged edge of the door frame as if reluctant to leave.

Carrie poured herself a cup of tea. She needed to pull herself together if she had to deal with John's parents. The hotel was out of the question. John would install his parents to babysit her until her own mother arrived. Then what would they do—watch her in shifts?

She went upstairs and put the photo boards and caterer's notes and playlists in the master bedroom. She made up the guest bed, put fresh towels and new soaps in the bathroom. She brought up two bottles of water and an extra box of tissues. She was losing her mind, perhaps, but not her manners. She'd be ready for company soon. But first, there was someone she had to see.

The former parish house was an attached row home, so it was never considered large. But it was even smaller than Carrie remembered it, the porch narrower, the steps shorter, uneven, cracked. In this part of town, near her old house, just beyond the reach of the tonier Main Line suburbs, houses could look peeling and sagging, on the verge of becoming slums, or be bright and cheerful as oversize Monopoly houses, depending on what street you were on. This block, not far from the commercial district, had been home to the maids and livery men for some of the larger, older houses, and the people who owned them tended to them carefully, as if trying to overcome their heritage. Mrs. Harrison had told Carrie that once, and her husband had come downstairs at that moment, smiled, and said that was what drew him there—that he was a servant too. A servant of God.

Reverend and Mrs. Harrison still lived there, even though they'd retired from the parish a long time before; Carrie knew that. She had kept track of them all these years just in case they moved or, God forbid, changed professions and took her secret like a suitcase to somewhere more worrisome to her, more prone to leaks.

She walked up to the house nervously, palms sweating, worried that he'd changed, that he would regret forgiving her. She told herself she was being silly, but her body didn't listen.

She knocked a few times before she heard footsteps. A man she didn't recognize answered the door. He wore a collar and dark pants, and when he offered his hand, she hesitated; she didn't want to take it without knowing exactly who he was.

"I'm the new priest," he said as if he understood. "Are you a former parishioner? I don't recognize you from service."

She smiled. She supposed priests weren't as up on local news and infamous residents of the county as other people were. *Or maybe he's just being nice.*

"I moved away," she said. "I go to another church nearby."

John's parish had always felt safer than her own. There weren't any girls from high school at John's. And there was no Father Paul, who knew too much.

Carrie glanced at the electronic chair mounted to the stairway.

"He needs a little help getting around," the priest said. "But he's in denial about it."

She nodded and said she'd love to see him, if he was up to a visit.

"He's in his study," the priest said. "I'm sure he'll be glad to have company."

A few minutes later, the electronic chair buzzed, and she watched as her old priest descended the stairs, the younger man walking slowly alongside him, as if he needed even more assistance than the chair could provide.

Reverend Paul Harrison had a small, impish face; even in his dotage, he looked a bit like a mischievous boy. He smiled broadly when he saw Carrie, and she couldn't help smiling back.

"Carrie," he said.

"Father Paul."

"Oh, I do so love to be called that again. Everyone is so formal these days. So few of you left who I know well."

Carrie couldn't imagine that was the case. Did anyone on the Main Line really move far? But she humored him, hugged him when he stood, and let him grip her arm as they walked into the small sitting room. The other priest murmured his

good-byes and closed the narrow door after offering tea, which
Carrie declined.

It took Father Paul a while to sit down, which made Carrie
worry about how long it might take him to get up. She asked if his
wife was home, and he said yes, and she was glad there were two
other adults nearby in case she needed help.

"I was wondering when you'd come," Father Paul said quietly.
"Given your troubles."

"Well, you know I go to another church now."

"Saint David's."

"Yes."

"Reverend Carson is a good man."

Carrie nodded.

"But he doesn't know you like I know you."

She started to tremble. Something sinister about the truth of
those words.

"No," she whispered.

She thought of that night she'd come to him, a few days after
giving birth. Shivering in the rain as she'd knocked on the door
to the cottage that was his office. She'd waited until Friday, when
she knew everyone would be gone and he'd sit down that evening
to write his Sunday sermon. He always did that on Friday night,
alone. She'd almost felt she didn't need to tell him. He looked at
her as if he could see it all, feel the ragged flesh, still so tender,
hear the blood dripping down onto the extra-large pads she'd had
to send Ethan out to buy. At moments like that, Carrie could
believe that not only God was all knowing, but also that people
who believed were too. He offered to call a doctor, but she said
no. He insisted on taking her temperature and was visibly relieved
that it was normal. He asked the questions a nurse would ask: Had
she delivered the placenta? Were there clean towels and sterile
instruments? Worried about her health first and everything else
later. Never a question about the baby—she'd told him Ethan
had taken him to Safe Cradle, and he'd nodded. His questions

were only about her, her soul, her fresh start. He'd said a prayer over her head and told her she would be forgiven, but that truly, there was nothing to forgive. She still remembered his words: *A thousand other girls wouldn't have had the courage to do what you did.* And when she'd blubbered back to him, *But I lied to my mother. I lied to everyone,* he'd held up his hand to stop her. *You did not lie to yourself. Or to God.*

"The police were here again yesterday," he said, bringing her attention back.

Her throat constricted, and she tried clearing it, but everything she wanted to say was caught inside her.

"Again?"

"Yes. They came once before."

"Father, I hope that you—"

"Didn't tell them? Of course not, child. I don't know what they thought they'd accomplish—that I'd forget my duties to my parish? That retirement was relinquishment? It's your secret to tell, and you've already told God. All they have is a whisper of a rumor, from a few of those misguided girls you went to high school with. Said you were weird and started dressing differently. The last time I checked, that's not a sin or a crime."

"No, it's not that. I hope you still…believe in me."

"Oh, of course I do. I always did, and then, well…my faith was bolstered, you might say."

"Father, I, um, I've been having some very strange…visions."

"Visions?"

"Or visitations, I guess you'd call them."

"From God?"

"No. From…spirits." She explained, but in the barest terms. Leaving out the parts about who and what—like her dog, lest he think she'd lost her mind, as John did.

He nodded carefully, seriously. He said that although it had never happened to him personally, it had happened to other priests and lay people he knew.

"So it does happen?"

"Yes. Depending on who you listen to and what you believe, it happens with great regularity."

"Father," she said, "one of the people who came to me was... Ethan."

"Ethan Lawrence?"

"Yes."

He shut his eyes tightly, then nodded. "So he told you then? About your child?"

"What? Wait—you knew?"

"Ethan came to me right before you did. The very same day."

Carrie's skin felt hot; she wanted to tear it off, start over, walk away with a new facade. *Father Paul had known? And hadn't said?*

That night, when he'd walked her to the door of his office, he'd said something so cryptic, odd. He'd hugged her and said that he was sure she would move on from this, that she'd find the courage to go on to have children someday when she was ready.

"Me and Ethan," she'd said.

And he'd said, "No, you. I hope you go on." As if he hadn't approved. As if he preferred her to Ethan.

Now she knew; Ethan had told him. He'd told him first, a secret impossible to keep long, because his sin was larger.

"Oh, Father," she cried, "you have to tell this to the police. Call them back!"

"I beg your pardon?"

"Otherwise, I'm afraid they'll find out and go to Safe Cradle. They'll put two and two together and think *I* did it. And did it *again* with Ben!"

"Dear child, I can't share Ethan's secret."

"Yes, you can! He's dead! And he loved me. He wouldn't want me blamed for what he did!"

"I can't trade the sins of one member of the flock for another, Carrie."

She started to cry, softly at first, then harder. He touched her shoulder tenderly, held it there, like he was covering a wound, until she finally stopped.

"But I also won't tell them what you told me. No one will know," he said. "No one but you. And Safe Cradle won't tell them either, I assure you."

He picked up a box of tissues from the table and brandished it in her direction. She took one and wiped her eyes, dabbed at her nose, then held it tight in her fist.

"Can you...tell me how to make the visions stop then? Is there some prayer, some way, to make them stop? Like an exorcism?"

He blinked slowly, so slowly that his eyes disappeared in between.

"What you are referring to...it's a gift, Carrie. You just have to see it as such."

"So I should share them? Try telling more people about them? Because," she said as she screwed up her face, "so far, people just seem to think I'm crazy."

"Perhaps you can use them to your advantage without talking about them, my dear."

She blinked, and he reached for her hands.

"Don't give these damned Main Line snobs another reason to think you're different."

"Father Paul!"

He laughed at her shock, waved away her concerns. "I'm old enough now to say what I please. And when you're a priest, everyone hangs on your words, believes them. But not when you're a young, pretty girl. If I stepped up to the lectern and told people you were receiving communications from the beyond, they'd believe it. But you? You have to be more careful."

"I don't know how."

"To be careful?"

"No, to...make use of it."

He drew a deep breath in, and his smile grew as the breath filled his body. Carrie had always liked that about him, how he seemed to draw pleasure from the simplest things, like breathing, holding a cup of warm tea, or watching a bird fly overhead.

"You'll figure out a way."

She nodded and sighed. "I suppose you're going to tell me to be patient."

He laughed. How many times, over the years, had he told a young person to be patient, to wait it out, that it would all turn out all right, if they just waited and trusted?

"I'm glad you were listening," he said. "Now, I have to rest, but do you promise to come back once in a while and tell me how you're doing? Not wait a dozen years? Because let's face it," he said as he stood up on wobbly knees. "I certainly can't be as patient as I used to be."

She nodded her promise. They walked into the foyer and said their good-byes. When she leaned in to hug him, she was relieved to smell nothing but the lime of his soap and the metallic tang of tonic combed through his hair. Clean. He smelled clean, and he smelled well, despite his protests.

She walked down the steps, and when she turned at the end of the sidewalk and offered one more wave, his face was blurred through the last of her tears, faded, like an old fresco.

C arrie's mother, Danielle, wasn't surprised when John called her back. She also wasn't surprised when he offered to pay the difference to change her flight and to pick her up at the airport. She assumed they'd changed their minds, that they were taking her up on her offer to come early, that her daughter had realized she needed her before the memorial service. She didn't think anything suspicious about it until her plane landed and John appeared at the gate without Carrie in tow.

John's head bobbed above the others, but he was looking out the long bank of windows leading to baggage claim. Distracted, like a boy might be. Or worried. He smiled when he saw her and hugged her when she came up next to him, reaching for the strap of her carry-on, insisting. Nothing wrong exactly, as he asked if she had a good flight and she said yes, but he had trouble looking her in the eye.

"Where's Carrie?"

"Oh, she'll meet us at home."

He struggled to continue the conversation beyond the banalities he might say to anyone. She and John had never had trouble talking before. It had always seemed her son-in-law understood her better than her own child. Danielle could imagine their conversations at night, Carrie explaining the disagreements between mother and daughter, differences over the years, and John telling her it didn't sound that bad to him. It didn't sound that bad to anyone, Danielle thought; a single mother struggling to do the best she could was the way anyone else would look back on it. But Carrie had pulled away in high school and never fully come around again, and Danielle knew she was the reason. Something she did or didn't do.

They walked down the long white corridor toward baggage claim, John's loafers squeaking a little, like they were wet. Danielle's boots were light and quiet in comparison, even though she had to put in extra steps to keep pace with his long gait. No matter—she was short and used to hurrying, always running late, always stuck behind a slow Florida driver when she needed to get to an open house.

The conveyor creaked, the bags slid down their silvery path, and they waited for hers. Every possible shape and size of black bag was represented. An occasional green or blue to break things up.

"Mine has a pink ribbon tied to it," Danielle said, and he nodded. John didn't speak while they looked for the bag. She knew how things worked, how men worked in particular. Knew that she'd have the best chance when they got out to the car.

John shouldered both bags, and she let him, and they walked out to his car with only one of them overburdened. They exited the airport, an endless loop that felt like circling the sun, and when they were at last on I-95, she saw her opportunity and asked him gently what was wrong.

"Wrong?" he asked dumbly. Unspoken: *Wasn't finding our son's body wrong enough, Danielle?*

"Oh, I know everything must seem wrong right now. But I meant something wrong beyond Ben, beyond the obvious."

He was silent. If he hadn't been driving, he would have looked at his shoes.

"Maybe something wrong...between you and Carrie?"

"Oh, no. Not really."

"But, John, is there a particular reason I've come early is what I'm asking. Other than general support."

"Well…Carrie's really, really not doing well."

She sniffed, nodded. How could she be? It was one thing to lose your child instantly, from an accident or illness. It was another to get used to the idea, slowly losing every drop of hope, before it was confirmed, suddenly snapping into place. How did she ever get used to it?

"Is she still seeing the therapist?"

"Yes, but reluctantly." He glanced at his watch. "I think she's actually still with him now."

Danielle's eyes rested on John as he drove, taking him in. She knew he was holding back.

"I'm happy to help with anything that needs to be done, John."

"Oh, it's all done, Danielle." He sighed.

He rubbed one hand across his eyes as he drove, which made Danielle nervous. Her ex-husband Robert had always done that—rubbed his eyes, yawned, blinked widely as if he could fall asleep at the wheel at any second.

"What's all done?"

"Everything—the funeral, flowers."

"No, can't be. When I spoke to her last, she said I could help her—"

"No, she did everything months ago."

"*Months?*"

"Preplanned the whole thing. Yeah, the detectives had a field day with that."

"But she said—"

"Well, Danielle, she doesn't always tell the truth."

There was a heaviness in John's voice, a weariness tucked inside the word *truth* that she'd never heard before. She had to remember that he was grieving too. Putting one foot in front of the other, doing what needed to be done, like calling her and picking her up at the airport. But doing it all with an arrow in his back.

"Well," Danielle said, "I guess she needed something to keep her busy."

"Right," he said flatly.

"You have an office to escape to, John, and she doesn't."

He shrugged. He'd heard that excuse from Carrie too many times already.

"At its core, planning a funeral is just busywork. It's not very different from planning a dinner party or cleaning or running errands. Or making flight arrangements and driving out-of-town guests, John."

"But the timing." He shook his head. "Who would do that in advance?"

"She needed distraction."

"She could have gotten a job, Danielle. Or a dog."

"Those are both things you can lose, John."

He sighed deeply, slowly. Then he nodded. "Never thought of it that way," he said, then turned to her and smiled. "See, that's why you're here. You understand her."

She nodded slowly. "Yes, but I don't know that Carrie wants to be understood."

"What do you mean?"

She sighed, stopped, looked out the window. The leaves on the trees danced in the breeze, threatening to tumble. She thought there would be color by now. Autumn was something she missed in Florida, but it was like missing a comet—so damned fleeting. And you never, ever knew precisely when it would arrive.

"I mean she has trouble being close to people. Never had a gaggle of girlfriends in high school, not anyone close. And who does she keep in touch with from college, really, besides you? Carrie always pulls away from people who know her best."

"Danielle," John said, "you've just described women in general, don't you think?"

"Maybe," she said. Certainly she was describing herself as well.

C arrie's father hadn't told her he was leaving permanently; her mother had simply announced they were getting a divorce one morning before school, after her father had already been gone a week. Danielle had declared it as she'd been walking down the hall, like it was nothing, like she was telling her daughter there was leftover meat loaf in the refrigerator for dinner.

"Are you sure?" Carrie had put down her orange juice and asked dumbly, as if Danielle could have misinterpreted what her husband had said, as if he'd been so drunk he'd slurred his words.

"Yes, honey," she said.

"And it's…definite?"

Danielle blinked at her, as if not sure what her child was asking. Did Carrie think she'd have a chance at rebuttal? That he could be persuaded by a cogent argument?

"Yes, I'm afraid so. It's been a long time coming, Carrie. I'm sure you felt the tension between us over the years."

"I heard the tension. Anyone could."

"Well, yes. I suppose."

"So the house will be quieter."

"Yes, the house will be quieter."

"Better for doing homework."

Danielle smiled. "I'm glad you see the positive side. I'll be out job hunting today, but I hope to be back in plenty of time for dinner."

"Okay," Carrie said, and her mother kissed her on the forehead.

By the time Ethan arrived to drive her to school, Carrie had already wiped away the few tears she had shed and was making calculations of whether she could afford to pay for her own books at college, assuming she got a scholarship.

"Wait, wait, wait," Ethan said. "So you're telling me that good ole Robb and Danielle didn't sit you down at dinner, all serious, and tell you they both still loved you and it wasn't your fault and this way you'd get twice as many presents at Christmas?"

"No."

"Your father wasn't even here?"

"No, he's in Minneapolis trying to get a new job."

"Well, you know what this means." He sighed.

"Yes. It means he's going to move to Minneapolis with a new woman who doesn't consider him an item on her to-do list."

"Your mother told you that?"

"No, I overheard him yelling that a couple of weeks ago. Drunk, slurring his words. And that means we're going to be broke, because even if he gets a job and pays back his debts, his money is going to be split between her and us."

"You're wrong," Ethan said, shoving a Pop-Tart in his mouth. He usually ate one cold in the morning and the other one he warmed on the defroster of his car and ate it before he went into school. "Your father blames your mother, you see? That's why he made her tell you. Because it's her fault."

"Ethan," she said with a sigh, "if my father is moving to Minneapolis with another woman who doesn't care that he gambles and drinks, then how is that my mother's fault?"

"Carrie," he said. "You really need to read John Updike."

"My parents are getting a divorce, and you're assigning summer reading?"

"It's not summer."

"Winter then. Winter reading."

"Novels illuminate the inner life. It's a way to understand adults, since we have so few clues as to why they behave the idiotic way they do. Everybody goes on and on about the teenage mind and how it's not fully developed, and then you look at what adults do. I'll take my half-assed brain anytime. At least I have reasons for doing everything I do. Why do you think your parents got married, anyway? Was your mother pregnant?"

"No," she said. "I did the math the last time they had a huge argument. They had a good four-month overlap."

"Maybe they lied to you about their anniversary. Have you ever seen their marriage certificate?"

His blue eyes, so light they almost looked like water, were open wider than usual, as they always were when he tried to make a point. Ethan spent his whole life trying to be edgy and dark, but his ocean-like coloring betrayed him. He was a soft guy trying to be a hard-ass.

"Ethan."

"We could go down to county records and bribe someone for it."

"My parents did not invent their anniversary."

"Okay, okay. I still maintain that he blames her though, instead of the other way around," he said. They walked to the front door where Carrie's backpack sat on a bench near the hat tree and umbrella stand.

"See this, right here? This foyer? Empty except for your stuff? None of his? This is why you need to read those novels. It means something, like it's all waiting for your father's umbrella and that weird beret he wears in the rain sometimes. This is a sad metaphor of a room."

"It's not weird to wear a hat in the rain. It's a reason to wear a hat. Since you like your reasons."

"Men don't wear hats in the rain, because they don't give a shit about their hair," he said.

"Some men do," she'd said, and their conversation had continued on and on over nothing, as it always had, as he'd lifted the backpack onto her shoulders and let it down gently, one strap and then the other, as if they were going on a long, arduous climb.

SATURDAY

The night before, John had only come in for a few minutes. He brought Danielle's bags inside, carried them up to the guest room. Then he said he had to go to a charity dinner in the city with clients, and it would run late, so he would be staying overnight at a hotel. He delivered that news perfunctorily yet sheepishly. Carrie knew the whole thing was a lie, and judging from the look on her mother's face, she knew it too.

As he walked toward the front door, Carrie reached for his sleeve.

"Don't," he said quietly.

"John, how does this look?"

"To your mother?"

"No," she said, "to the police."

"What do you mean?"

"Don't be naive. They have the suspect they've been looking for, but they still think I'm involved! That's why Nolan was here! They'll take any opportunity to twist this into something I did! And if you leave me—"

"I'm not leaving you, Carrie. I'm just…" He trailed off, looked at his hand, then quietly opened the door. "Pictures of you? On his phone?"

"I don't know him, John!"

He sighed, shook his head.

"Admit it, John," she said. "You're just overreacting to every tiny piece of information that comes along. You're using it as an excuse now. You don't know what you're doing. You have no idea what you're doing."

He turned back toward her for one second, his large eyes conveying not warmth but distance, as if he didn't need any more information, didn't need to take any more in.

"Well, do you know what you're doing, Carrie? Have you ever?"

Carrie heard the click of her mother's suitcase upstairs.

"Did you tell her?"

"What?"

"On the way home, did you tell her about, about—"

"Jesus, Carrie," he said, shaking his head as he stood in the door. "How big of an asshole do you think I am?"

"I don't know," she said. "Maybe I should ask Lyndsey how big of an asshole you are."

"I did not stalk her," he said evenly. "I only followed her when she was drunk."

"And she was drunk all the time?"

"Don't change the subject, Carrie. My parents already know my secret. But yours belongs to you. It's not my place to tell Danielle."

She shivered. It was the same thing Father Paul had said. Of all the things she owned and tended and cared for, this was the most unique. This was the thing that defined her, not house, not car, not clothes. Her secrets.

The rest of the evening was spent in a charade of settling her mother in, offering to cook dinner but her mother insisting on doing it herself and then proceeding to clean up, ending with Carrie saying she was tired, even though she hadn't done any of the work. And she was tired—that much was true. Just watching her mother scurry, wiping up each crumb right after it fell, just being around her sometimes exhausted her. Her mother who always half ran up the stairs, who never let dishes drain by themselves. Danielle was always in motion, and it made Carrie more tired, not less.

But that hadn't kept Carrie from waking up early, well before six, and going down to make coffee only to discover, with disappointment, that Danielle was up first and had made a pot of coffee and a tray of muffins.

"So what do we need to do today, kiddo?"

"Nothing really."

"Surely there's something you need for the funeral on Tuesday?"

"No."

Danielle sighed. So John was right. She'd hoped he'd been exaggerating, but apparently not.

"How about a new dress? Shoes?"

Carrie shrugged. She couldn't think of anything more depressing than picking out something to wear to her son's funeral. She remembered Libby telling her once that she had bought two black dresses—one short-sleeved, one long-sleeved—and kept them in her closet for year-round funerals. At the time, she'd thought that was a little too organized, like something her mother would do. Now she saw the wisdom of it. The dress would already be there. She should have done that months ago too.

"Maybe something pretty and new, not black but in Ben's favorite color? Wasn't blue his favorite color, sweetheart?"

"Blue," she said softly, thinking of his blue tennis shoes.

"We could do a whole blue theme then. Napkins and tablecloths. I could call your caterer and arrange that, make a few tweaks."

"Okay."

"And you ordered the flowers already? What colors?"

"I just said not red."

"Okay, well, I'll call them back and order tones of blue, maybe lavender. See? We have plenty to do. Do you have a file in the office?"

Carrie nodded. "It's all in the master bedroom, the photo boards, everything. I did the boards on blue," she said, a little brightness coming back into her voice. At least she'd done one thing right. One thing that didn't have to be undone.

"Okay then. Should we hit the mall first or make the calls?"

Danielle looked at her watch. Carrie knew that movement by heart: the flick of the arm, the downward glance. Her mother's career had depended on that watch, which she wore constantly, even on the beach in Florida. If she ever took it off, there would be tan lines around the square chain links.

Danielle didn't wait for an answer; Carrie was sure she had probably made up her own mind. The mall would be crowded soon; Danielle knew her daughter didn't like being in crowded places anymore. Not where people might recognize her and whisper. Sitting there at her kitchen counter, Carrie watched her mother wiping up invisible crumbs, rinsing out coffee cups. Always doing something. Wasn't that the problem with them both? If only Carrie had done less, maybe she'd have noticed more—more about the guy at the Y who always seemed to be on his phone. That had to be him. His dark glasses, his shaggy hair that was sometimes, maybe, pulled into a small, low bun. How she thought he must be another parent because he was always taking pictures with that white phone. Why hadn't she told anyone? Why hadn't she paid more attention? Why had she been so busy running errands and signing Ben up for classes and drinking coffee that she hadn't opened up to what could be happening around her?

"Mom," she said suddenly. "I have to tell you something."

"What's that?" Danielle continued scouring the sink.

"Stop," Carrie said. "Stop cleaning."

Danielle turned around. Her face was always light bronze, and the wrinkles around her eyes had gotten deep. But now her brow furrowed too; she looked frightened, Carrie thought. And was that what all this cleaning and the constant doing was for? To keep out the worst possibilities?

"I, uh…don't know where to begin."

Danielle put down the sponge carefully but kept her fingers on it, as if for ballast.

"Is this about…Ben?" She said the words as softly as she could, as if they could barely make it out of her mouth.

Carrie's heart fluttered. *Dear God, what did her mother think? John, the detectives, not her own mother too!*

"No, Mom," she said. "It's about me."

"Darling, I know about the funeral planning. John told me. And I just want you to know, I understand. I do. I explained it to him too. It's…something I would have done. Honestly."

Carrie smiled. Of course she did. Her mother would understand that.

"Mom, I… There's no easy way to say this."

"Then just say it, honey."

"I had a baby in high school," she blurted out.

"What did you say?"

"Please don't make me say it again."

Carrie's eyes filled with tears. She felt something pulling deep within her, sinew and muscle twisting, as if her body remembered giving birth. How it had hurt, with nothing to ease the pain but the whiskey Ethan had forced her to drink.

"The day before Thanksgiving break, you stayed home from school with cramps," Danielle said suddenly. "I had the open house on Lincolnwood."

Carrie sniffed, nodded. "It was the night before," she said. "I told you I was sleeping over at Monica's."

"You never stayed home from school with cramps," Danielle said.

"No."

Danielle blinked, thinking back, searching the sky. "I'm sorry, honey. I knew something was off that day. I did. I can picture the look on your face right now. But I…how did I miss…your stomach, the weight gain? Was I that oblivious?"

"I was skinny. I wore sweatshirts. You were busy."

"No," Danielle said. "I mean, yes, I was, but I…was so afraid of the teenage years. I was so relieved that you were like a little adult, I can't even tell you. And I was so sad, after Dad left."

"You didn't seem sad."

"I hid it, I suppose. So you took the baby to…what was that place called on all the billboards? Something Cradle? You and Ethan?"

Carrie burst into tears.

"He said he did—that was the plan—but he didn't. I didn't find out for years, but he, he—"

"Oh dear God, Carrie," Danielle said. "Are you saying what I think you're saying?"

Carrie nodded and sniffed, and Danielle folded her into her arms.

"He wanted me to have an abortion," she cried. "But I couldn't. And I couldn't lose the scholarship."

"Oh, Carrie. So this is what you've been shouldering all this time." Danielle rocked her daughter back and forth gently, a rhythm that seemed to live in her limbs. "I'm sorry, honey. I'm so sorry you had to go through that alone. Does John know? Is that what's going on?"

"He…only knows part," she said softly. "I couldn't tell him the rest because I don't think he'd trust me ever again."

Carrie started to cry as she leaned into her mother. Danielle was thin but she was steely, which was its own brand of comfort. A doer, not a dreamer. A fixer, not a hugger. But this was not something Danielle could fix.

"Before we go to the mall, honey," she said with a sigh, "I think we need to go to a church."

After Carrie's father had left, there hadn't been much time for church. It suddenly became an elective activity, like scrubbing the copper bottoms of pans or color-coding closets. She did the things that mattered, that showed, that counted. And church wasn't going to get Carrie a scholarship to college or help her mother pay the bills. No, quite the contrary; the church would expect their money and steal their time. But once Carrie was ensconced in college, alone and often lonely on the enormous campus, the chapel was one of the few refuges of comfort. She'd gotten back in the habit of attending every week, like she and her parents had done when she was young.

Carrie and her mother drove to Saint David's. Danielle had suggested going to another church where no one knew her, but Carrie had said no, that would be worse—what if someone recognized her and made a big deal about her being there? No, she was safer here, where she was known. That and she wanted to talk to Libby. Libby would understand. Libby, whose daughter's bedroom was like a shrine, even all these years later. There were only a few cars in the lot, Libby's Subaru being one of them. But no one was in the church, although the lights were on and candles were lit. They slid in to the last pew and bowed their heads. It had been a long time since Carrie had said a prayer next to her mother. Finally, they finished, crossed themselves, and left.

As they stood outside near Libby's car, Carrie glanced at her watch, wondering what was taking her so long.

"You seem nervous to see this Libby person," her mother said.

"I'm not nervous," she said.

"Well, you look nervous."

"Mom," she said with the exasperation of a much younger person. "I'll wait in the car for you."

"Fine."

She leaned against Libby's Subaru and thought about going down to the basement but knew Anna, Joan, and possibly others would be there, and she didn't want to see them all.

Finally, Libby came out the back door, cocked her head when she realized who was standing by her car, then hurried over.

"Carrie, dear," she said. "How have you been?"

"Good."

"Good?"

"Well, okay. I've been okay, I guess."

"I'm baking you and John a lasagna tonight and bringing it over."

"Oh, you don't have to, Libby, honestly."

"You'll have lots of out-of-town company, and you'll be glad for the food. Trust me."

"All right." Carrie breathed in deeply, testing her nerve, going over different phrases in her mind. The last time she'd broached this topic, it hadn't gone well. But Father Paul said to see it as a gift. And what could be more of a gift than what she was about to say?

"Libby," she said slowly, "I saw your daughter."

"I'm sorry, lovey, what did you say?"

"I saw Mary. A few days ago. When I was driving down Birch Lane, near my old house. Did she have a friend who used to live there? A boyfriend maybe?"

The blank look on Libby's face hardened into a shape Carrie didn't recognize. "I don't know what you're talking about, but—"

"She had the same haircut, like the one in the photo on your mantelpiece."

"No," Libby said, shaking her head vigorously.

"She looked happy," Carrie said.

"Carrie," Libby said, digging her keys out of her purse, "I know you've been through a terrible time, a dreadful time, but this isn't funny. Dragging me into this...this dream state or this fugue of mental illness—"

"Mental illness?"

"Or game, this game, whatever it is you're doing... John doesn't want it, and I—"

"John? What on earth do you—"

"It's not—I want no part of it. Do you hear me, Carrie? I want no part of it."

Carrie swallowed hard, faced her friend. Two stubborn tears sat at the corners of Libby's eyes. Her mouth turned down so hard Carrie barely recognized her.

"No part of it," Libby repeated as she got in her car and cracked the windows. She started to pull out of the parking space.

"Libby," Carrie called to her, "she was wearing the belt! The same belt!"

She watched as Libby drove through the lot, shaking her head quickly, as if wiping Carrie away.

Carrie walked over to her car. Father Paul was wrong; she would never learn how or what to do with the information. Ever.

In the car, Danielle remained quiet. She'd already been admonished for saying too much, for acting like a mother, and she didn't want to make that mistake again.

She looked out the window while Carrie drove, admiring the picturesque land the church occupied.

"I miss autumn," Danielle said finally. "I'd so hoped the leaves would have turned by now."

"They're late this year."

"Although when I lived here, I preferred spring."

"That's because it's the best time to sell a house."

"Maybe."

"Mom, I don't really want to go to the mall," Carrie said. "I don't want to shop. I don't want to talk. I—"

Danielle nodded. "We don't have to go."

She passed the turn at West Gulph Road that would take her toward the mall and went the other way, toward home. She drove faster than normal, almost as fast as John. She made little adjustments the entire way—fiddling with the mirrors, seat, windows, vents, anything to avoid talking more with her mother.

"You go, Mom," Carrie said as she pulled into the driveway.

"What?"

"You go to the mall and pick out something for me."

"No, honey, I shouldn't—"

"Shouldn't let me be alone? Is that why you're here, so John doesn't feel guilty about leaving his depressed and crazy wife at home? Is that why he told Libby I was mentally ill? Is that why he convinced you to come early, to keep an eye on me?"

"Carrie, no, that's not it."

"Isn't it?"

"No."

"Then prove it. Go to the mall," she said. "Go to the mall and get me a blue dress. Please."

Danielle looked at her daughter carefully. Her eyes were clear, her voice strong. There was nothing about her that seemed disheveled or confused. But could she trust her own instincts anymore? After what Carrie had told her, how could she trust that she knew what was going on with her daughter? Still, her radar didn't even ping. *That was years ago,* she told herself. *I was too wrapped up in my own problems then, but not now. Not now.*

"Okay," Danielle said quietly. "If that's what you want, honey."

Carrie nodded. Danielle watched her daughter walk to the door. Part of her knew damn well she shouldn't leave her; the doorjamb was cracked and unstable, and John would be upset if he found her alone. But part of her also knew that Carrie would be fine. That she was strong, like her. And in the end, depending on how one looked at it, hadn't what she'd confessed proved that all over again? That she was strong beyond measure?

Danielle rolled down her window. "Lock the door!" Then she drove to the mall but hedged her bets by calling John's cell phone. She insisted that Carrie was fine, just tired, and that she had asked her mother to run the errand for her.

"What about church—was it her idea to go?"

"No, it was mine."

Danielle frowned; she didn't remember mentioning to John that they'd stopped by the church. Carrie had told Danielle the detectives were following her—was John following her too?

"I guess she'll be okay for a little bit," he said.

"Well, I didn't have much choice, John," she said. "It would be completely out of character for me not to go. She would know that something was up and pitch a fit."

"You're right," he agreed. "I'll check on her. Make sure she's okay."

Danielle hung up the phone and headed out to the mall, past all the developments she'd watched spring up, all the homes she'd tramped through, judging their wallpaper, their carpet, their aging pipes and chipped roofs. Their cherry front doors and emerald shutters. *Cobalt*, she thought suddenly, as if holding a paint chip in her hand. Her daughter would look beautiful at the funeral in a deep cobalt blue.

The day she'd found out she was pregnant the first time, Carrie had taken a bus all the way to City Line to buy a pregnancy test from a drugstore where she'd been certain she wouldn't run into anyone she knew. Whether that said more about her or about the Main Line, she couldn't tell you. She took the test in the cramped dark bathroom in the gas station next door, waiting for the telltale sign to appear while another patron pounded on the door. When she finished, she wasn't surprised, and she wasn't scared. That would come later. She threw the kit away, went outside to wait for the bus, and waited three days to tell Ethan, because they both had to study for a chemistry exam.

That Friday, after school let out and chemistry was at last in the rearview mirror, Ethan slumped over a plate of cheese fries and mused that he had probably failed the test.

She sighed. "You always say that, and you never do."

This was part of his ritual, his need to discuss and worry and be the center of attention even when there was no reason or need. It was also, she was certain, part of some kind of reverse voodoo prayer, something that would bring him good luck by being too cool to ask for good luck.

Carrie waited until the booths on either side of them were empty. High school students came here early, college students came here late, and moms occasionally grabbed takeout in between, but there was always a lull. Carrie wanted to nestle her secret into that space, somewhere public and private at the same time.

Ethan slurped his Coke and scraped a large fry against the plate, getting the last dribs of ketchup before he bothered to pour any more, as if hoping he could make it last.

"Ethan," Carrie said, "my period is late."

"Wait, what?"

This wasn't something she usually discussed with him; she was private, decorous even when they were having sex, careful about covering up, closing the door when she went to the bathroom. She had never even passed gas in front of him that he knew of.

"Late. My period."

"But it came, right?"

"No. And…it's not going to."

A fry dangled from the corner of his mouth. He looked like a cat with a fish hanging there, not caring what he looked like. He blinked, then pulled the fry out of his mouth and put it back on the plate.

"Are you saying what I think you're saying?"

She nodded. He scanned her face, trying to read it. She didn't look happy, nor did she look like she was about to cry. She looked serious, like she looked when she told him she had to go to work or to study. She looked the way she looked when she knew what needed to be done.

He let out a long sigh.

"You're sure it was me, right?"

"Ethan!"

"I mean, you weren't roofied by a football team one weekend or anything?"

"If I'd been roofied, I wouldn't remember. Isn't that how that works?"

He sighed. "Well, luckily, I have some money."

"Money?"

"Yeah. I mean, I assume it's not free, even at Planned Parenthood."

Carrie's mouth fell open, just a half inch. He didn't seem to notice this and just leaned over and continued to talk, whispering but loudly, filling up the space with his own voice.

"I mean, if you haven't called them and asked the price yet, I'd be happy to do that. I'll do my part. Comparison shop! We should comparison shop, to get the best situation. There're probably a lot of places where you can have it done, and we'll find the doctor with the best track record at the Better Business Bureau. The lowest rate of infection, the fewest number of protestors outside—"

"Ethan," she whispered, but he didn't hear her.

"I think I know a guy from camp whose girlfriend had to have one last year. I can ask him what he thinks—"

"Ethan!"

"What?"

"That's…that's not… I mean, I can't. I can't do that."

His face turned gray in the low, buzzing fluorescent light.

"Carrie, what are you saying? I mean, we're in high school. You're fighting for a scholarship. Plus, Jesus, my parents would fucking kill me!"

Her face still held so little emotion. No tears, no worry lines.

"Well then, we won't tell them."

"What, we'll run away?"

"I'll have the baby secretly, and we'll give it up for adoption."

"Carrie, seriously. How can that fucking happen?"

She stood up and pulled her large gray sweatshirt out in front of her dramatically. Fifteen to twenty pounds, she estimated, at her height, if she was careful, if she didn't drink milkshakes and eat junk like other people did. There was room for way more than twenty pounds in the clothes she often wore.

Ethan's eyes narrowed, and he motioned her suddenly to sit down.

"What?"

"Your neighbor just walked in. The guy you used to babysit for."

"Probably getting pizza for his kids. He wouldn't recognize me from behind anyway."

"Well, he was looking at your ass kind of funny."

"Don't be ridiculous."

Ethan was nervous while the man was in the shop, told her not to talk, not to say anything about "the situation" until he left. Finally, the door jingled, and Ethan nodded that it was safe.

Carrie's stomach growled, and she suddenly wished there were more french fries, hot ones, crisp ones, on the plate. Then she admonished herself: this was exactly what she needed to be careful about.

"But how can you hide, keep a secret for, what, nine months?"

"Eight."

"What?"

"The average gestation is forty weeks, which is ten months, and I'm already two months along."

He pulled his hands away from the fries and started to count. "April, May, June, July, August, September, October, November."

"November." She nodded.

"It won't work. Someone will find out. Someone will know."

"No, they won't."

"November," he'd said finally with gritted teeth. "Hopefully you can do it over Thanksgiving break."

"Why?"

"Because we won't have any tests to study for."

Carrie went upstairs and lay on her bed, pulling the pale yellow throw across her feet. It was getting colder this month, with all the windows ringing this room. She remembered before they bought the house, how the real estate agent had trumpeted those three walls of windows, and Carrie kept hearing Danielle's tempered voice warning her: *It will be too hot in the summer and too cold in the winter.* She was exhausted suddenly, just as she had been the night before. As if just talking to her mother and thinking about her required more energy than she had.

She turned on the television, flipping through the channels, settling on a home decorating show that used flea market furniture. She'd always meant to do that, to go to flea markets around the area, like she used to with her grandmother. A tear rolled down her cheek, thinking of what Gran would say: *Then get off your keister and let's go!* Maybe after the funeral was over and the other people had gone, she and her mother could go do something like that. Something to bring them closer.

A thud near the front door, like a paper landing, but they didn't subscribe. Had a package come? Had someone sent food? That was probably it—Libby with her lasagna. Other people with casseroles. Chelsea or Tracie. They hadn't kept in touch much, but surely they'd heard by now. The moms from the Y? But she hadn't heard the UPS truck or a car in the driveway.

She went downstairs to the door. The frame was bent, but the dead bolt still turned. She looked outside. A fat yellow phone book on the welcome mat. She shook her head. Who used these things anymore? She unlocked the door, went outside, and picked it up, carrying it toward the garage, straight to the recycling.

As she pushed the code in at the garage, a man stepped out between her house and her neighbor's.

"Carrie," he said. "Ah, it is you. I'd know you anywhere."

She blinked. "Mr....Shepherd?"

He'd lived a few streets away from her and her mother. He looked older than she remembered. Grayer, paler. His hands were shaking like he'd been drinking, even this early in the day.

The Shepherds had two little girls she used to babysit—Emma and Rose. Mr. Shepherd had driven her home a couple of times when he'd come back from a party, insisting it was too late for her to ride her bike. And he'd leaned in too close, asked too many questions about her life. Sometimes he'd watched her house a few seconds longer, after she'd gone inside and turned out the light.

She tried to stay calm as she pushed at the garage buttons quickly, to change the code, keep the door from opening.

"You look...the same," he said.

He had to be there for a perfectly logical reason. To express his condolences? To see her mother, having heard she was in town? But still, her eyes were fixed over his shoulder, praying one of her neighbors was home, watching. Then, seeing his hands shake, wondering if he was drunk, like he had been those nights. Was he always drunk, like her father?

"Do you and Mrs. Shepherd still live in the old neighborhood?"

He laughed. "Ha, live in the old neighborhood? That's a good one."

Carrie's heart sank. Good God, *another one*? Mr. Shepherd was clearly unhealthy—he drank too much, and he drove too much. He'd been asking for death for years. She breathed in deeply, looking for the earthy undertones, the clue. Was his joke proof that he was dead too? But how? When? And was it all connected? How was she supposed to know the goddamned difference when he'd looked half dead his whole life?

"Why are you here?"

"Why do you think?"

"I have to get going," she said and turned away.

He grabbed her by the arm firmly, too firmly for a skeleton. He was strong, wiry.

She tried to fling him off, failed.

"Oh, you think you're tough, do you? Well, you were always a little wild one, weren't you? Always a little tease," he hissed in her ear. "Practicing the splits in your backyard, fucking your skinny boyfriend in the basement, pretending not to know I was looking through the window!"

He reached up and grabbed her breast, and she screamed, broke away. Ran up the street with him following on her heels. He tackled her at the corner, pinned her down.

He leaned his face into hers, and she turned her head furiously from side to side to avoid his mouth, the sidewalk scraping her scalp.

"That's the thing about staying up all night, taking midnight walks. You see and hear everything. You see boys running to their cars with a bundle of rags, and you open the door and hear a baby cry as he tosses the rags in the trunk!"

"No, he put it in the car; he changed his—"

"Please. You think I don't know what you are?"

"No!" she cried. "I didn't know. I—"

Tires screeched; a door slammed. Her view blocked by Shepherd's body, her eyes squeezed shut as he raised his hand. Then suddenly, John's hands pulling on Shepherd's coat, ripping one sleeve. He yanked him off, but Shepherd squirmed out of John's grasp. John lunged for him but missed and tumbled to the ground.

"John!" Carrie cried.

He scrambled back to her, leaned over, his breath holding together in the cold air, streaming like clouds.

"Carrie," John said breathlessly. "Are you okay?"

"Don't go after him, John. Don't!"

"I won't. I'm calling the police."

"No!"

She covered her face with her hands. She was so tired of trying to explain. Of having to worry about what she saw or how it looked or what anyone thought. Tired of no one understanding what was plain and obvious as day.

"No? Carrie, I—we—"

"John, just…let him go. It's over, and I'm fine now. Just…stay with me."

Tears streaked her cheeks. He ran his thumb across each of them, wiping them dry. He couldn't bear to see his wife cry. Not again. Not more. And staying away from her, never knowing where she was, not following her, trailing her for the first time, it had been torture. Torture, the not knowing.

"Stay with me, Frog," she cried.

"Okay, babe," he said. "I'm here. I'm here."

He pulled her up to a seating position, cradling her head. She glanced nervously in the direction Shepherd had run. But there was no trace of him. He was gone, and John was the only one with her, his arms circling her, his head bending down, blocking the clouds, the wind, the cold, swirling air.

He is my home, Carrie thought. *He is the lock on my door.*

Everybody looks at my clothes like they are trying to figure out what I am underneath. You don't see people like me every day.

If I left the store and followed someone for real, they would notice me right away, with my gypsy skirt and bright scarf. But I don't need to do that.

I just shut my eyes and see.

So I saw the little boy riding in the car, stopping at the corner where the Starbucks was. It's not like a camera; you can't zoom in and pan through your vision until you find what you need to see. It just comes to you, limited, sometimes in pieces. And this time, I saw the boy, waiting, dangling his feet, kicking them until one blue sneaker fell off.

And then the man, the man with the shaggy hair in the back, clothes rumpled like a homeless veteran, lifting him out of his seat, running across the street and behind an idling bus painted red, where his gray car was parked.

The bus blocked the view of the car. But I saw. I saw the first three letters of the license plate—BMT—before he left.

But I never saw the boy's mother. I never heard her scream.

Where were you, Carrie Morgan? I see you everywhere: on the covers of newspapers, on the local news. Anyone who wanted to memorize your face, the way you walk, could do it on YouTube, with all the clips they have of you now. Your pretty hair and your blank expression, like a pale chalkboard.

Am I the only one who knows you weren't there?

Everyone says if you can see it before it happens, you can stop it.

But all I can see is the after, always.

That's why hardly anyone wants to pay for the after. And why they'll pay almost anything for the before.

When was the last time John and Carrie had spent a Saturday afternoon just talking? She couldn't remember. Her mother had called from Nordstrom, wondering if Carrie preferred short sleeves or long, and John had told Danielle to take her time, not to hurry back, that he was there, and Carrie was fine. Better than fine.

Carrie probably hadn't spoken this many words since the last double session with Dr. Kenney, months before. *Why, she hadn't spoken this much or listened so hard since those days with Ethan,* she thought with a smile, as they ate leftover fajitas for lunch and opened a bottle of Pinot Noir.

She told John what it was like when her father left them and how she had to go straight from school to the restaurant, work until eleven, ride the bus home, and stay up doing her homework until two or three a.m. How she had to set her alarm for five thirty because her mother had already left for the office and the house had to be vacuumed every morning before she left for school, in case someone wanted to come by and look at it. She told John how she was so tired she cheated nearly every day, vacuuming the first floor only, since no one ever did anything messy upstairs, unless you counted an occasional thread dropping from an errant hem. How she had to quit the cheerleading squad because she was so exhausted after studying all night that she fell asleep during practice, head nodding while stretching in a split, waiting for the music to queue up.

She told him about Ethan and how they studied together and ate meals together, even breakfast some days, because she never had any spare time to actually go out on dates. How one night before a big geometry test, she secretly set an alarm before they had sex, allotting him only ten minutes for the task. "But he only needed three minutes!" She laughed, and John laughed too. It felt so good to laugh, Carrie almost forgot to feel guilty.

Her mother came home from the mall and was surprised to find her daughter half drunk and laughing. Danielle put the packages on the counter and kissed Carrie on the cheek.

"I got you a beautiful dress," she said.

"Oh, good. Thanks, Mom."

"And some blue napkins and paper plates."

"Perfect," Carrie said. "We're doing everything at the funeral in blue," she said to John.

He nodded without understanding precisely why. Blue for a boy? Like a baby shower?

"So, Mom, the creepiest thing happened today after you left."

"Oh no," Danielle said with dread. She locked eyes with John briefly, but he didn't look angry. He looked almost as drunk as Carrie did. His hair, a little long in the back and sides, tickling his ears, made him look younger, like when Carrie had first brought him home.

"Remember Mr. Shepherd from our old neighborhood?"

"Of course."

"He came here today."

Danielle blinked at her daughter. "Oh no, that couldn't be. Ralph Shepherd died five years ago, maybe six."

John's eyes widened a little, like a door swinging open on a breeze, but not Carrie's. No, Carrie was learning what she could and couldn't say, even with her eyes.

Without missing a beat, she said, "Well, it sure looked like him. Maybe he had a brother?"

"Maybe."

"Well, whoever he was, he attacked Carrie," John said. "I tackled him, but he ran away before I got a good look at him."

"Good God, are you all right?"

"I'm fine," Carrie said. "Just a little shaken up."

Danielle looked at both of them, blinking, suddenly seized with comprehension. The things John worried about were the wrong things—Carrie's mental state, her seeing things. The things she had worried about were wrong too—the dress, the arrangements, the food. She felt both a deep sense of shame and an utter call to arms. She could fix this!

"Where's your phone book, Carrie?"

An electric current ran up Carrie's spine, remembering the book's call to her, its warning. Its curse, really.

"It's...out in the recycling bin. Why, Mom?"

"Because I'm going to call an alarm company." She sighed. "We're going to make this place secure and safe for you, Carrie. For you both. Once and for all."

John blinked back at her. He had enlisted Libby and the neighbors and his mother-in-law to help—he should have known that a woman couldn't protect another woman from a man.

"I can't remember the name of the one I used to recommend all the time," she continued. "But if I see their ad in the Yellow Pages with that old photo of a man in armor, I'll recognize it straight off. They'll remember me and come out right away." Danielle walked toward the door, shaking her head. "This was always such a safe, welcoming hometown," she exclaimed.

Carrie frowned. Had it been? Safe, maybe, but welcoming? She didn't remember her mother having friends on their block, getting together for a drink or a coffee klatch.

Danielle went outside and came back brandishing the book in the air like it was the Bible. She sat down at the kitchen table and started thumbing through it. "And I thought Florida was full of crazies." She sighed.

"I tried to convince her," John said softly. "I got estimates and everything afterward."

But they'd fought over it, Carrie refusing, screaming, anguished. She'd believed the lack of impediment—no alarm, no gate—had facilitated Ben's return. And she'd failed to understand that John had only been trying, once they had Ben back, to keep him there. To lock him in for good. And when he'd said to her, gently he'd thought, "Carrie, you can't rely on faith to keep you safe," how she'd turned away from him, as if he'd impugned her character and not just her habit of prayer. But she couldn't argue anymore. This latest episode was proof that she was unsafe and unlucky.

Carrie started to clear their plates. As she passed her husband, she reached up and tucked a shaggy lock of hair behind one of John's ears. He needed a haircut before the funeral, and she was sure if she said something, her mother would find someone who could do that too.

SUNDAY

T he knock was heavy and startling, like a man's. Despite the recently installed alarm system, Carrie jumped in the kitchen. That vibrating fist seemed to shake the whole house. She did the math: John was in the shower, her mother was getting dressed, Nolan couldn't possibly be coming back again, and Shepherd was both dead and gone. This was probably an overenthusiastic Boy Scout selling an autumn wreath. She wiped her hands on the striped kitchen towel and walked into the living room.

Through the front window, she saw the phone first, up against an ear, short hair, shorter than she remembered it, a profile. Heard the throaty voice giving someone directions. Then the person turned and blinked at Carrie through her black-rimmed glasses. Maya Mercer.

"What do you want?" Carrie said through the door.

"I want to talk."

"See, that's the problem. You talk too much and listen too little."

"If you answered my questions, I'd listen. The world would listen, Carrie."

"No."

"So you'll just let things play out, let the whole awful story unfurl, let people think the worst of you, even if it isn't true?"

Carrie's right hand went to her throat.

Maya raised her eyebrows.

Carrie twisted the dead bolt, opened the door, and let her in.

Maya's high heels clattered on the wooden entry. For a wiry woman, she stepped almost as heavily as she knocked. She sniffed the air as if expecting the coffee she sensed, but Carrie didn't offer any. Maya walked farther into the house, and instead of sitting on the sofa or asking for that coffee, she took a few steps into the kitchen.

"I don't remember your kitchen from when we filmed."

"The opening was draped. There were cables and lights and things in here."

"Huh," she said, looking around the kitchen like a real estate agent. Lingering on the *Eat* sign on the wall, the small wooden island, the red chairs against the nook in the corner. "It's cute, the way you've decorated it."

"Thank you."

The door to the pantry was open, and Maya stepped closer.

"Look, if you're really that hungry, just ask, Maya. I'm sure we have—"

"No," she said. Her eyes lingered on the door frame. She knelt down and looked at the low pencil marks of Ben's height. The careful handwriting and all the unused space about it. She reached out her hand to touch it, then stopped. Pencil. Pencil didn't last forever.

She stood up abruptly. "Can I see his room?"

"No. No, you cannot."

"Because you've changed it already?"

"What is wrong with you? You show up here, you make these accusations—"

"Carrie, let me interview you again. For real this time."

"Why? They have the guy."

"Yes. But can they convict him? Because I've heard the forensics don't quite match up."

"What are you saying?"

"I'm saying they *think* they have the guy."

"Well, maybe he'll confess."

"Yeah. And maybe, on the way to getting that confession, he'll tell them everything he knows about you. Every last little thing."

"You mean…the photos he took?"

"No, Carrie, I do not mean the photos he took."

Upstairs, the water turned off. The slide of the shower curtain, yanked so confidently, filled the air with a metallic ring they could almost taste.

Carrie glanced up at the ceiling. "I don't know what you're talking about."

"You just keep telling yourself that," Maya said. "Repeat it to yourself over and over until you believe it. Carrie, you are in control of this situation—how people perceive you. Don't let rumors from when you were seventeen years old color the truth. Don't let some crazy person be in charge for you. Don't let John tell you what to do."

"Crazy?" Carrie said, but Maya didn't answer.

She walked into the living room, looked around. "We could do it now. I have a camcorder in my car," she said.

"I have to go to church," Carrie replied.

"Catholic?"

"Episcopal. Why?"

"I was hoping you'd confess to someone. Although I'd prefer it to be me. Call me if you change your mind, Carrie. About anything."

The kitchen was clean when John and Danielle came downstairs, but Carrie kept scouring the sink as if it were stained. "Darn it, I was going to wash those dishes for you," Danielle said. "Now I'll have to think of something else to help. Maybe I'll just have to mess up the kitchen again cooking a big breakfast so I can clean it," she said and smiled.

John straightened his tie, and his mother-in-law asked him if he liked French toast. Said she'd learned the best way to cook it, and it involved whiskey. He laughed. Of course she would know the best way, just like she knew the best alarm company. Carrie had always said she and her mother weren't particularly close, but when they'd moved into the house and Danielle had lifted as many boxes as the movers they'd hired, John had told Carrie that sometimes love wasn't milk and cookies. Sometimes it was a strong back and a wrench. And Carrie had said that sounds like a father, not a mother. But Danielle had had to be both.

Carrie managed a small smile as she rinsed the sink and wrung out the sponge, grabbing her coat where she'd draped it on the chair. John punched in the new security code before they walked outside. The air was heavy and wet, pulling at the leaves.

As Carrie opened her car door, something turned her head in

the opposite direction. A crow? A dog? She lifted her nose suddenly and sniffed. Wet leaves. Moss, loam.

Her husband and mother were in the car, had buckled their seat belts. John looked out. Carrie stood in profile, arm draped across the open door.

Down the street, between their house and the end of the empty lot next door, in the opposite direction of where they would be driving, a car seat sat alone on the sidewalk, rocking lightly in the breeze, as if being pushed by an unseen hand.

"Is this a trick?" Carrie said.

"What?" John replied. "Is what a trick?"

Carrie walked toward the car seat and the scent in the air, unmistakable. Dead leaves. The sharp compost of fall.

"Carrie?" John called, but she didn't turn.

Danielle turned in her seat, twisting her neck to watch where her daughter was going. She blinked, squinted in the bright light, then unbuckled her belt.

"Carrie!" she called, running after her daughter.

"Shh," Carrie said, as if she knew the child would be asleep.

She stood over the ordinary seat, rocking without its base, the sensible navy blue that anyone could have chosen anywhere. The baby inside was tiny, bent like a lima bean in a simple cotton onesie and socks, and so pale you could see the veins pulsing in its head.

Danielle looked up and down the street, shielding her eyes with one hand, as though if she looked hard enough, scanned the horizon, the reason for the baby being alone would emerge, walk out from between the shadows, jingling keys.

Carrie crouched down, and Danielle's knees bent automatically, following her. Behind them, the car shut off. John stepped cautiously toward them on the sidewalk. They heard his confusion with each halting step as they whispered over the baby's head.

"A newborn," Carrie said.

"Looks like a C-section."

"How can you tell?"

"He doesn't look like he struggled." Danielle sighed. "His head is so smooth, not smooshed. Enjoy it while you can, little one. From the looks of it, the rest of your life may not be that easy." She stood up, turned back to John.

"I think she put it here," Carrie said suddenly. "Like a test."

"Who? Carrie, what are you talking about?"

"Maya Mercer. She came by while you were in the shower."

"Carrie, that's crazy. Why would she do that? Lure you?"

"I don't know. I—"

"Any of your neighbors pregnant? New parents? Or grandparents?" Danielle asked.

"No," Carrie said firmly.

"I don't really know." John shrugged. "We don't know any of them very well."

"None of them had a baby. We would know that."

"Would we?"

"All the big boxes for the crib and the high chair put out in the recycling. The blue banner and the balloons on the door welcoming him home."

"I didn't notice that," John said.

"I know."

"It *is* hard not to notice a baby," Danielle said. "On a warm day, you'd certainly hear him crying, what with all the windows open on this block."

"We should call the police," John said.

"Or child services," Danielle added. "Probably both."

"Yes," Carrie said.

She lifted the carrier and started walking toward the house. John touched her elbow as she passed him, but she pulled her arm away, as lightly as if she were shrugging off a coat.

Danielle and John watched her walk for a minute.

"Who is Maya Mercer?" Danielle asked.

"A reporter."

Danielle nodded. "Well, I don't think even a crazy, aggressive reporter would plant a baby in the street."

"Yeah," John said with a sigh. "No kidding."

They fell in step behind Carrie. A procession, with a swaddled baby in the lead. Like church.

J ohn had always liked running errands. When Carrie handed him a list, he never folded it in fours or crammed it in his pocket. He looked over the items excitedly, then carried them jauntily, as if they were important. Even when the list was spoken—*Can you run downstairs and get the Advil, please? And find the hot-water bottle?*—he always treated her requests with a kind of reverence, as if he would be tested on it all later, and he really wished to get a good grade. But in the days when Ben had first been taken, this had almost become a charade between them: John wanted to leave, to do anything but stay home, and Carrie wanted him gone so she could clutch Ben's belongings and cry without him watching her, wringing his hands. She gave him something to do so he wouldn't have to figure out what to do or what to say to his own wife.

Danielle was the same way. Carrie still remembered how badly she had wanted to be a cheerleader in eighth grade, and how, when she'd confessed this to her mother, Danielle had immediately pulled out a pen and paper and made a to-do list to help her succeed. *Go to library and get book on cheerleading. Go to community college and watch older cheerleaders practice. Ask Norma, who used to be a dancer, for choreography advice.* Lists weren't drudgery; lists were accomplishments waiting to happen.

And so, the day they found a baby on the sidewalk, Carrie distracted her mother and her husband with lists. A list of things they needed from the grocery store—diapers, formula, bottles, infant vitamins. And a list of steps to be taken—talk to the neighbors, check the Amber Alert website. Steps she promised to take if they would just let her move this baby inside. *If they would just relax and listen and please let her have this moment with a baby again! Please!*

In the quiet hush of the living room, John and Danielle had exchanged looks over Carrie's head as she hummed a lullaby. Their tacit agreement formed in the air. How could they take this small moment away from her? No, they could not. The calls could be made later. The exact timing didn't matter. *Let her have this*, they both wrote in the air with their glances. *The world owes her this much.*

But it wasn't until John was gone, the sound of his tires on asphalt fading away slowly, that Carrie told Danielle that this was her baby.

"*Your* baby?" Danielle said with alarm. How long had John been gone? Thirty seconds? A minute? And she already wished he would come back. This was worse, worse than he'd let on. First she imagined a reporter was trying to mess with her mind, and then this. She fingered her phone in her pocket.

"Yes," Carrie said. "The one Ethan and I had."

Danielle swallowed hard. John had told her how easy it was to set Carrie off, to push her over the edge with a word or a look. She had to be careful. Find her moment, like she did with her clients, ruminating over a house that needed too much work. She stepped forward and put her hand on the baby's delicate skull.

Carrie glanced up at her mother, eyes shining, as if Danielle were anointing the child, acknowledging it as family. The baby's heartbeat pulsed in her palm.

"When they're this young, they're like another species. Alien, you know? Sometimes I forget that, with no child in my life."

"I didn't forget," Carrie said softly.

"Well, he's certainly beautiful," she said and sighed.

"He *was* beautiful," Carrie said. "We had a flashlight, so no one would see the light in the window from the street. I thought candles would be more relaxing, but that seemed dangerous to Ethan, you know? And I think he'd read enough to know that nothing about it was going to be relaxing. He was always so cynical, so negative. Do you remember that about him, Mom?"

"Yes," Danielle said, but she didn't. When she thought of Ethan, tried to conjure him, with his light eyes and sandy hair, he always came up muted and vague, like a faded plaid. She knew he'd been important to her daughter. That much was clear from how long they'd dated and how badly she'd missed him when she first went away to school. But she couldn't even picture his face or the sound of his voice, let alone summon his personality. Like a lot of things during those years, Ethan was a blur.

"He just couldn't see the positives in any situation, ever. Did you ever know someone like that, Mom?"

"Yes."

Carrie started to cry. Danielle took her hand off the baby and put it on her daughter's shoulder. This was her moment.

"Is that why he didn't want to keep the baby, honey?"

Carrie nodded, and the tears fell more heavily.

"He wanted me to have an abortion."

"It's okay, sweetheart."

"I know," she said and sniffed. "It really is okay now, isn't it?"

Danielle looked away from her daughter's earnest gaze. She didn't answer; she didn't want to be misinterpreted.

"I went to church on Friday evenings all that last month, when you thought I was at the library. I didn't know why I was going really. I just felt like I had to, you know?"

"Sure."

"I didn't know what he was planning to do. I just… But now… now I wonder if I wasn't praying for forgiveness for lying to you, but…praying for the baby's soul, praying that he be…preserved. So I could meet him again. And now I have."

Danielle bit the inside of her lip. So much she wanted to say but didn't dare. Like that all newborn babies look alike. Like that whatever a teenaged girl in labor, sweaty and exhausted, might have thought she'd seen in the pale yellow glow of a flashlight wouldn't be accurate. What Carrie held in her head wasn't a snapshot, even though it felt like one. Time played tricks, memory, light. It was like remembering a sidewalk drawing in the pouring rain.

"You know what I think? Going to church is never the wrong thing to do," Danielle said.

"See, and we were on our way there just now," Carrie said. "That's...symbolic."

Danielle patted her daughter's hand. "Still, honey, there might be someone looking for this baby. Missing him. Crying for him. His mother."

"I already told you," Carrie said. "I'm his mother. He's come back. Just like the others."

The carpet beneath Danielle's feet suddenly felt swampy. She steadied herself on the rounded arm of the green sofa.

"The others?"

"First there was Ben, then Gran, Ethan, and Mr. Shepherd. Oh, and Jinxie! Gosh, I almost forgot Jinxie. And I feel awful saying this, Mom, but Jinxie was the most...the most thrilling of them all."

Danielle swallowed hard, then took in a deep, audible breath.

"Did...you tell anyone else about this?"

"I tried to tell John," she said, "but he didn't listen. He just kept calling Dr. Kenney and telling me to rest."

Danielle tried not to panic. This was what John was talking about, what John hadn't been able to name. Carrie was seeing things, believing things, that made no sense to him. Did he think they would make any more sense to Danielle? Or was he just tired of dealing with a crazy wife all alone?

"Well, John cares deeply about you, honey."

"Aren't you going to ask me about Gran?"

"What?"

"Gran. Don't you want to know how she was? If she asked about you?"

Danielle felt something twisting into a knot in her throat. Her mother. Her only family. The most positive person she'd ever known. Danielle could still conjure her mother's bright clothes, loose on her small frame. She saw clear blue eyes, heard her distinct, singsongy voice that caught every now and then on one of her multisyllable words.

Danielle had taken great care to hide her grief over her mother's death from her daughter. Didn't want to admit how unmoored she'd felt. After the funeral, during Carrie's senior year of high school, Danielle had called in sick for a week but pretended to go to work, for Carrie's sake. She started her day with breakfast at that old diner, then read magazines at the library. When the library closed, she sat in the bar down the street, a blue-collar pub where she was sure she wouldn't run into any clients, and nursed a single beer until it was seven p.m., the time she usually left the office. She hadn't wanted Carrie to know she'd felt afraid to work, to speak to people, to negotiate. Afraid she'd open up her mouth and only sorrow would come out.

"Of course," Danielle said, biting her lip.

"She looked great, Mom. Not dead at all. That's the thing—they aren't like holograms or anything, you know? Not filmy and see-through the way we've been conditioned to think. They're...solid. Her hug felt exactly the same."

"Hug?"

"She hugged me and rocked me, just like she used to. Like that picture you have."

Danielle looked away, wiping involuntary tears onto the heel of her hand. On her nightstand at home, she kept a two-sided frame: in one side, a photograph of her mother rocking Carrie; the other, a photo of her rocking Danielle.

"Oh, and Mom?"

"Yes, honey?" Danielle sniffed, looked back at her daughter.

"She says she hears you."

"Hears…me?"

"When you talk to her at night."

Danielle's shoulders started to shake. "No," she cried softly.

"No, you don't talk to her, or no, you don't think she hears you?"

Danielle walked over to the kitchen and splashed water on her face. She was standing in a house on a cul-de-sac admiring a dead baby while discussing a dead grandmother? She pulled a tissue out of a box, blew her nose.

"Mom, maybe if I remembered what I said, I could get her to come ba—"

"No."

"No?"

Danielle knew her daughter was offering her a kind of lifeline. But if she started leaning on the idea of her mother now—when she was feeling strong—she believed she would crumble. Crumble into dust.

"Gran died a long time ago, but I still miss her, Carrie. Every day. I'm not going to deny it. And God knows I would love to see her again. But…"

"But what?"

Danielle answered carefully.

"My mother's soul… It—it's so hard for me to imagine her in the—in the in-between. I can't bear to think of her as not being at rest. At peace."

"She was peaceful," Carrie said simply. "It wasn't like she was trying to be somewhere she wasn't. She knew what she was doing."

"Well, good then. Good."

She watched as Carrie stroked the baby's cheek. It was hard not to see a found baby as a miracle. Wouldn't anyone take it as some kind of sign? Still, it was a coincidence, surely. There had to be a reason. Danielle imagined that someone looking for him would be knocking on their door any minute.

She went to the window, looked outside. A thin line of spent twigs danced in the gutter across the street. A flag flapped against a pole. No cars, no people.

"Carrie…you didn't also see…your father, did you?"

"No," she said softly. "Why? Was there something you needed to know about him? Or any reason you could think of that he'd come back?"

Their eyes met. They both knew he'd left because he'd fallen in love with someone else. There was no mystery there, nothing to unravel. Or was there? The last fight before he left. *I don't want to be another to-do item on a list.*

"An apology would be nice," Danielle said with a small smile. She thought of what her own mother had said when he'd gotten cancer and died: his death was his apology. For everything he'd done to everybody.

The word *apology* caught in the air, like in a dialogue bubble. Carrie looked down at the baby. There was no apology Ethan could ever make for what he'd done. But this day, this moment, was Carrie's apology to the baby. For being stupid enough to have trusted Ethan. She traced the outline of the downy hair on his cheek and thought, for just a moment, that he almost smiled.

The two of them sat side by side on the sofa, but Carrie's eyes remained on the baby, as if she could fix him there, lock him down, with her gaze. Danielle listened to the sounds of each of them breathing, the different rates and rhythms, proof they were all alive, that none of them were dead. *Couldn't Carrie hear it too?*

"Carrie, honey." Danielle spoke quietly, but she hoped, with enough warmth that her daughter wouldn't turn away. "If what you say is true, why don't they stay? Why do they come, only to leave?"

"Because," she said, "all I ever asked for is one more day."

"But what about them? What…do they ask for, do you suppose?" There was a dreamy look in Danielle's eyes that Carrie had never seen before.

"I don't know, Mom. But Gran said they come back because they need to. They have a reason."

Danielle nodded her head slowly, as if she understood. Did that mean she was a success? That her life was steady and upright, with nothing her mother needed to fix or adjust? There was something comforting about the idea of her mother floating above the earth, ready to swoop down and straighten out someone's life like she was leveling a crooked picture frame. She smiled, thinking of it this way. And then she wondered if John would think she was crazy too, mother and daughter and grandmother and father too, the whole bunch of them, absolutely cuckoo.

John came back with everything on the list and spread it all out on the coffee table, as if making a statement that it wasn't prudent to put things away, to make things more permanent than they were. His cheeks were pink, like they were in the winter, like when he rushed. He hadn't left the two of them alone with that baby for very long. And who could blame him, really? Danielle loved her daughter, but she had a newfound respect for everything that John was juggling in addition to his own grief. As he folded the paper bags, crinkling them, the baby woke up with a noise that was more like the squawk of a bird.

"That's quite a distinctive cry," Danielle said. "Something you'd remember."

Carrie filled a baby bottle but said nothing. She'd stopped expecting people to believe her. When she thought back to the sounds the night of that first birth, all she could conjure was the quiet hush of the basement, the whoosh of the heater blowing, the tick of a grandfather clock above them in Ethan's hallway, the catch of her own ragged breathing as Ethan pulled the baby out and cut the cord. After Ethan had left the house, she hadn't heard a thing. Not the frantic crying, distinctive or not. Not the trunk slamming shut. Her lip quivered. Had she even said good-bye? Had she said she was sorry? So no, she didn't remember the sound of his cries, and she thanked God for that. But the baby's paleness, his almost-blue skin, his otherworldly hands—oh, those were precisely, exactly the same.

Danielle pulled John into the kitchen.

"So how long are we going to let her do this? A couple of hours, or—"

John breathed deeply. "I don't know. It's the first time I've really seen her happy since Ben disappeared again."

"It hasn't been that long, John."

"I know. But…days seem a lot longer when they're unhappy ones."

She nodded. "Still, John, we can't just keep a strange child in the house indefinitely. We have to tell someone."

"I know. I know it would look bad, but now that they're close to making an arrest—"

"They are? They told you that?"

"Yeah, Forrester told me."

"So they must have enough evidence finally? They're pretty sure?"

"I guess so. They have his license plate apparently, and a witness. So no one's looking at her anymore. The car is gone—"

"Car?"

"They were following her for a while," he said. "I saw them."

"But…this still looks bad, John. They might change their minds about following her and making that arrest if they find a missing child in your house!"

"I checked the Amber Alerts, and there was nothing."

"Are you sure?"

"Yes, positive."

"Well, if it's an abandoned baby, I guess an hour won't matter."

"I think we should let the baby spend the night here."

"That's too long, John."

"One more day won't hurt."

Danielle winced at the phrase. But she didn't want to tell her son-in-law what Carrie had told her. She watched John watching Carrie, his gaze tender and hopeful. How could she spoil the beautiful mood with her matter-of-fact talk of ghosts and of death? If he knew what she knew, what would he do? Have her committed? Call the police? Or just struggle to stay awake all night, watching his wife, guarding the crib.

What could the harm be, after all, Danielle thought, *of giving her daughter one more day when one more day was all she ever expected to get?*

MONDAY

The night before, Carrie was the last person to leave the baby's room. John was not surprised by that; he was surprised she was willing to leave at all. The three of them stood over his crib before they went to bed themselves, saying their own form of prayer or blessing for a day of peace. And while they didn't discuss what they would choose to do the next day, Carrie knew in her heart she would not have to make that decision.

At five forty-five a.m., Danielle bolted upright to the sound of a scream from the room next door, followed by the baby's squawk. She grabbed her robe and ran into the nursery.

Her daughter stood next to the crib, hand over her mouth, sobbing.

"Carrie, honey, what is it?"

"He's…here!"

"Well, of course he—"

Danielle stopped talking, swallowed hard. So this was the moment of reckoning, the proof. The terrible evidence when her daughter learned she was wrong. When her daughter learned, perhaps, that she was crazy.

The baby cried out again, but Carrie made no move to pick him up. *Of course*, Danielle thought. *She knows he's a stranger now.* The bond, the spell, was broken. But hunger, need, loneliness, those continued. Carrie reached in and picked up the baby, cooing to him, walking him around the room.

"Why is he still here?"

"Carrie, I—"

"What does it mean, that he stayed and the others left?"

"Honey, you need to face the possibility that—"

"That what, Mom?"

"That you were wrong about all of this."

"All of this?" She screwed up her face. "You don't believe anything I said either?"

"That's not what I said."

"You don't believe your own daughter? You don't believe your own mother?"

"Carrie, calm down. What I'm saying is…"

"Yes, what are you saying?"

"I'm saying isn't it possible…that you were right about the others and wrong about the baby?"

Carrie blinked in the low light of the room.

"No," she said. "The only one I was wrong about was Nolan, and he—he tricked me, because he was sick. I know he was sick. That's why he came to me, so I could save him."

Danielle's mouth was a straight line, her lips disappearing. A signal, sure as birds on a wire, that she held words inside she was afraid to say.

"We have to get the baby to Ben's pediatrician," Carrie said suddenly.

"Carrie, honey, it's been long enough. We need to get this baby somewhere safe before this goes any—"

"No, see, I'm thinking that sickness gives off the same kind of signal…I sense it around someone's body, like heat waves off a grill. It's a kind of half-dead smell, it's like…a predeath, I guess. So it confuses me."

"Carrie," her mother said, grabbing her hands. "Listen to me."

"What?"

"Carrie… Your father. He—"

"What, Mom?"

"He...saw things too."

"Things?"

"After he came back from Vietnam. Post-traumatic stress. The people who died, that his unit killed...they...sometimes came back to him."

"What are you saying? That I'm crazy like he was? That it runs in the family?" Carrie's eyes flashed. The idea of it—and that her mother might believe it and might have told John, and John told Dr. Kenney, and someone told Maya Mercer.

"No," Danielle said, but quietly, guiltily. "I'm saying there was a reason he drank, and a reason he gambled, and a reason he couldn't stay with the people he loved. And I'm saying that stress can do terrible things to a person's psyche."

Carrie shook her head. The room felt smaller than it had a few minutes before. Her mother, the ultimate skeptic. Who believed only in the power of one foot in front of the other, of tackling the list, of getting it done, nothing else. *If this, then that.*

Well, she thought, when they went to the pediatrician and found out that something was wrong with this child, then it would all become clear. She'd show her. *She'd show everybody.*

John, Carrie had learned as soon as she'd had Ben, was uncomfortable around babies. He'd held his newborn son awkwardly, all elbows and shoulders, too delicate with him, never sure where to put his hands. But as soon as Ben had started moving, when he'd learned to crawl and roll a ball, John had stopped being afraid he would break. Quite the opposite. He'd toss him repeatedly in the air, making him laugh, throwing him so high it had made Carrie nervous, made her cry out. She supposed it was John's sporty upbringing—everyone in his family an athlete—that made him like that. The whole clan would be arriving soon for Ben's funeral, staying in a hotel together, a bank of rooms on the same floor, as if they couldn't bear to be apart. They'd done the same for John's grandfather's funeral, for a cousin's wedding. It was how they operated: separate but together, a team. And inevitably, someone would bring a Nerf ball and the hotel pool would be transformed into a leaping, shrieking mass of them. *Moving*, Carrie would think, watching them. *They were all about motion.*

So when John came into the kitchen while Danielle and Carrie were warming bottles and making coffee, they were both surprised by what he had to say.

"I guess we could find a way to keep him, right?"

"No, John," Danielle said sharply, barely containing her horror.

"But no one's looking for him," he said.

Carrie measured coffee grounds, poured water, her back to the others, saying nothing.

"Doesn't matter," Danielle replied. "There will be questions eventually, questions you can't answer. Haven't you had enough media attention?"

"We could move," he said simply.

"John, really," Danielle said. She'd been summoned because Carrie was losing her grip on reality, and now... Was something in the water? What was happening to John?

The house phone rang shrilly. It was used so seldom, but John insisted they keep it for safety. John walked over to the handset to look at the caller ID.

"Maya Mercer," he said.

"Don't answer it," Carrie said.

"She'll just keep calling. You know she will."

"You can't talk to her," Danielle said. "What if she hears the baby? What if he cries?"

John blinked. "You tell her a friend is over."

The phone stopped ringing, and in a few seconds, the message light flashed. Danielle picked up the car seat. "That's it. This baby is going to Safe Cradle. Now, one of you, hand over your keys."

John looked at his wife for a second, just a second, before he reached in his pocket and fished out his car key.

T he day Ben was born, Carrie had gone on a hayride. She'd been more than a week past her due date and hadn't had any Braxton-Hicks contractions, and unbeknownst to John, she had already tried eating spicy food and driving down cobble-stoned streets in Philadelphia. John didn't believe in that level of intervention; he was firmly in the camp of Carrie's gynecologist, of being patient, of letting nature take its course. He would have been furious if he'd known, would have seen it as risk taking.

But Carrie was tired of being pregnant, tired of the weight hanging so low inside her she half waddled. The man driving the tractor didn't give Carrie a second glance when she climbed into the bed of the truck and sat down on a bale of hay. The other moms, dragged excitedly by their kids, smiled at her and nodded, completely understood. They rode over the hills, circling the farm, past scarecrows and bushels of pumpkins and flapping ghosts in the haunted house display. She thought nothing of those white sheets with the mournful long faces, made no connection between her past and her present, didn't see it as a sign.

Afterward, driving home, sitting at a traffic light still ten miles from home, she felt water trickling out, over the seat, onto the floor, and felt a sense of accomplishment and control. She called

John, who tried to get her to wait and have him pick her up, but she refused and drove herself to the hospital.

"What were you doing in Willis Township?" he asked when he met her in the lobby at preregistration.

"Just driving around," she said, wincing between contractions. They were coming faster than she remembered. Or did she remember at all?

Everything was different the second time. Speedier, flashier. The lights were so bright, she squinted, covered her eyes, cowering in a ball on the table. They kept moving her, trying to get her in position, manipulating her feet, her legs. Unnatural. No squatting, no moving intuitively the way she had the first time with Ethan, without guidance. Between pushes and contractions, she curled up on the hard table, wishing for the low light of Ethan's basement, the flashlight in his hand, the candles in case they needed them. She hadn't seen the terror on his face, and she didn't want to see the concern on John's, the focus of her doctor, the efficient blandness of her nurse. She didn't want to see anything but her baby, safe and sound, healthy. Hers to keep this time.

Proof that she'd been given another chance. But who knew if she'd be given a third?

Safe Cradle wasn't on the outskirts of town anymore. When Carrie was growing up, it had been just off Reservoir Road, down by the river, where the asphalt curved and took you out to nothing but water treatment plants, welding companies, factories. She thought of Ethan that night. Had he driven down there and just kept going? Got on the highway because it was near, because it spoke to him?

Perhaps that was why they moved it, why it was in town, near the firehouse. Safer, not near any ditches or bodies of water. Danielle had looked it up online, and Carrie was surprised to see the address. She'd driven by it a million times and had never noticed a logo or young women lingering outside.

Danielle insisted she be the one to surrender the baby. Just in case someone was watching. Just in case someone saw her go in. The car wasn't following Carrie anymore, perhaps, but people were every-where. And they would happily spill their story to Maya Mercer.

"I'll go alone," Danielle said. "It's the only thing that makes sense."

"No," Carrie said. "Absolutely not. I'm going with you."

"Well, as long as you stay in the car," John said.

Danielle got in the driver's side of John's car, and Carrie sat in the back with the baby. They drove through the neighborhoods, Danielle glancing at gardens, lawns, houses, Carrie's eyes fixed on the baby.

Danielle pulled into a parking spot adjacent to the fire station, put the car in park, and turned around to Carrie, holding out her arms.

Carrie unbuckled the seat quietly, the first time she'd touched a car seat buckle in a long, long time.

"It's the right thing to do," Danielle said. "No matter who we believe this baby is, honey, this is the right thing to do."

"I know."

"I know you know."

"Closure." Carrie sighed.

Danielle thought of a million other things she could say but shouldn't. Like that Carrie was still young. That she and John could have another baby. That she could move to another town, under another name even, and no one would ever know she was the mother who lost her child. John had said his parents wanted them to move farther east, where they lived. She would encourage that. She would help her find a house they could afford there, help them fix it up. She could spend spring and summer with her, doing whatever needed to be done. Florida was too hot in the summer. *I miss my daughter*, she thought with a pang. *I miss being a mother. I want to be here, grandchild or no grandchild.*

Danielle felt Carrie watching them as they exited the car. She approached the door slowly. Nondescript, except for small red type with a roof design floating above the words. A doorbell and a door knocker too, as if for good measure, and a camera mounted to the right, trained on the stoop. They had been right not to let Carrie go to the door.

As Danielle reached the stoop, a young girl came up the sidewalk from the right, holding a bundle in a blanket. Her eyes were red and her steps were slower than Danielle's. When she saw her, she hesitated, as if to let Danielle ring the buzzer first. But her eyes were less polite. They burned into Danielle as if to say, "Yes, I'm young and stupid and frightened. But what the hell is your excuse, lady?"

Danielle jumped when the door buzzed open, and she realized she didn't have a good excuse or a good story or even a plausible one. She turned back and looked at her daughter. In the backseat, shielded by the glass, Carrie raised her hand and waved. Danielle reached down and lifted the baby's arm and waved back.

She stepped inside and walked to the simple desk on the right of the lobby. Painted above it were the words *No questions asked*.

The neon Budweiser sign buzzed in the window. From behind, it appeared rusted and cracked, and whenever someone at the pool table broke a gaggle of balls, it rocked against the glass, threatening.

John had never been there before. It was on the edge of the city, well outside his township and the police district, and if the pool table was ringed with men younger than he was, the bar stools were occupied by men far older. As if someone had given up seats on the bus, out of respect.

He wore a cap low on his head, nursed a beer, and waited. He'd arrived earlier than he was supposed to, leaving Carrie and Danielle to clean up the dishes after lunch. He felt jittery, on edge, although he didn't know why. He was doing nothing wrong. He wasn't the one worried about being caught. Finally, the door opened, and Forrester came in. He gestured to the bartender, who opened a bottle and brought it over without a word, just a nod.

"You're a regular?" John asked.

"He's my uncle," Forrester replied.

"Ah."

"I wouldn't trust going anywhere else."

"I thought cops always drank at a bar together."

"Not the smart ones," he said and smiled. "Although plenty of cops drink to avoid talking about the job."

"It's a hard job."

"Thanks for acknowledging that." Forrester drank his beer, swallowed. He looked John right in the eye. "Look, I thought you should know, we're very, very close to making an arrest."

"Really?"

"Yeah. He's still in for questioning, just letting him stew a little."

"How?"

"I found a witness who gave us a partial license plate, tracked it down. Just have to, well, break him now."

"Wow, that's great. That's...great."

Forrester lifted his glass, clinked John's.

"Yeah. A couple things don't quite add up, but the guy's jumping out of his skin. He'll talk. He wants to tell someone what he's done."

"Like what doesn't add up?"

"It's...a little delicate, John."

"I want to know."

"I'm not sure you do."

"I do," John said firmly.

"Well, the body was...pretty decomposed."

"But...it was him? It was Ben?"

John had almost gotten used to saying *was*. The past tense of being a parent once but no longer. A friend of his mother's, whose son died in a car accident, always told people that she had two children. One in New York, and one in heaven. Her son was gone, but she would always be his mother.

"Yes, yes, of course. The dental records matched. DNA too. But the decomposition doesn't...match the time frame, the theory. It's been a mild fall, but...well, the water simply wasn't warm enough for it to happen that quickly. Unless something was added to it or done to the, uh, remains... I...well, I just don't know."

John's face turned pale.

"I've said too much. I'm sorry. It's disturbing, I know."

"So this guy could get off because of that. Is that what you're saying? On a technicality or something?"

"I don't want you to worry. We have his car. We have an eyewitness who fingered him in a lineup. We even have the motive. It's just the one piece that we can't figure out."

"I don't think I want to know the motive," John said. He swallowed hard, the beer suddenly swelling in his throat.

Forrester nodded. "It's important to the prosecution but not always to the family. Sometimes the why is worse than the how or the…when." He threw up his hands. "That came out wrong. I'm not explaining it very well, am I?"

"No, no, I—I get it. And I—we—appreciate all that you've done. All the information. It means a lot to me, to us. To Carrie."

John finished his beer in one long swallow and stood up.

"One more thing," Forrester said as John slid a dollar under his coaster. Those were the words Nolan always said to Carrie. To make her nervous, pay attention. Did both of them know that?

"What's that?"

"It looks like…the guy might know Carrie."

"You mean because of the photos? I thought he took those at the Y—"

"Beyond that. There are connections. But we're not 100 percent sure how well he knew her. Also, I have to mention something else, just to be thorough. The reason Nolan keeps circling back to Carrie."

John blinked. He stood in the middle of the dark room, halfway between the table and the door, like he wasn't sure if he should stay or go.

"The Google search history," he said.

"She was helping a friend," John replied quickly. "She told me."

"Which friend would that be?"

John swallowed before the name came out, garbling it. "Chelsea. I…don't know her last name."

Forrester nodded. "John, I would be remiss if I didn't say to you what Nolan would say to you right now: that if you know something and you tell us now, we can, well, we can offer you immunity."

John breathed as deeply as he dared to. He feared his breath and his panic might become audible, that he'd be panting, if he let it go too far.

"You know I always thought someone was after her, not Ben. I always thought that."

"But why, John? Why?"

He shrugged. "I can't explain it really. Just…well, people look at her. Notice her when she walks by."

"Attractive women on the street and all?"

"Yes. But…I don't know. She… It's like she has a light on her, you know? She just…shines."

Forrester smiled, took another drink.

"Well, I guess I should get home," John said finally, turning away. Through the window, he could see that it was darker outside, and the traffic was less heavy than when he'd arrived. Just like that, everyone had gone home.

Forrester nodded. "How well did you know her?"

"What?"

"Before you got married? How well did you know your wife?"

"We dated for six years."

"You met in college?"

"Yeah."

"But you didn't know her in high school?"

"No," John said. He reached for the door, the old metal knob cold in his hand. He opened the door, then turned back.

"But I know her now," he added.

Forrester kept nodding his head. Even after John left him alone at the small wobbly table. Like he was reminding himself to stay positive.

TUESDAY

F ive hundred people attended Ben's funeral. They filled the soaring church behind Carrie and John, and she could hear their breathing, whispering, quiet coughing, the rough clearing of their throats. But she didn't turn to take it all in as John did, swiveling around and back, waving and smiling to people he knew.

In the first pew, next to them, John's family and Carrie's mother. One mother crying into a monogrammed hanky, the other into a tissue, grieving for their grandchild. John's brother, Luke, and sister, Nan, red-eyed and sniffling behind their dark glasses. But no glasses for Carrie and John. John looked the same way Carrie did: pale and exhausted. He had made his own calculations about the number of attendees, comparing it to a baseball stadium, then marveling at it. Would that many people come to an adult's funeral? To his, to his wife's? Then he shelved the thought, deep in the back of his brain, as being too sad. He was tired of being sad, as she was, surely, but he needed to deflect it as much as he could to get through his life.

But Carrie believed she would always be sad, in a low-level, constant way, something she carried around in her bones. Not the big, showy displays anymore; those were in the past. She'd had plenty, more than her share, and now she just had this permanent condition. That was why she was tired. Not because she continued to have nightmares of abductions, not because she saw ghosts, but because she couldn't sleep. She was tired like a villager carrying water over mountains, a person who'd lost too much and had too little and had been carrying grief like a millstone forever. This wasn't the kind of grief people wanted her to have; she'd never had the right kind, she knew. No, she'd gone from shrieking maniacal breakdown to weariness and missed the phase that looked best: sniffing back tears, mouth downturned, eyes half closed. Where John's family lived, eternally.

When the reverend finished his eulogy, Carrie crossed herself, and before they slipped out the chapel door for a private moment alone with Ben's ashes, she turned around to look at the crowd behind her. What did a wall of grief look like? Finally, she allowed herself a glance at the full church, just to appreciate it in case she never saw such a spectacle again. A sea of the expected faces, the TV news version she'd never summoned. John's hand pulled her forward, propelling her toward duty, and she did what his hand told her. She met the reverend's half smile with one of her own, the one that signals seriousness, not joy, before she could think about who those people in the church actually were, who'd come early to get a good seat, who came because they felt guilty, who came because Reverend Carson was such a great orator, who came because they were gathering evidence still, and who sat on the aisle not to weep for a child but to observe other people less lucky than themselves.

In the chapel, John closed his eyes as they stood over the silver urn. Carrie put her hand on it, warming the cold surface, and thought of how Ben had looked in the morning light, his eyes so happy to see her walk into the room. How John had always looked to her. She lifted her face toward the stained glass windows, throwing dappled light across the room, the pale colors dancing across her husband's face. She thought of their honeymoon in Italy, paid for by his parents, walking through the streets, touring the churches. Their first day in Florence, she had asked John what he thought of it, and he had squirmed a little and said, "I don't know. It's awfully religious." John, always looking for lawn over stone, for trees, not buildings. His faith was outside, not inside. She squeezed his hand to open his eyes. He smiled and said they should probably go join everyone, and she nodded. They had mourned their child everywhere. They would mourn him every day. They didn't need to stay here and do it.

"We'll get past this," he said.

"Will we?"

"We'll take a vacation," he said. "Somewhere sunny. Somewhere Ben would have liked."

She smiled. But then she wanted to ask if Dr. Kenney would be coming with them, or if she'd awake one morning to find her mother in the suite down the hall. *Will you ever be able to handle me alone again, John? All these years of following me, on my trail, and now what will you do, alone with me?* But she said nothing. Not now.

They walked out the back door and down the stone path slowly, slower than John usually walked. They passed the small cemetery, the stands of linden trees, to the rectory. The reception room was large and high ceilinged, swollen with people. Painfully loud, like an auditorium. Carrie looked at the blue plates and napkins, the trays of cheese and shrimp and finger sandwiches, the blue frosted cupcakes she probably hadn't ordered enough of. She looked at the food first and then the diverse crowd of people waiting to say how sorry they were and to gently remind her and John that it was a blessing, at least, to have closure. Closure? The word made her ill. Carrie knew better. Things were never, ever closed.

Everyone from Saint David's was there, from the reverend's wife to the day-care coordinator to the janitor. John's family, of course, but also his coworkers—his fellow salespeople, his assistant with her mascara running down her face. The mothers from the Y, still wringing their hands with guilt, especially now that the suspect had been identified. All the teachers and parents from preschool. Carrie's college roommates, Tracie and Chelsea, standing near twenty of John's fraternity brothers. Dozens of couples Carrie remembered vaguely from her wedding, who had to be friends of John's parents. Libby and Anna, holding hands as if to steady each other. Nolan, standing at the corner of the room, silently eating skewers of cheese. And the man with the dog—Neil—running up to shake John's hand, paying his respects. The dog was tied up outside in the shade, being pet by a small group from the ladies' guild, and Carrie's mother, nuzzling it close, just in case her daughter was right.

They split up to work the room, John going left, Carrie going right. Dark clothes balanced by bright eyes, white smiles. The timpani of whispers and blowing noses.

When Forrester walked in with a dark-eyed little girl wearing red clogs and a quilted skirt, Carrie assumed she was his daughter. She smiled as they approached her, thinking they were headed for the cupcake table, which was at her elbow. No one else had dared to bring a child, but children were exactly what the occasion called for. Life. Hope. The future.

They stopped short of the dessert table.

"Mrs. Morgan," Forrester said, "there's someone who wants to meet you."

Carrie smiled, but the little girl didn't smile back. She simply cocked her head as if curious.

"And who might this be?" Carrie broadened her smile, thinking the girl had to be nudged further. Such a solemn, formal occasion; she needed permission, perhaps. Funny that it had never occurred to Carrie that Forrester might be married and have children himself. Shame on her for not wondering. John probably knew this, knew everything she didn't.

"This is Raina," he said.

"Hello, Raina."

"Hi."

"That's a pretty name. Is it a family name?" She looked at Forrester quizzically.

"Oh, no," he said. "I mean, I don't know. You see, Raina's the witness who was across the street from the Y."

"Oh," Carrie said, blinking. "Oh my goodness. I thought…well, I assumed—"

"I'm not married," Forrester said.

She nodded. "I'm sure I knew that. I just…well…"

He shrugged. "Well, now you can see why there was some initial skepticism about her. Though not on my part. I always thought she was credible."

"I appreciate you staying on top of things," Carrie said and smiled, and he smiled back. Forrester had done it all; Forrester had always believed she was innocent. She glanced across the room at Nolan, who took in the crowd as if he trusted no one. Didn't it work better when you did things Forrester's way? When you listened to your gut? But Carrie remembered Nolan bent over, ailing, at the doorway of her house. Being eaten alive from the inside out. Something was wrong with his gut. Stomach cancer, she thought with terrible clarity. She must find a moment to hint at this later to Forrester, so he could urge his partner to see a doctor.

She bent down to talk to the girl. "You were very, very brave to tell what you saw."

"You are brave too," she said.

Carrie's eyes opened wider. She exchanged a glance with Forrester, who offered a small smile.

"What…do you mean, sweetheart?"

"It's brave to say what you believe. Especially when people don't want to hear it," she continued.

Carrie swallowed hard. Was this just coincidence? What was she talking about exactly?

"I'm afraid I—" Carrie felt tears threatening at the corners of her eyes.

"Now's probably not the best time to talk, and of course she can't discuss the case with you or anything," Forrester said. "But Raina wanted to meet you, and her mother had to work, so I said I'd bring her here."

"Well, that's very kind. My mother worked too, when I was your age."

"I know."

"You…do?"

"Raina's mother runs Psychic Connections," Forrester explained. "Family business."

Carrie's mouth formed the word *oh*, but she wasn't sure if she spoke it out loud. Her body felt a kind of electric current that had rendered her temporarily numb.

"Well, surely you're too young to be put to work," she said finally.

"I greet people at the door sometimes. But I can't see what's going to happen, only what has already happened. And everyone who comes wants to know the future, not the past."

Carrie put a hand over her mouth.

"She's a firecracker, isn't she?" Forrester said and smiled.

"Your son was beautiful," she said solemnly. "I saw you in the parking lot sometimes."

"Raina," Forrester cautioned. "We can't talk about that, remember?"

Carrie's right knee started to shake. "Thank you," she whispered.

"And that man—I saw him too, before, but I didn't know, you know? My mother would have known, but I didn't know or I would have told. I swear to you, I would have told."

Tears sprang to Carrie's eyes. She crouched down, took the child's hands in hers, and pulled her into an embrace. "Of course you would have." Her new dress brushed against the wooden floor, then blew up slightly from an unseen vent.

Raina's lips were nuzzled close against Carrie's hair. "But I didn't tell them everything," Raina said.

"What?"

Her breath was hot on the shell of Carrie's ear. Like Ben trying to whisper, breathing too much, talking too loud.

"I didn't tell them that you weren't there," she whispered.

A group of people, wearing their grays and blacks, started to swim and swirl in front of Carrie's eyes. She tried to stand. She

ONE MORE DAY

clung to the small ballast of the girl while the hem of her dress swayed to and fro and her knees threatened to buckle beneath her.

"I feel sick," Carrie said, and Forrester knelt beside her.

"Sit down," he said. "Put your head between your knees if you need to."

"My dress," she said dully.

"Doesn't matter," he said. "Take some even breaths now."

He radioed to Nolan, told him to call an ambulance.

Carrie sat cross-legged on the floor, her head hung down, her hair forming a curtain on either side.

"You should come visit me sometime," Raina said. "Maybe we could help."

Carrie raised her head and wiped her eyes with the edge of her cobalt sleeve. Help? Help with what? What would this child do with what she knew? Who else might she tell? And would it matter now, with the man in custody?

Her spaniel posture, looking at Carrie as if she were the only person in the room. What was this child offering to help her with? Was she saying that seeing ghosts, experiencing the dead, was something she needed help using? Was she offering Carrie some kind of job? Or giving her a lifeline—a way to predict that nothing this terrible was ever going to happen to her again?

"My mother could tell you whether you're going to have another baby."

Even on the dusty floor, surrounded by feet and legs and crumbs, Carrie felt something rising in her chest, bubbling, a mixture of hope and fear. She felt the buzz of the crowd, the fizz of the drinks. She smelled the chocolate cupcakes in their hands, the sugar on their lips.

They were alive, all of them. They were alive, and they still had time. Time to help each other, time to change. Time to go on, accomplish, remember. Time to heal and forgive each other.

Her head swam with the truth of this; she looked over the girl's head for John's face in the crowd. Across the room, in a cluster of

285

blue blazers, listening and not listening, he raised his eyes to meet hers at the exact same moment. *Run after me*, she wanted to call. *Follow me. Don't let me go.* But he was already moving. Already on his way to her, wherever she needed or wanted to go.

At the funeral, the lady got light-headed and had to sit down. Mr. Forrester thought I said too much. That's my mother's problem too, my father says. That if she said a little less, people would come back and pay her a little more.

But there was so much I hadn't told her yet. Like that I know why dead people come back. It's because they miss having bodies. They want to be touched. They would give anything for one more hug.

And that I knew what she wished for in the back of her mind as she lay alone in her bedroom when she was young. Another soul to keep her company. Another being just like herself. And that she felt all the more guilty because of it, because she believed she had wished that first baby into being.

And maybe she had that power. Maybe she had others. Time would tell.

Like maybe when I get older, I'll be able to look forward, not just back. Because people can change, you know?

You can leave a baby and find one. You can grow up a Boy Scout and end up a murderer.

Things happen.

FRIDAY

I t felt good to get out of her house, away from the Main Line, even if it was just a twenty-minute drive to the airport. Carrie rolled down the windows and tried to pretend she was someone else, a person with no past, no ghosts trailing her, her whole bright future ahead. She wondered if she'd always have to pretend or if she'd actually feel that way someday—that there was more to see through her windshield than in her rearview mirror.

John had a sales meeting scheduled in Philadelphia and was going to cancel everything for another week to be with her, to help her rest, but she had told him no. He'd already taken off Wednesday and Thursday, and they'd had dinner with his parents and her mother. Afterward, they'd looked at vacation sites online, trying to plan something fun for Carrie and John, a gift from his family. Everyone had a different idea of where they should go and what they should do. Carrie just let them talk. *Let them decide for me*, she thought. *I'll just close my eyes and pick something on a map.* What did it matter where she went? There would be children everywhere. Babies, toddlers, boys. She didn't need to find a new setting; she needed to grow a new skin.

Her mother offered to stay longer, through the weekend, and she'd told her absolutely not. They'd already booked three appointments with Dr. Kenney for the following week, and Carrie was tired of everyone's fawning concern. She'd blamed the fainting spell on the heat of the day and the smell of the food, the crush of the crowd. But she hadn't told anyone that her head started to swim again every time she picked up a paper or listened to the news. First, she learned that the baby they'd found was a pawn in a custody battle, abandoned to punish its mother. The mother finally reported it, and Safe Cradle returned the child. It should have made her feel better, but it didn't. It didn't because she'd been *wrong*.

Then her mother showed her an update in the morning paper— that an arrest was imminent in Ben's case, that the suspect was cooperating. The memory of Nolan appearing at her door again, asking questions, always one more thing, trying to trip her up, made her feel sick all over again.

She and her mother dropped John at the train station and continued onto the highway, heading for the airport and the US Airways drop-off—always a drop-off, because her mother wouldn't let Carrie walk her inside.

When they curved around the long approach to the departure gates, the road was clogged with unloading cars, a bus, skycaps. Carrie put on her blinkers in the middle of the lane, but a cop whistled at her and told her to keep driving.

"I'll just park in short term and walk you over, Mom."

"Oh, you can let me off at another gate."

"Don't be ridiculous. I'll park and help you with your bag."

"It's not that heavy."

Carrie sighed. "You know," she said, pulling up to the short-term gate arm and plucking a ticket, "the next time Dr. Kenney asks why I'm such a loner, I'm going to say it's hereditary."

"Well, that's true enough, I suppose. Your father was that way too."

"Was he?"

"Yes," she said. "He was always going off to be alone. That's why it was so hard for me to realize when he started going off to drink and then to be with someone else. I never suspected. He'd been that way since the war."

Carrie nodded. "I think the same thing about John and his sales meetings. How would I know?"

"John loves you, sweetheart," she said. "It's plain as day. And John doesn't have a secret war past."

"Everyone has secrets, Mom."

"Such as?"

"Well, if I knew them"—Carrie smiled—"they wouldn't be secrets."

The night before, John had been so thankful for Danielle's help. Carrie had felt guilty over those years when she'd been so ashamed of her mother and, with no father around, of having no money. She remembered the meanest girl in high school, Lauren Stein, watching her swing and miss during softball practice. Lauren batting her eyelashes and saying sweetly, "Why don't you ask your dad to help you bat? Oh, right, your dad's gone." The laughter of the other girls who didn't know how to do anything but play along.

Back then, she'd blamed her mother for her father leaving, for having to work, for not being around to do the things other mothers did: bake cupcakes, drive them to museums on school trips. But glancing over at her mother, it was easier to remember how tired Danielle had been, how accommodating—buying Jinx to keep Carrie company when she was alone, even though they could hardly afford the vet bills.

When Ben went missing, her mother had flown up from Florida and spent three weeks with them. She was, Carrie realized, always happy to help, but Carrie hadn't always been happy to let her. Being around a mother reminded her that she wasn't one anymore.

The first short-term lot appeared to be full, and the tiered design of it was in the shape of an *H*, making it hard to see what spaces were open. Carrie thought she finally found one, only to see that a motorcycle had slipped into the slot.

"Damn it," Carrie muttered.

"We have plenty of time," her mother said. "Just go back out, loop around, and drop me off at another gate."

"No," Carrie said. "There's more parking at the adjacent gate." She had to exit and enter again, but the walk would not be that much longer. This lot was only one level, open to the air, and wasn't much farther to the US Airways entrance. Carrie found a space between a van and a Vespa, and they headed inside.

Carrie led her mother to a self-check-in kiosk.

"I already have my boarding pass," Danielle said.

"Of course you do."

"And I'm not checking my bag."

"Of course you're not."

They went up the escalator together in single file, on the right. As they approached the security line, Danielle suddenly dropped the handle of her rolling suitcase and reached for her daughter's hand.

"Are you sure you don't need me to stay?"

"Yes, why?"

"Because, well, you're dragging out our time together. Circling the lot, stopping at the baggage desk."

"That's coincidence."

"Is it? Or don't you want to say good-bye to your mother?"

Tears fell onto Carrie's cheekbones so suddenly that they seemed to have leaped out of her eyes like small fish. Danielle folded her into a deep hug as travelers streamed around them, rolling their bags to one side or the other to avoid the elbow edges of their awkward embrace.

"What if," Carrie whispered into her mother's shoulder, "the next time I see you, I don't know? What if I can't tell if you're really here or if something happened? What if, you know, you were in an accident and then suddenly—"

"What's more alive and real than a mother, Carrie? Can you think of one thing more real than that?"

"No." She sniffed.

"Here's how you'll know," Danielle said and smiled. She licked her thumb and wiped at Carrie's mascara beneath her eye.

"Ew," Carrie said.

Danielle laughed. "If I do that, I'm alive, all right? I promise. Now, I'll be back in a month, okay?"

"Okay," Carrie replied with a small smile.

As Danielle turned to leave, Carrie grabbed her hand. "You feel good, right? I mean, you're not sick or anything?"

"Why, do I smell funny?"

Carrie smiled and let her mother's hand go. She watched her turn and join the other travelers in the long, snaking line, then headed back down one of the wide corridors that laced the parking garages to the gates. She didn't see that Danielle turned too and watched her daughter walking farther and farther away down the concourse, until she was as small as a child.

As Carrie went back to her car in the far lot, the blue sky clotted with gray. The parking spaces on either side of hers were empty, and she had the vague thought that her car looked lonely as she walked toward it.

Behind her, bus doors and tailgates opened and closed, hissed and squeaked. What gave her pause was not those sounds but something smaller and yet larger—the clearing of a throat.

She turned. He looked vaguely familiar, with his aviator sunglasses and shaggy hair, lighter at the tips than the roots. She didn't see the airplane arcing over her head, gaining altitude, but she smelled something foul in the air, like jet fuel or garbage, half sweet, half sharp, as his steps grew longer, faster. Too fast.

She lunged for her car door, fingers scrabbling for the indent of the handle—but his hand was suddenly there, larger, long fingered, snapping it shut. His entire handprint, the deep grooves and whorls of his skin, sank into the light layer of road dust. A chill moved deep into her spine. All those fingerprints on her car they couldn't lift. *And here was one. Clean.*

His hands moved onto her wrists, squeezing, twisting, so different from the way her mother had just touched her. John had always thought the man at the Y might have been after her, not Ben. Was he right?

"Why did you lie?" he growled.

She started to scream, but his hand covered her mouth. He wasn't that tall, wasn't that wide, but he was strong and quick, and she hoped—she prayed—that he had been quick with Ben too. He had killed her son, yes, but let it have been quick. Before Ben knew what was about to happen.

"Did you do it to save your own skin?" he asked through gritted teeth. "Or just so no one would know what a terrible mother you are?"

Carrie closed her eyes and felt her body start to go limp. The scenes of that day played out across her eyelids, like the hazy moments just before she fell asleep.

The smell of chlorine in the car, the wet beach towel rolled in the passenger seat.

"Look, Ben," she'd cried when she'd found the parking spot next to Starbucks. "Aren't we lucky?"

Ben had tried to say "lucky" back to her, but it came out all consonants, all hard edges.

As she'd closed her door and walked around to the parking meter, she'd carried that lilt, that spinning luck, whistling until she'd opened her purse and found nothing but a penny at the bottom.

Was that the moment it all turned?

She'd looked down the street and had seen the parking attendant coming toward her. She glanced into Starbucks, noted the long line—imagined the people telling one another "but it moves fast, really"—and then her eyes kept going, looking farther up the block, until she saw the bank on the other corner. And so she walked. Not whistling anymore, not sauntering. She half walked, half ran, as well as she could run in a tight maxi skirt and sandals, toward the teller who would give her change for a dollar, who would give her quarters for the meter so she could have a cup of coffee.

But she never made it all the way there. Something made her turn back just as she reached the revolving door, the bright, squeaking floors inside, the uniformed guard, the basket from which she would grab a lollipop to take back to Ben.

It was guilt; it was knowledge. Or it was the smallest sound only a man makes, of clearing his throat.

The man at the Y. Who knew she hadn't locked her car. Who knew she hadn't just been fumbling in her purse. Who knew she hadn't stayed with her son.

And she hadn't said good-bye.

His breath on her face felt stale and dusty, like he'd eaten hot sand. With her free hand, she rooted around in her brown shoulder bag, scrabbling to find something sharp, stinging, fiery.

He leaned in closer.

"I hate bad parents who don't even know how beautiful their little boys are. My mother was like that too. Never knew the value of what she had. You always let him run around, talk to strangers. And then you leave him alone in an unlocked car?" He laughed so hard it came out like a honk. "That was the last straw. People like you don't deserve to have children."

Tears stung her eyes.

"Oh, you cry for him now? Now you cherish him? Too late. You threw away one child, but I forgave you for that. I gave you the benefit of the doubt. But I was wrong to do that. You disappointed me. So I took him away, and I strangled him before you hurt him even worse. Just like I strangled the others. With the laces from that itty-bitty sneaker."

She yanked a pencil from her purse and raked it through the air, aiming for his neck. He bobbed away but stumbled with the effort, sprawling, and Carrie didn't hesitate. She didn't look, and she didn't think, and she didn't see anything but her feet on the ground. This time, she ran.

She sprinted toward the terminal, the busy lane of buses and cars. Behind her, he screamed.

"Don't you know you can't hurt me? Nothing you do can hurt me!"

Carrie kept running, past her mother's gate, past the next one, searching the crowd for a police officer, a police car. Where were all the uniforms when she needed one? Up ahead, a Hertz bus idled. She banged on the door, surprising the driver, who opened it with equal parts concern and annoyance.

"You all right?" she asked.

Carrie ran up the steps, gasping for breath. "Please," she croaked. "Please don't let anyone else on. Please drive. Someone's after me. I need to—"

The woman blinked at Carrie, taking in her messy hair, a scratch across her cheek. She swung the lever, shutting the door. "Okay," she said. "I'll drive you around a little till you calm down. But I can't leave the terminal, you understand?"

"Yes," Carrie said, trying to catch her breath. "Just...don't let anyone on."

As the bus pulled away, Carrie looked out the window in every direction, looking for the man. He could be hidden, in a car, on his way. She kept her eyes open for police as the driver continued on their route. Shouldn't they have an office somewhere on-site? Should she call 911 and give them a description?

The driver turned on the radio, and after a few seconds of weather, a news report blared throughout the bus: *Suburban Philadelphia police are under increased scrutiny today as a murder suspect in custody hangs himself in the interrogation room...*

Carrie's hand went up to her mouth. Strangled her child. Strangled others. And then, when it was clear he was going to be arrested, strangled himself. *Of course*, she thought. *Of course. That wasn't garbage or jet fuel she smelled. That was him. Him.*

She closed her eyes, relieved and yet...ashamed. For all she still didn't know, all the little mistakes she kept making over and over again. Why hadn't she taken a second to lock the door? Why hadn't she scooped Ben up and carried him with her for the block-long walk to that bank?

She thought of the little girl, Raina, who said she could only see the before, not the after. Carrie could smell the before and the after, but she hadn't recognized it in time. It had been in her car all along, she realized—at the Y, at Starbucks—sweet and moldy, a blue, rotting vein. And she thought it had been the chlorine from the beach towel.

The bus had almost completed its loop, and she needed to make a decision. To get off or keep going. Her phone rang in her purse, and she fished it out.

"John," she said.

"Have you heard?"

"Yes," she whispered. "How did it happen? How could they, after all the work they've done?"

"Forrester left him alone for a minute, to get a pencil, I guess—and Nolan was supposed to be watching through the one-way but wasn't because he wasn't feeling well."

"He needs to see a doctor," Carrie said.

"What? Who?"

"Nolan." She thought about him, the baby they'd found, the shoe at the pond. Could it be she knew the middle of things, if not the end or the beginning? She pictured herself in waiting rooms, sitting in the cracked yellow seats in hospital corridors, knowing. Could she know? Could she help?

"I have a call in to Dr. Kenney for you, speaking of doctors."

She didn't answer. The idea of having all this happen to her and no one she could tell it to made her feel even queasier.

"Are you okay?"

"No."

"No?"

"I'm not sure. Is there any way you can come drive me back, maybe?"

"Sure. I'll…grab a cab."

"I'll be…at the Hertz rental lot. Okay? Meet me there?"

He didn't ask her why. He just said fine, to wait for him there, and not to go anywhere else.

She sat in the small enclosure with the rental agents and

customers, watching for John's cab through the window. She ran outside when it pulled up, and she opened the door and slid all the way across the seat, pressed against him, refusing the seat belt.

"Oh, Frog," she said through her tears.

"It's okay," he said. "It's all going to be okay."

Together they drove back to the parking lot. He paid the driver, and she waited for him to open the door and get out first.

The cars around hers looked different from the last time she'd been there, but some of them could have been the same; she wasn't sure. Other than the Vespa, she hadn't really noticed. Was he still there, waiting to cause more trouble? Would he show himself in front of John?

She felt a wave of guilt for not telling John what had happened, for not warning him. She glanced in the backseat before she got in. She sniffed the air like a dog, looking for rot, fearing it, yes, but also searching for the thrill of recognition. But then they were out of the lot. Then they were on the highway. And nothing—no dark ghost or dark car—followed them anymore.

"It's really over," he said as he pulled onto the highway.

She blinked at him like she wasn't sure what he meant. The circus? The accusations? Or them?

"Is it?"

"Of course it is. He confessed, Carrie."

"But what else did he tell them?"

"You mean about the…murder?"

The word caught in his throat and came out strangled. It was one thing to say it about a stranger and another to say it about their son.

"No, about…me."

"Carrie, the man was mentally ill, okay?"

"Tell me."

"Well, nothing, really. Just a lot of crap about people who are bad mothers, who pay more attention to their phones and their coffee than they do their kids. He's also wanted in two other unsolved murders near Pittsburgh. Both young boys with pretty mothers. Forrester said he hated his own mother," he added. "She was a model apparently. Traveled the world, left him alone."

"It's always the mother's fault," she said quietly.

"What? No. No, no, no. It's just—"

She waved him away. "It's all right, John. I know you didn't mean it like that. He didn't say anything else though? Because Maya Mercer told me he knew Ethan."

"Yeah, they met in a mental health outpatient facility years ago, okay? So what does that tell you? Wait, Maya told you that? When?"

"It doesn't matter."

"How did she know that?"

"I don't know, John. Maybe you're not the only one Forrester is feeding information to."

John took a new route home, leaving the expressway a few exits early, trying to avoid traffic, and after they exited, there was a long stretch of strip mall that seemed to go on forever. It was the type of neighborhood that was all proximity; you could turn left or right at any point off the boulevard and find a house that would inspire longing, part of your neighborhood technically, but not part of your world, with a quiet, lumbering grace that marked nobility, remove, *other*. Carrie was separate from all those people, she knew, and always had been. Not more deserving or less, just different from everyone else.

At the corner was a car wash, flashing a neon sign. John looked at her, raising his eyes for permission, and she nodded.

Together they watched Carrie's car through the glass, watched as it was gripped by the metal clamps, moving slowly, grinding, until the first shelf of water came down. The fat foam fingers slapped the doors and roof, the hard water pounding the dust, the prints, the residue. She watched the gray spumes of water fall off the car, waited until they turned to transparent steam when they hit the cold pavement.

Outside, the conveyor spat it out, half dry. A man in a gray uniform appeared with a folded brown towel. He wiped the car steadily, in even strokes, patient in a way that reminded her of someone. He looked up at her for just a second, and she was sure, for a moment, that she was looking into the eyes of her father.

The man walked behind her car and back into the vaulted garage, disappearing behind a cloud of steam. She ran back to the viewing room, craning her neck around the train of cars going through the steam. But no one was there. The man who looked like her father was gone.

She closed her eyes. *I'll be different*, she thought suddenly. *I'll do better. I'll keep my car cleaner. I'll lock my doors. I'll work harder. I'll pay more attention. I'll be more like everyone else.* That could be her promise. Her exchange. Because after all, if Ben came back once, couldn't Ben come back again?

When she opened her eyes, John still lingered at the counter, looking at the products, paying the bill. She walked outside and watched other men, men in the same gray uniforms but who looked like no one, wiping the doors and roof and trunk with their cloths, men who could be anyone, criminals or workers, alive or dead.

The sprays of water, the grind of the conveyor belt, and above them, suddenly, the honk of geese. Carrie watched the dark dotted V traveling south, the slate clouds behind them auguring rain, change, autumn. The birds' pathway through the mist, the heavy air that hung just below the clouds, was a route known only to them. Wasn't migration of anything, living or dead, always part mystery to anyone else who happened along the way? How could she explain what she knew, that small part, to anyone, even herself?

They got back in their car and headed home.

"You know what I was thinking?" John said as he eased onto Sugarland Road. "I was thinking that when we're ready to have another child, we might try for a girl. Maybe do that thing where you spin the sperm. It would feel like a true new start."

In the air between them, the memories of all those boyish nights in the backyard with Ben. All those Saturday afternoons of John with his own father and brother, doing the same thing.

Carrie blinked. "Really?"

"Well," John added, "of course, she'd have to be a tomboy."

Carrie smiled and squeezed his hand. They passed properties so large they looked like farms. Farms with barns but no crops. Places with no reason for being the way they were anymore.

"And...could we have a dog, maybe?"

"I don't think that's genetically possible." John laughed.

"I mean in addition, Frog." Then she added softly, "A girl and a dog." As if testing out the sound and the weight of that sentence.

"Why not," he said.

"The dog can be a boy."

As they idled at the next red light, John reached in his pocket. He pulled out an air freshener in the shape of a tree and hung it on the mirror where Ben's shoe used to be. And from his other pocket, he took a fat roll of quarters and nestled them in the console.

"Just in case," he said. "Just in case."

Reading Group Guide

1. For Carrie, one of the most frustrating recurrences is the unwillingness of her family and friends to believe that she has been visited by the dead. Have you ever had a supernatural experience? How did others react to your description of it?

2. To what extent does their faith and upbringing drive Carrie and John? Does it support or conflict with their actions and reactions?

3. How does Carrie's past influence her relationship with John and her choice of John as a husband? Do you think Ethan was a better match for her?

4. John and Carrie have very different ways of grieving their son's kidnapping. Which do you relate to more?

5. Young women who give birth in secret and are in denial about their pregnancies are frequently in the news. Do you think Carrie was in denial about her pregnancy? Or about Ethan's intentions the night she gave birth?

6. Many people return to their hometowns after college to raise their families there. In Carrie and John's case, do you think this was a mistake?

7. Carrie and her mother's relationship becomes distant during Carrie's teenage years. How does this impact the choices each of them makes? How well do they actually know each other?

8. Much of the novel is told from Carrie's point of view. To what extent, given her supernatural experiences, does this make her an unreliable narrator?

9. Does the loss of Carrie and Ethan's child foreshadow the loss of Carrie and John's? How?

10. It could be argued that there are multiple people stalking others in the book—the killer, John, the detectives, the ghosts. Discuss the themes of obsession, control, and privacy.

11. Spiritual, emotional, and intuitive advisers are sprinkled throughout this novel—from priests to therapists to psychics. What role did Dr. Kenney, Father Paul, Raina, and Carrie's grandmother each play to move the plot forward?

12. The metaphor of a clean versus dirty car bookends the novel. What other metaphors or symbols did you find throughout the book?

13. As more and more dead people seem to appear in the story, Carrie struggles to determine who may or may not be alive. Did you find yourself doing the same thing? What clues did you use to help decide who was alive and who was dead?

14. After a loved one's death, the sentiment "If I could have only one more day with them" is often expressed. How does this wish affect Carrie's time with the people who visit? How does it work against her?

15. The grief showcased in the story is also surrounded by people who could ostensibly help diminish it—the community, the congregation, two families, and a clinical therapist. But Carrie has very few friends and no grief support group. How did each group help or hurt Carrie and John? Would they have fared better if they'd chosen to lean on different types of support?

16. Does Dr. Kenney strike you as someone trying to help Carrie or trying to help John? Is there any evidence he is involved in the investigation or aiding the detectives?

17. Dr. Kenney, John, and Detective Nolan seem to believe that Carrie is losing her grip on reality and perhaps sliding into psychosis. Which other characters grow to share that belief? Which ones grow closer to believing her? What do you believe she is experiencing?

A Conversation with the Author

Supernatural elements figure prominently in the plot of *One More Day*. Have you had experiences with ghosts, séances, and sixth sense? Do you believe in them?

One of the worst things about being over forty is that people's parents start dying. And so many of my friends and coworkers would say things like "Oh, my mother came to me in the form of a red cardinal" or "My mother spoke to me last night in a dream" that when my own mother passed away, I truly expected her to come back and say "hey" somehow. It's been one of the central disappointments of my life that this has never happened.

So I am both fascinated—and jealous. To be open to a whole other realm? That's just really cool to me.

My mother, interestingly, always claimed to be a witch—and she did possess a strong kind of intuition. My only personal gift seems to be that I can always tell when my kids are lying. It's useful, but let's face it: I'd rather be able to talk to my mom.

One of the central themes of the book is religion versus belief. What drew you to that material? What kind of research did it require?

I grew up in the Episcopal Church, and my kids are all baptized (by a female priest, yay!), but I'm not much of a churchgoer. So

I had to dig back in to the teachings of the church, as well as take a peek at the intuitive community, which I knew even less about.

It sounds ludicrous to some, but in my mind, they are connected. Part of me believes that if I went to church more often, I'd be allowed into the intuitive realm! Guilt!

It could be argued that there are several "stalkers" in the book—as the character of Maya recognizes something in John's behavior that Carrie clearly does not. Were you making some kind of statement about men, obsession, and privacy?

I don't think of it as a statement, exactly—although social media and technology make it something I'm vitally aware of as a woman and a mom. But I've certainly known quite a few men who walk a very thin line between protecting and controlling the women in their lives. That line was interesting to me. And the media stalking people—that added a whole other layer.

Carrie and Ethan both make choices as teenagers that, while different, are chronicled in headlines every day. What made you choose that plotline as their backstory?

As a writer, I try to err on the side of empathy. To shine a light on actions that seem impossible to understand and help people see the motivations, the humanity. And to showcase how those actions can impact a person's life going forward—especially if they all remained a secret. All of that dovetailed perfectly with Carrie's loss going forward. Two losses, each compounding the other.

What are you writing next?

I'm finishing one new novel and dabbling with the outline of another. I have two other completed manuscripts I'm not sure about. I'm also developing a TV show with a producer. And in answer to your next question—I drink a lot of coffee.

Acknowledgments

I couldn't have written a novel that involves crimes and ghosts without a lot of help (and a lifetime spent with Nancy Drew and Ouija boards). Thanks for the keen insights of Anne Bohner, Anna Michels, and Shana Drehs; the eagle eyes of Sabrina Baskey, Heather Hall, and Patricia Esposito; to the entire team at Sourcebooks; and the weekly cheerleading and suggestions of fellow authors Beth Kephart, Merry Jones, and Greg Frost.

My writing friends in the Liars Club and the lively Philadelphia writing community propped me up with all kinds of other important things, like craft beer. (Don't judge me. Try writing something outside your comfort zone, and you'll be at a bar by nightfall.)

In short, I thank everyone who ever encouraged me to keep trying something new. (Except my hairstylist in 1992. You were wrong. I cannot pull off short baby bangs.)

About the Author

Photo by Bill Ecklund

Kelly Simmons is also the author of the novels *Standing Still* and *The Bird House*. She is a former journalist and advertising creative director who divides her time between writing, teaching, public speaking, vacuuming up dog hair, and refereeing her three daughters. Visit her website at www.bykellysimmons.com or follow her on Twitter @kellysimmons.